AMPHETAMINES AND PEARLS

THE GERANIUM KISS

AMPHETAMINES AND PEARLS

THE GERANIUM KISS

Two Scott Mitchell Mysteries

JOHN HARVEY

MYSTERIOUSPRESS.COM

OPEN ROAD
INTEGRATED MEDIA
NEW YORK

Cover design by Julianna Lee

978-1-5040-3887-4

Published in 2016 by MysteriousPress.com/Open Road Integrated Media, Inc.
180 Maiden Lane
New York, NY 10038
www.mysteriouspress.com
www.openroadmedia.com

THE SCOTT MITCHELL MYSTERIES

An Introduction

Growing up in England in the immediate postwar years and into the 1950s was, in some respects, a drab experience. Conformity ruled. It was an atmosphere of "be polite and know your place." To a restless teenager, anything American seemed automatically exciting. Movies, music—everything. We didn't even know enough to tell the real thing from the fake.

The first hard-boiled crime novels I read were written by an Englishman pretending to be American: Stephen Daniel Frances, using the pseudonym Hank Janson, which was also the name of his hero. With titles like *Smart Girls Don't Talk* and *Sweetheart, Here's Your Grave*, the Janson books, dolled up in suitably tantalizing covers, made their way, hand to hand, around the school playground, falling open at any passage that, to our young minds, seemed sexy and daring. This was a Catholic boys' grammar school, after all, and any reference to parts of the body below the waist, other than foot or knee, was thought to merit, if not excommunication, at least three Our Fathers and a dozen Hail Marys.

From those heady beginnings, I moved on, via the public library, to another English writer, Peter Cheyney, and books like *Dames Don't Care* and *Dangerous Curves*—which, whether featuring FBI agent Lemmy Caution or British private eye Slim

Callaghan, were written in the same borrowed *faux* American pulp style. But it was Cheyney who prepared me for the real deal.

I can't remember exactly when I read my first Raymond Chandler, but it would have been in my late teens, still at the same school. Immediately, almost instinctively, I knew it was something special. Starting with *The Big Sleep*—we'd seen the movie with Bogart and Bacall—I read them all, found time to regret the fact there were no more, then started again. My friends did the same. When we weren't kicking a ball around, listening to jazz, or hopelessly chasing girls, we'd do our best to come up with first lines for the Philip Marlowe sequel we would someday write. The only one I can remember now is 'He was thirty-five and needed a shave.'

I would have to do better. The Scott Mitchell series was my attempt to do exactly that.

I'd been a full-time writer for all of eighteen months. Spurred on, to some extent, by tales of Chandler, Dashiell Hammett—another formative influence—and others, writing for the pulps at the rate of so many cents a word, I had given up my day job as an English and drama teacher to try my hand as a hack for hire. Biker books, war books, westerns: 128-page paperbacks at the rate of roughly one a month. One of the editors I got to know was Angus Wells, with whom I would later write several series of westerns, and it was he who gave my proposal for a new crime series the green light.

Scott Mitchell: the toughest private eye—and the best.

American pulp in a clearly English setting—that was the premise. A hero who was a more down-at-the-heels version of Philip Marlowe and Sam Spade. A style that owed a great deal to Chandler and a little, in places, to Mickey Spillane. Forty years earlier, I could have been Peter Cheyney selling his publisher the idea for Lemmy Caution.

Amphetamines and Pearls—the title borrowed from Bob Dylan—was duly published by Sphere Books in 1976. John Knight's gloriously pulpy cover design showing a seminaked stripper reflected in the curved blade of a large and dangerous-looking knife. 144 pages, 50,000 words, £500 advance against royalties. You do the math.

But, I hear you asking, is it any good?

Well, yes and no. Reading *Amphetamines and Pearls* and the other three books again after many years, there were sequences that left me pleasantly surprised and others that set my teeth on edge like chalk being dragged across a blackboard.

Chandler is a dangerous model: so tempting, so difficult to pull off. Once in a while, I managed a simile that works—"phrases peeled from his lips like dead skin" isn't too bad—but, otherwise, they tend to fall flat. What I hope will come across to readers, though, is how much I enjoyed riffing on the familiar tropes of the private-eye novel—much as I have done more recently in my Jack Kiley stories—and how much fun it was to pay homage to the books and movies with which I'd grown up and which had been a clear inspiration. Inspiration I would do nothing to disguise—quite the opposite, really.

As an example, quite early on, there's this:

What I needed now was a little honest routine. I remember reading in one of Chandler's Philip Marlowe novels that he began the day by making coffee in a set and practiced way, each morning the same. It also said somewhere that Marlowe liked to eat scrambled eggs for breakfast but as far as I can recall it didn't say how he did that.

What I did was this. I broke two eggs into a small saucepan, added a good-size chunk of butter, poured in a little off the top of a bottle of milk and finally ground in some sea salt and black pepper. Then I just stirred all of this over a medium heat, while I grilled some bacon to go with it.

They say that a sense of achievement is good for a man.

And later, this:

I didn't know whether she was playing at being Mary Astor on purpose, or whether she'd seen The Maltese Falcon so many times she said the words unconsciously.

But I had seen it too.

Intertextuality. Isn't that what they call that kind of thing? Metafiction, even?

Much of the success of the book depends on how the reader responds to its hero. In many respects, Scott Mitchell fits the formula: men are always pointing guns at him or sapping him from behind; women either want to slap his face or take him to bed or both. When it comes to handing out the rough stuff, he's no slouch. Anything but. He's the toughest and the best, after all. But, personally, I find him a little too down on himself and the world in general, too prone to self-pity. On the plus side, he does immediately recognize Thelonious Monk playing Duke Ellington, he knows the difference between Charlie Parker and Sonny Stitt, and he has a fondness for Bessie Smith.

The scenes in the novel that work best, for me at least, are those in which the attempts to sound and seem American are pulled back, letting the Englishness show through. That only makes sense: it's what I know, rather than what I only learned secondhand. And what I know, of course, London aside, is the city of Nottingham, destined to be the home of the twelve novels featuring Detective Inspector Charlie Resnick.

It had been so long since I last read *Amphetamines and Pearls* that I'd forgotten that's where quite a lot of the book is set. And in the chapter where Mitchell visits the city's new central police station, there's a description of urban police work that points the way pretty clearly towards the world Resnick would step into a dozen or so years later.

Men in uniform and out of it moved quietly around the building. Policemen doing their job with as much seeming efficiency as men who are worked too hard and paid too little can muster. From room to room they went, sifting the steadily gathering detritus of the city night: a group of drunken youths with colored scarves tied to their wrists and plastic-flowered pennants on their coats; the first few of the many prostitutes whose soiled bodies would spend the remainder of their working hours in custody; a couple of lads—not older than fifteen—who had been caught breaking into a tobacconist's shop and beating up the owner when he discovered them; a sad queen who had announced his desires a little too loudly and obviously in the public lavatories of the city center; and the car thieves, the junkies, the down-and-outs.

You couldn't work in the midst of all this without it getting to you. It didn't matter how clean the building was, how new. The corruption of man was old, old, old.

And down these mean streets . . . well, you know the rest.

—John Harvey
London, December 2015

AMPHETAMINES
AND PEARLS

This book is for Leanne and Tom with all my love.

-1-

The streets wound their way listlessly, as though they had made the journey too many times. They were cracked, uneven; the product of a private estate which could no longer afford their keep. The houses were large and dark. Once they had testified to the wealth that was to be made from hosiery and from coal—now they were divided into flats. Expensive flats, true, but still flats.

It was an early winter evening. The weather report had promised a fine, mild night, but no one had bothered to tell the sharp November wind which sniped round the blackened corners.

I pulled my overcoat collar up higher and hunched my head down inside it, searching for warmth. I thought about Candi.

When first I had known her she was just plain Ann. The more exotic name had come later, when she was wrapped and packaged and sold like so much confectionery. She had been Ann and she had been sitting on the stage in front of the band, shaking a tambourine and smiling nervously. She was wearing a white dress punctured at intervals with small holes; her eyes were surrounded by the blackest of black make-up; she was very young and very nervous.

Yet later, when she stood up to sing, with gawping faces seeking as much of her young flesh through her dress as they could steal, she was something different. The first song I ever saw her do was 'Lovers' Concerto', a piece of ripped-off Bach with lyrics about rain falling gently into meadows. But it wasn't the song. It wasn't even her—it was the voice. There was a strength in it, an intensity which transformed what she was singing into something personal. From where I watched it was difficult to associate that voice with the slender girl, forlorn in the revolving lights.

She had clung on to the microphone with her left hand and during each chorus she made a circular waving gesture with her right. It was as though someone had told her to project and this was her attempt: it was mechanical, unnatural, awful. From the rear of the hall, behind that sea of faces bobbing up at her, I wasn't sure if she was waving or drowning.

Ann. Candi. Whoever she was, I had got to know her after that evening. Had thought I got to know her. For a time I had even thought that what I felt for her was more than sexual attraction and sympathy: when I had been sure I had gone beyond feeling that much ever again. There had been a pale brightness in her flesh that had sung when I touched it; a glow of truth around her eyes. But they had changed more than her name.

And with every taste of success she had needed me less and less. There were others with more to offer than an ex-cop trying to make a half-way honest living as a private eye. Maybe she really did prefer the faster cars, the quicker cash, the glittering flotsam of the lush life: maybe she just got fed up with the sad stink of second-rate hotel bedrooms which clung to me like a second skin.

Whatever it was, she had no longer wanted to know. Whenever I had phoned her she had been out; if she ever phoned me, which I doubted, I had not been in. Apart from the odd occasions when I switched on the radio and by some accident heard her unmistakable voice, what relationship we had had was finished.

Ann. Candi. Whoever she was.

Or so I had thought.

Last night she had phoned me once more. I was in. At home, late, sitting in the room with the lights out and a bottle of Southern Comfort losing its fight for survival. I was miserable. I was lonely. I had just spent seven hours tailing some rich sexpot who was supposed to be providing me with evidence so that her even richer old man could divorce her without losing too much in the settlement. Sexpot! The way she passed her time would have brought the Archbishop of Canterbury out in dimples. Maybe she was on a losing streak. Her and me both.

There wasn't even a late-night movie on TV. Nothing to do but drink myself to sleep. Then the phone had rung. There was no doubting her voice at the other end of the line. But changed again, frightened, nervous, more like the little girl who was trying so hard to steady herself in the spotlight. I saw her once more on stage as she spoke to me, her right arm circling in that same despairing gesture.

She wanted me to go and see her. As soon as possible. It was important but she couldn't say why over the phone. She wasn't in London any more: she was in Nottingham. She gave me the address. I said I would catch the evening train the next day. Today. Before putting the phone down she said she was really grateful. From her tone she might even have meant it. I poured myself another drink.

The house corresponded to the number I had written in my notebook. All those years of police procedure had left me a methodical man. Her name was typed in red on white card and had been slipped into the greening brass holder: Candi Carter. Obviously, she had an agent with an alliterative ear. There was a large bell-push alongside the card which looked as though it wouldn't work. It didn't. The ornamented wooden door appeared to be unlocked. It was.

The light inside the hallway came on, to my surprise, and I saw the name cards were repeated on one wall. This time the bell-pushes looked more functional. The only thing was, no one answered. I kept ringing and looked at the cards; there were four of them and Candi's was the third from the bottom. I figured out that her flat would be on the third floor. It was decisions like that which kept me working—just. I stopped pressing the bell and climbed the carpeted stairs.

I didn't need the light on the landing to show me that her flat door was painted white, but it did show me another of those cards on the wall beside it. Cheaper by the dozen. I rapped the paint gently with my knuckles: the door gave slightly.

Immediately I felt a coldness creep across the tops of my thighs and into my stomach. Doors. You never knew what was behind them: or who.

I had a sudden vision of a man entering a room. A detective, in a movie, Frank Sinatra or someone like that. As though a projector inside my head was flashing out the clip for me. Anyway, he walked through the door into this room.

It was richly furnished: *objets d'art* were everywhere. Along one wall there was an expensive-looking Japanese screen; in a central position the statue of a naked boy in black marble rose up out of the carpet. The carpet—deeply piled, warm to the bare foot, but no longer warm to what now lay upon it. A body, outstretched, mutilated; someone had attacked him with a blade, had ploughed drunkenly across him as though were would be no tomorrow. Deep ruts crossed and recrossed the flesh and along the edges the blood that had been thrown up had started to coagulate.

I shook my head clear, but the door was still there in front of me. Still slightly ajar. I didn't like stepping through doors, especially when something gave me an uneasy feeling about what was going to be on the other side. Sure, in my job I had been through a lot of doors even though I hadn't taken too kindly to the idea beforehand. But I still didn't like being sapped from behind; I still didn't like being shot at; I still didn't like finding dead bodies—especially when some maniac had carved them up with all the finesse of a crazed Jackson Pollock.

I could always turn around and get right away, walk back down the stairs and along the streets to the station. I walked back along the landing, put out the light and came back to the door. No sense in making an easy target. I stood on one side of the door frame and edged the door open with my foot. Nothing happened.

Stepping lightly into the doorway, I pushed the door right back as far as it would go. There was nobody standing behind it. Quickly I went into the room, shut the door and felt for the light switch.

I found myself staring at the carpet. There was nothing there—except carpet. Everything in the room was white, except for a long settee and an armchair, both of which were in black leather. The room was big, big enough to take a baby grand piano. Above the fireplace there was a blown-up, framed photograph of Candi, which I recognised as one of her publicity shots.

Candi herself was sitting in the leather armchair. Like the room, she was in white. Her dress was simple and beautiful, revealing the curve of her breasts before taking them into a swath of satin. Her arms along the sides of the chair were quite still. Her hair was very precisely pulled back off her face and held in a plain black velvet band. She was very pale. Only the thinnest trickle of blood disturbed the whiteness of her face as it traced a slightly meandering path from the corner of her mouth down on to her chin. From there it snaked along her neck and over the top of her right breast until it disappeared beneath her dress.

Very still; very pale; very dead. And very beautiful.

I don't know how long I stood there, in the centre of that room, looking at her. But when I could look no longer I went to the chair and slipped my hand down between her back and the leather upholstery. There was yet a trace of warmth in her body which gave a lie to the iciness of her skin. When I drew back my hand the fingers were sticky with blood. Whoever had shot her had been careful and close; if he—or she—had used a larger weapon half of her back would have been blown away.

I went into the bathroom. In the mirror I caught a glimpse of a grey face and a pair of empty eyes that I might have claimed for mine. If I had to. I washed my hands slowly, easing the blood from the corners of my nails into the flow of warm water. Then I looked around the flat.

Either she had kept little that was personal there, or whoever had been before me had cleared the place out thoroughly. Apart from the photograph, the cards outside—and her body—there was nothing to show that the flat was hers. Although there were two things which might have been Candi's.

The first was a single record on the stereo turntable. It had no label and I guessed that it was a test pressing. I had never heard the song before, but I knew the voice. Her voice. I sat on the settee across the room from her and listened to her disembodied voice as it filled the room. As I did so the crazed line of blood darkened on her face, so that it looked like a crack in a piece of fine china. I stared at it and listened to the sound of someone who had passed beyond whatever help she had thought I could give her.

'Baby, I reach for you in dreams,
The more I reach for you it seems
As though these hands of mine just pass right through you.

I try in vain to kiss your lips,
But find your dear face only slips
Past my reach and I just can't get close to you.

Oh, tell me lover, why must it be so?
When I want to come to you,
Why must you tell me to go?

The ghost of your love haunts me now,
And I will always remember how
You breathed a new kind of life into me.'

It was some time before I got up and lifted the stylus from the tracking groove in which it had stuck. I didn't want to take the record with me; I didn't think I would ever want to listen to it again. I would not be able to hear it without seeing that delicate line of blood disfiguring her face. And I didn't want that: I had memories enough already.

But I did take the second thing I found—or, rather, things. They were in a shoe-box at the bottom of the wardrobe. A number of small, cylindrical pills in a bottle; a quantity of what smelled to be good grass; an envelope with a few round pills, dark red in colour; and, on a piece of paper folded and re-folded into the smallest size possible, what appeared to be a telephone number.

All these I put into my jacket pockets. Then I put out the lights and stepped out into the hallway.

After taking so much care about getting into the room through that door, you might have thought I would have given some attention to the manner in which I went back out of it. You would have been wrong.

As soon as I had set foot outside the flat and into the darkness of the landing whoever was there waiting swung at me. I don't know what with exactly. But I do know that it was hard and cold and it was aimed at my head with a lot of force. I must have sensed something just ahead of the swishing sound behind me for I had begun to leap to one side when the blow landed. Instead of taking away a sizeable section of my scalp, it merely bludgeoned into the side of my head just above the ear and cannoned into my left shoulder with sufficient force to numb it

As I fell to my right I tried to see who it was who was hitting me so lovingly but it was too dark. Too dark to distinguish anything other than the kicking shape which now drove me hard against the wall. I grabbed at the foot, too late, and rolled across the floor, dimly aware that he was above me. This time his boot was more accurate and it caught me under the ribs and sent the breath spinning out of me. I reached up again and succeeded in catching hold of an arm.

The wrong arm.

The right one came crashing down on top of me and whatever it was wielding found its target properly. The top of my head felt as though it was being slit in two like a brittle coconut. I had a last thought about hanging on to the arm at all costs and then I became one with the darkness.

When I came round my head still felt brittle. I must have let go of his arm, though, for there was no one else on the landing. Hesitantly, I levered myself to my feet and leant against the wall.

I really didn't need to feel in my pockets, but I did anyway. It was wasted effort all right. The things I had taken from the shoe-box had gone. If it wouldn't have hurt my head too much I would have shaken it. Instead I tried to keep it very steady as I walked down the stairs and out into the street. Maybe I would find the right size dustbin, and then I could just throw it away with all the other old trash.

I had only walked some fifty yards down the street when I saw the car parked against the kerb, waiting.

-2-

It was not a marked car. It just sat by the kerb, sidelights on, waiting. The two men inside the car looked big from their shapes through the windscreen; when they got out of the car they looked even bigger.

They got out slowly as though they had all the time in the world, as though they knew that I wasn't going to make a run for it. For what? A bullet in the back? No way. They didn't have guns: I didn't have a gun. It was just a cosy little English arrest in a quiet English street.

Well, almost. Even the ordinary English cop isn't exactly like Dixon of Dock Green any more. Perhaps they can't afford to be. Perhaps they didn't know I wasn't carrying a gun. I mean, how could they?

They came up on either side of me, two men in their late thirties, in raincoats. They moved slowly, confidently, without bothering to speak. They didn't need to—they had done this before.

One of them wore a hat: he hit me first. Hard, with the flat of his outstretched hand into my solar plexus. While I was bending forward the one without a hat rabbit-punched me from what seemed to be a great height. Then one of them tripped me. I don't know which one—by this stage in the proceedings I had lost interest in their wardrobe.

Together they hauled me from the pavement where I was quietly retching and slung me into the back seat of the car. Somehow they had managed to slip the handcuffs on me during the same brief moments. Real professionals!

With timing like that they should have been in variety. Except that variety had already died when I was a kid and God knows when that was. If you were a variety artist you either died with it or television embalmed you shortly after. That is, unless you are a genius like Max Wall and even he's had to go straight.

I glanced at the two cops and wondered if that was something they'd had to do lately. For a moment I even thought I might ask them. But I decided against it—I had been hit enough for one evening.

With little fantasies like that we keep ourselves going.

The one with the hat was sitting in the front of the driver's side, making notes in a little book. I wondered what resemblance his report bore to what had happened. I might as well have wondered who would be the next British heavyweight champion of the world. The warm-blooded one sat beside me; he was taking more than his fair share of room, but it wasn't because he wanted to hold my hand.

'That house you came out of. We heard there's a singer called Candi Carter living there. You know her?'

Easy now, Mitchell, I thought to myself, you've got to play this one cool. I looked up at him. 'Maybe,' I said.

He wrenched hard at the cuffs and scraped several layers of dirt, sweat and skin off my wrists. Before he slapped my face.

Very good, I thought to myself. Very cool.

He repeated the question, his mouth close to mine. He stank of beer, stale cigarettes, hamburgers with sour onions.

'I used to know her.'

'Meaning?'

'Meaning I don't know her any more. Meaning she's dead. Now nobody knows her.'

His partner turned round from the front seat and stopped writing fiction. I must have said something interesting.

'What kind of dead?' he asked.

'The usual.'

He looked as though he was going to clip me as well, but his intentions were interrupted by the car radio calling for a report on his position. Tersely he told them where he was and what I had said about Candi. The station told him to wait until more officers came, then bring me in.

While we were waiting, we got real friendly. They even asked me my name: just when I had begun to think that they didn't care. The only thing was—when I told them I got the impression that they had known all along.

The central police station was quite a new building. Outside and in the fabric was impressive, strongly made and clean. The rooms were sparsely furnished with upright chairs which never did seem to be the right height, pearl-grey filing cabinets, wooden tables barely marked by cup rings and cigarette burns. On the walls there were the usual posters: missing since last July; tickets for the Police Ball; wanted in connection with the murder of a publican in Sutton-in-Ashfield; measures to take against potato blight; watch out, there's a thief about; dull it isn't.

Men in uniform and out of it moved quietly around the building. Policemen doing their job with as much seeming efficiency as men who are worked too hard and paid too little can muster. From room to room they went, sifting the steadily gathering detritus of the city night: a group of drunken youths with coloured scarves tied to their wrists and plastic-flowered pennants on their coats; the first few of the many prostitutes whose soiled bodies would spend the remainder of their working hours in custody; a couple of lads—not older than fifteen—who had been caught breaking into a tobacconist's shop and beating up the owner when he discovered them; a sad queen who had announced his desires a little too loudly and obviously in the public lavatories of the city centre; and the car thieves, the junkies, the down-and-outs.

You couldn't work in the midst of all this without it getting to you. It didn't matter how clean the building was, how new. The corruption of man was old, old, old.

And yet it was not the petty and the unsuccessful who really corrupted. It was those who made it big outside the law and stayed outside it. Easy money and good times just for the asking. Just for turning an eye in the other direction, just for overlooking a piece of evidence, just for picking up a guy and shaking him down hard. A guy walking along a darkened street one November night, a guy who had been looking at the murdered body of a girl he might once have loved, who had been sapped and booted, then hit and hit again.

The room I was sitting in held no surprises. By the door stood a uniformed constable, his mind firmly on other things. Across the table from me a C.I.D. Inspector was checking through my statement. The only sound was a steady hum which seemed to come from nowhere and fill the heavy air.

Since the law had found out that what I had told them about Candi being dead was true they had been treating me a little more carefully and a lot more seriously. The two heavies who had picked me up first had obviously been working on a quick tip-off that I might be worth turning over and a request that they did it hard. But murder made it all different. Maybe.

At least the Inspector had asked my name first.

A call to Tom Gilmour at West End Central had brought me a certain credence, even a little grudging respect. What it didn't bring me was any love. Cops who left the force and opened newsagents shops they could understand, cops who crossed the line and went bent full-time even, but a cop who wanted to do the same work by himself and probably for less money . . . ?

He had finished reading my statement—for the second time. A methodical man: or maybe he just didn't read too well.

He was not far off retiring age, I guessed. Maybe he even had a little calendar somewhere on which he ticked off the final months. He had a small moustache of the kind that had long since gone out of fashion, one eye was slightly runny and he dabbed at it from time to time with a handkerchief. He looked tired: he had been tired for a long time now.

When he spoke his voice sounded far away, beneath the hum that still permeated the room.

'You've made a full statement, Mr Mitchell, and what we have been able to check so far substantiates it. The marks which the police doctor found on your body correspond to your assertion that you were attacked by persons unknown after leaving Miss Carter's flat.'

The phrases peeled from his lips like dead skin.

'You say that you were shocked by what you found in the flat and did not think to call the police from there. That you were on your way downstairs for help when you were struck from behind. All that is not necessarily admitted by us to be so. Not yet. So you see, Mr Mitchell, it is most likely that we shall want to speak to you again.

'However, I can see no reason for holding you here any longer at present and you may return to London as soon as you wish. I must ask you to report to West End Central police station in the morning and to keep them informed of your daily whereabouts until further notice.'

He paused and looked up at me, till a stream of rheumy fluid caused him to turn his head away.

'You have been very co-operative. Thank you for that. There is still a train for London tonight, if you don't mind travelling up with the mail. If you ask at the desk, there may be a patrol car going towards the station. You could get a lift.'

I hesitated for a moment, thinking he was about to stand up. He was not. When I turned again at the door, he was still sitting behind the table, notebook open in front of him, eyes open, staring at the blankest of bare walls.

I went out of the station without talking to anyone. I had had enough rides in police cars, had spoken to enough policemen, had seen enough of humanity for one night.

I crossed the empty square where the fountain no longer played and headed for the railway station. It was still cold.

There was a guy once who told his wife that sleep was the balm of hurt minds. Well, it didn't do too much for him and, since she turned out to be some kind of insomniac, it didn't help her much either. As for me, I usually find it soothes the body and sometimes brings a pleasant memory or two. Usually some old movie with a heart of gold. But not this night.

In my dream I awoke in the small, plain room of what had to be a motel. Dressed and went outside. It was night, I guess, but there appeared to be a lot of light. I suppose I should have looked for a full moon, but it didn't seem important at the time. Maybe it wasn't.

I walked through this batch of scrubby trees towards a tall, battered-looking house. My movements were slow, as if stepping through invisible waves. Inside the front door I hesitated, not knowing at first which way to go: there was a staircase leading up to the floors above and another which went down to the cellar.

Then I knew which way I was to go; knew also that I didn't want to go that way; didn't want to follow those steps down to the basement. But something drew me down, something which left me no choice.

A door. Again, a door. A door which creaked slowly, then swung wide. I wasn't aware of stepping inside, but somehow I had.

And suddenly it flailed at me. It. Something. Something large and whirling, like a giant bird, flapping its black wings across my face. Then a blade, huge, shining strangely and swinging at my body.

I threw myself at the thing, whatever it was. My hands touched nothing but sticky, cloying dampness. Strangely swinging—shining—a single bare light bulb. A face. An old woman's face approaching me, smiling, toothlessly, invitingly. The mouth opening till I could see the pulp of the gums seeming to swallow me up. The sickly-sweet stink of over-ripe fruit was everywhere.

Then the face was that of a young man, high cheek bones, small dark eyes staring. I summoned all my strength into one punch and drove my fist at that face. As I did so it changed into the mask-like features of Candi, the line of dried blood a hair-line crack in the white plaster. I tried to pull back the punch but it was too late.

My knuckles drove through the unearthly surface of Candi's face, passing through bone and flesh as though delving into some strange fruit.

From somewhere, Candi's voice singing:

'The more I reach for you it seems
As though these hands of mine just pass right through
    you.'

I shouted and shouted for release but no sound came, only a blackness into which those flailing wings disappeared until they tore and tore at the inside of my brain.

At some time my nightmare must have ended and allowed me to sleep, though when I eventually woke it was still imprinted on my mind. When I could lay in bed with it no longer I got up and pulled on some clothes and walked unsteadily into the kitchen.

What I needed now was a little honest routine. I remember reading in one of Chandler's Philip Marlowe novels that he began the day by making coffee in a set and practised way, each morning the same. It also said somewhere that Marlowe liked to eat scrambled eggs for breakfast but as far as I can recall it didn't say how he did that.

What I did was this. I broke two eggs into a small saucepan, added a good-size chunk of butter, poured in a little off the top of a bottle of milk and finally ground in some sea salt and black pepper. Then I just stirred all of this over a medium heat, while I grilled some bacon to go with it.

They say that a sense of achievement is good for a man.

After breakfast I had a bath and examined my bruises. Then I made a second pot of coffee and thought about opening the morning's mail. From the nature of the envelopes it didn't seem too good an idea. Then somebody rang the doorbell. I wasn't sure how good an idea answering that would be, but I went anyway.

She was standing a couple of paces back from the doorway, smiling a smile which would have thawed out the frostiest of November mornings. Her face was beautiful and I stared at it for what seemed a long time. A fine face, without a disfiguring line of blood: Candi's face.

–3–

I stared at her for what seemed a long while. Mouth, eyes, bone structure: all the same. The hair was the identical colour, but was cut shorter and turned up just above her shoulders. When I took in her whole body I could see she was shorter by several inches and when my eyes swept back to her face they found it lacking the hardness that Candi's had developed.

She had frowned at the coldness and surprise in my stare. Until she guessed the reason and then she smiled at me again. I should have known then that smiles like that meant trouble for men like me. But then I never did learn that kind of thing until it was too late.

'Hello, Scott. It's a long time since we saw each other.' She wrinkled her nose in a way her sister would never have done. 'Are you going to invite me in?'

By way of answer I stepped aside and watched her pass by me, on into the living room.

'Coffee?' I asked.

'Please. White with sugar, if that's all right.'

It was and when I brought it through from the kitchen she was reading the newspaper, opened out at its centre pages.

'They don't waste much time, do they?'

I put down the two cups on the small glass table and sat beside her. The middle of the spread was taken up with a large photograph of Candi Carter exposing as much flesh as her manager could persuade her would be good for her record sales. She was draped around the mast of a yacht, wearing the smallest of small bikinis. On the pants, slightly to the right of centre, were her initials, one C running through the other. Her mouth was parted and her tongue poked out, as it were, provocatively. Meat for the world's meat market: now dead meat. Dead at the world's table.

The inch-deep headlines to the left of the page shouted out her murder. The text underneath said nothing in great detail, while it suggested a good deal more. Had she been waiting for a lover? Had she known her killer? What was the mystery of the woman in white alone in an anonymous flat?

The right hand side listed the facts of her career—from teenage band singer in the provinces to international recording star— and gave the names of her currently available albums. For those who wanted to climb aboard another cult wagon.

'Tasteful, isn't it? Someone must have worked hard through the night to put all this . . .' she held the paper up between two fingers as though it might be contagious . . . 'muck together!'

She stood up and flung the pages across the room. I looked up into her face, looking for the saving smile. This time she could not manage it. The tears fought their way past her will into the corners of her eyes, then sprung out on to her cheeks.

'Scott!'

The cry was despairing: as though she could hold in her anguish and her fears no longer. She half-fell, half-dived down into my arms and I was holding her tight, tight; her breath was warm against the inside of my neck and her face was damp and small against my shoulder. I sat like that until her breathing eased and the chest that pumped a plea through me had calmed; I sat and stroked her hair and all the time part of me wanted to be more than a million miles away.

But when I had stepped aside at the door to let her through I had already made my move.

I took her by the arms and held her away from me.

'Would you like a drink?'

She wiped at her face with a tissue, yellow and already over-used. Again the smile.

'Maybe another cup of coffee. If you've got the time.'

Time. I had all the time in the world and then some. Time to live and time to die: time to get suckered into a few more beatings: time to be a fall-guy for murder even. What I didn't have time for wasn't worth having. And what I sensed Vonnie was going to offer wasn't worth having either.

'Why were you there, Scott? It says in the paper that you found the . . . the body. I didn't think you had been seeing her. Any more than I had.'

I was putting the coffee down as she said it and something about that last sentence made me spill it over into the saucers. Only slightly, but enough to notice. Why did she need to tell me that? I knew they hadn't been on speaking terms for years.

I went back into the kitchen to find something to wipe up the mess. Methodical. Neat, tidy . . . and suspicious. I'd been in this business too long.

'She phoned me the night before last. Said she needed help— she wouldn't say what over the phone.' I went up to see her and . . .'

Vonnie looked at me: 'It must have been horrible!'

'Dead bodies are never nice. Especially when they were people you knew.' She was stirring her coffee absent-mindedly. 'What do you want, Vonnie? Why did you come round?'

She sat back, a little startled, and stopped playing with her spoon.

'Scott! That doesn't sound very nice. It makes it seem as if I wanted something from you.' A pause. A smile. 'I suppose I do . . . a little sympathy. I mean, you used to know her so well, and . . .'

'. . . And I just happened to find her body.'

The room struck very cold. I wanted to ask more questions but she was too close and the memory of her crying in my arms was too fresh. I got up and walked over to the sideboard; poured myself a whisky; drank it down. When it hit my stomach I spoke.

'If you wanted sympathy what was wrong with your husband? All you had to do was roll over in bed and there he was. Instead you get up early, make yourself up smart, wear your most appealing clothes—while allowing for a little sisterly mortification in honour of the recently deceased—and get round here hotfoot so as to weep your pretty little tears all over my morning coffee. Why, Vonnie? Why?'

At first I thought she might be going to start wailing all over again, then I thought she might try and smile her way out of it. But she was good. She stood straight up and came right at me.

'Look, Scott The first I knew of Ann's death was when I went downstairs early this morning and picked the newspaper up out of the hall. Nobody else had thought to tell me, though I suppose there was no reason why they should and I can't think who would have done it anyway. I bring the paper back upstairs and then I find out she's been murdered and that you, of all people, found her body. Martin's still in bed sleeping—he had a late night. So I got dressed, left him a note, and came round to see you. I wanted someone to talk to, damn it!'

'And more . . .' I suggested.

'All right! And more.' She sat down, but she wouldn't let me off the hook of her stare. 'I want you to take the case.'

'The case?'

'Yes, the case. Isn't that what you call it?'

'Call what?'

'What you do.'

'Vonnie, all I do is try to make a living from walking round with my feet dragging in the sewers and my head even lower. If that's what you call a case, then I guess that's what I do.'

'Then if that's what you do, I'll pay you to do it.'

I went over to the easy chair and lowered myself into it, slowly. My bruises from the night before still hurt me; my head was singing out inside with warnings and snatches of old songs about dying; when I looked over at her still young body I felt suddenly old.

'I'll say it again, Vonnie. Why?'

'Why? Come on, Scott, I thought you were the detective. I'm asking you because you were the one who found her and because you used to know her. Know her well.' The look cut through me. 'Surely if anyone can find out what happened, then it's you.'

I hauled myself forward in the chair. 'Maybe. But why not just let the po . . .'

'. . . The police don't exactly have a very good record for solving murders at the moment, do they? And besides, there may be things they wouldn't turn up, things they . . . Oh, Scott, I don't know. I just feel that if you were looking as well then there might be more chance of getting to the truth.'

'The truth?'

'Yes, the truth.'

I had a horrible feeling that we were about to go into one of those Marx Brothers routines again. Only I had no doubt in my mind who was Groucho and that the dope who was being fooled by the dollar bill on the end of a piece of thread was me. The thing was I couldn't see the face on the bill and I didn't want to grab the thread yet for fear of breaking it.

'If I agree, there's the money. Your old man may not like the idea of his hard-earned cash going into my pockets.'

'Don't worry about that. I have some money of my own. I won't even tell Martin.'

I looked at her quizzically. For a girl who had come through my front door under the pretext of being all dewdrops and roses, she was rapidly becoming decidedly thorny.

'Martin wouldn't care. He's too wrapped up in his own business to pay much attention to what I do.'

It was said in a matter-of-fact way, without a trace of sarcasm or bitterness. But it was said. I filed it away under possibly useful information and went on.

'I thought he was a librarian. I'd never thought of that as a totally absorbing occupation.'

'He is a librarian. But lately he's gone into partnership with somebody in the book trade. Rare editions, special bindings, that sort of thing. They do a lot of export trade. So, since he began doing that, he's been twice as busy. Some weeks I hardly see him at all. But . . .' She shrugged her shoulders and twitched her nose again. '. . . as long as he's happy . . .'

Vonnie's voice trailed off. If she was playing for sympathy, then she sure as hell wasn't going to get any. Only I didn't know if she was—playing, I mean. I didn't know what she was doing. I just wondered if she did.

She was sitting down again and one of her smooth hands was holding the sleeve of my shirt.

'Will you help?'

Now was the time to be definite: now was the time to say no. To look her back straight between those smiling, pleading eyes and say no—politely, yet firmly—and show her back out of the door.

Instead I heard myself saying, 'Fifty pounds as a retainer. Then ten pounds a day, plus legitimate expenses.'

She said, nothing. After a few seconds I got up and went over to the filing cabinet that served as desk and flower pot stand. Not that I had any flowers. But the stand gave the room an air of hope, at least. At least, that's what I thought. Sometimes.

I gave Vonnie her receipt and took her cheque. It was made out in a small, neat hand to Scott Mitchell. It was for fifty pounds only and at the bottom, in the right hand corner, was the signature—Veronica Innes.

When she had gone I had got two-thirds of the way through making yet another pot of coffee before I realised that I didn't want any more. I sat on the stool in the kitchen and looked idly at the pattern on the tiles. Martin's name was Lambden. Her married name was Lambden. So why had she signed the cheque with her maiden name?

-4-

The room as at the back of an amusement arcade in Old Compton Street. From where I was standing, idly playing pin-ball and trying to look as though that was how I usually spent my lunch times, it appeared to be locked. At least, when a greasy looking drifter in a soiled afghan had tried it there had been no response. And there was no light showing through the glass above the door. It might have been the middle of the day, but if Maxie was in there he would have needed some light. In his moleish world he needed every bit of light he could get.

I pulled back on the table and tried to jerk the ball on to some promising numbers. All I got was tilt. Still, I wasn't the only poor player around. The guy across the room wasn't having much luck either.

Worn leather bum-freezer jacket, leather cap on his head, gloves stuck into his trouser belt. He sure was intent upon his pin-ball machine. Or was it the fact that he would be able to see me reflected in the glass behind, just as I could see him?

Whatever the case, he sure as hell couldn't play.

Someone else tried Maxie's door. They must have been in some kind of a hurry, for they kicked it real hard when it wouldn't open. I figured the noise gave me an excuse to look round.

When I saw him I wondered that the door had not given way. I had seen big men before but he was ridiculous. He had to be all of six foot eight and he weighed enough to start a whole new class of heavyweights. He wasn't wearing over-much considering it was still what most normal people would consider cold; the only concession to the temperature was a brown woolly hat that was pulled down tight over his skull. He was as black as ebony and looked as if his idea of a little light exercise might be tearing telephone booths in two.

I noticed that my fellow pin-ball devotee was looking at him in a rather awe-stricken way, too, but I guessed there was nothing surprising about that.

He didn't bother to look down on either of us; just once back at the door, then out.

I wondered whether Maxie would be glad or sad he had missed his visitor. Maybe he'd be sad. Perhaps he was one of those happy giants you read about who are just like happy children inside: full of friendly fun. Only they often don't know their own strength.

I went back to my game; my interested companion went back to his. A few Greeks drifted in and then drifted out again: waiters without a table to serve: hairdressers without a head to work on. A young woman ran in, looked round breathlessly, swore once, then ran out. Apart from that it was quiet. Only the click and occasional buzz of the machines.

When Maxie came back from what I guessed was his lunch-time drink, he shambled through the brightly lit arcade without apparently noticing either of us. Or anything else. His wispily balding head stuck out from the dirty collar of his coat like a disease. The scalp was pitted and scabbed under the few strands of greying hair. His puffed-up eyes were almost totally closed and little light showed from the slits that remained. Maxie was a walking sore, but he had worked this patch since before I had been a copper on the beat. He knew everything that happened in and around his arcade, whatever it might appear to the contrary. When he shuffled round, giving change or jabbing at machines with a screwdriver, he heard more than anyone thought he could, saw when others thought him almost blind.

It wasn't only the coloured prostitutes from South London who plied their trade in the evenings inside the warmth of the arcade. There were the pushers, also, using the freedom of movement that the place afforded. An envelope, a small roll of plastic, a phial: here anything could change hands for the right price.

And the coppers on the beat kept on walking by, eyes averted, hands outstretched. Nothing changed.

I gave Maxie time to scratch himself, then I went in. He hadn't seen me for a long time but he recognised me straight away. I couldn't tell whether or not he was pleased. Not that it would have mattered. Only the notes inside my wallet did that.

"Ello, Mitchell. Long time since you was this way. Thought you might 'ave give it all up. Become a salesman or somethin'.'

His cackling laugh broke into a spluttering cough, which he quenched with a dirty piece of rag from his coat pocket.

'Only one of us is a salesman, Maxie.'

'You're right there, Mitchell. No one would buy anything from an ex-copper.' He laughed at his own joke and shuffled his feet. For a moment I thought he was going to break into a dance. Instead he came towards me and I took a step backwards to avoid the smell.

'It's information I want, Maxie. Not a close-up. Christ! When did you last have a bath?'

'Bath, Mitchell?' he chortled. 'Bath? Why, none of me friends would know me.'

'Okay, Maxie.' I reached for my wallet and laid it on the table in front of him. Immediately he stopped laughing; money was no laughing matter.

'Anything I can do, Mitchell, you know me.' The words sounded like claws.

I took out one note, then another. I held fast to them with my fingers pressed down on to the dirt of the table top.

'If I wanted to get a steady supply of dope, where would I go?'

'Well, that depends, don't it. I mean there's all kinds of dope nowadays. Depends how much money you got, too. But if you come in about ten tonight, then I'll . . .'

I reached across the table and lifted him off the ground by the collar of his coat. It was like running your fingers into thick grease. I pushed him away against the wall.

'You heard me, Maxie. I said a steady supply. Not a quick jump from one of your friendly neighbourhood pushers that you're busy getting a cut from. Good stuff, clean and reliable. Delivered quietly and respectably and without any awkward questions being asked. Maybe amphetamines, maybe something harder. Maybe heroin. I'm not sure.'

He had pushed himself back from the far wall and was wheezing breath all over the table: but his tiny eyes were focused on the notes. I added another two. Already that was two days of Vonnie's money I had spent and I hadn't started yet.

He didn't want to tell me but he didn't want the notes to find their way back into my wallet either.

'It's difficult. Things are changing. There's a lot of new muscle about. People are getting eased out and others are moving in. Some of the small-time blokes who use my place have stopped coming. Someone is out to tighten up on the market.'

Maxie looked up at me and although I could not see into his eyes I knew that they were worried. Even frightened.

The notes were on their way back inside the wallet and I was on my way to the door.

'Wait. Give me a day. Come by again, say tomorrow. Around closing time. I'll do what I can for you.'

The last promise was accompanied by an outstretched, dirty hand. I put one five pound note into it and watched the fingers close round it as though they were starving.

'The rest tomorrow, Maxie. If you've got the information.'

I went out through the door. My friend in the leather jacket was no longer to be seen. Half way to the entrance I thought of something and went back.

Maxie did not appear to have moved. Maybe he was drinking. Maybe not

'Someone called to see you while I was waiting. About seven foot of Negro, all sewn together in one neat package. Anyone you know?'

This time I didn't need to see his eyes to know that he was afraid. The grubby fingers tightened round the note and screwed it tight into the palm of his hand.

For a split second I almost felt sorry for him: then I went out.

When I got out on to the street I saw the guy who had been playing pin-ball sitting across the way drinking coffee. He tried very hard to look innocently at the passers-by and not to notice me. I just wondered who was paying him and if they knew what a cheap deal they were getting for their money.

My office was in Covent Garden. It had been there in the days of the vegetable market and when that had been moved out so that the site could be redeveloped I sort of got left behind. Somebody gave the orders to somebody else and all around me old buildings were sent crashing to the ground to make way for new bomb sites.

I guess the building which housed my office they left because it looked as if it was going to fall down of its own accord. But it hadn't yet. Though there were days when I wished it would; as if sending the bricks and mortar and glass of that office smashing to the ground would somehow release me from the web I had wrapped myself up in. Whereas all it would do would be to take me with it.

Today I had a drink and even then things didn't look any better. I climbed up the stairs to the first floor and looked gloomily at the chipped paint of my name on the door. I gave an involuntary jump as the phone bell started to ring from inside the office. I took out my key and put it into the lock. I didn't turn it. The phone still rang. I removed the key and put it back in my pocket.

When I got downstairs to the front door the bell was still ringing.

By the time I got to Sandy I had swallowed several more scotches and was feeling none the better for it. But at least things had stopped ringing in my ears.

She came to the door of her flat and let me in. She didn't look surprised and she didn't look particularly pleased either. Just stepped back out of the way to let me in. I put the half-bottle of whisky I had just bought down on the table beside the bed. Sandy went back over to the dressing table and continued to put on her make-up. I went into the small kitchen, brought back two glasses, poured two generous shots, put one on the dressing table top and took the other over to the bed. I lay across it and looked at her.

Ten years ago she had been a slight figure ducking back into doorways, avoiding my approaches as I patrolled the streets. One evening she had been thrown out by her pimp; she had not been bringing in enough money. Not just thrown out, though. He had beaten her up, leaving bruises as deep as they were colourful all over her body—and a three-inch cut alongside her right ear which he had made with his razor.

I had found her, crawling on her hands and knees along the gutter, her face a mask of blood, grime and tears. Still she had had the strength to spit into my face.

I took her back to someone I knew would look after her and went looking for her pimp. At three in the morning I found him in a West Indian drinking club in Paddington. There were too many of his friends there so I waited until gone five, when he came out with two of them. They had walked around the corner towards their car, laughing into the morning air. It was just starting to get light and they saw me moving towards them but even so it was some while before they realised who I was. One of them turned and ran. I let him go.

The one I wanted stopped and reached inside his overcoat pocket for what I guessed was his razor. His companion raced for the car. He reached the door a fraction of a second before me:

enough time to get the key in the lock. I flung him back across the pavement and into the wire fencing that ran alongside a used-car lot. As he bounced back off it I caught him in the middle of the back with my boot and he cannoned into it again.

He began to slump down to the floor and I turned to face the razor which streaked before my eyes. I shot up an arm and knocked it high and lunged in beneath it. My right fist hit something hard, drew back and hit again. This time it punched against something softer, like an eye. He shouted and swore and the hand holding the razor tried for my face once more. It found the edge of my ear but nothing more. I grabbed upwards with both hands and took hold of his arm on either side of the elbow. Then I brought down the back of the arm, held taut, against the upraised top of my thigh. There was a splintering sound that echoed across the early morning and was followed by a scream of pain.

Behind me I heard his friend trying to get to the car again. Some friend! He was more successful this time and got half of his body inside the front before I grabbed him and pulled. In his fear he clung fast to the steering wheel, while I wrenched his neck backwards. Still he clung. I swung the car door hard. It caught him across the top of his shoulder blade and he let go and dropped to the floor. He fell with his head between the sill and the bottom of the front seat. I swung the door again.

Razor Boy was still holding his right arm and whimpering. I wrenched him round and threw him back against the wire fence. As he flopped back at me I hit him hard under the jaw with the heel of my hand, caught him, turned him and slammed his face against the fence. I held him there while I went through his pockets. There was still over sixty pounds in his wallet. I pushed it down into my jacket and rammed his face hard into the wire with my other hand.

'Right! Now listen and listen good because I'm only going to say this once! If I see you round on my patch any more I'm going to take you in and ram every charge in the book right up your black arse! And that's before I get you alone in the station house with no witnesses and a nice piece of rubber hose. And you can tell the same to any of your friends who have an inkling to carve young girls up just for the fun of it. Understood?'

I jammed his face further into the fence and held it there; when I released him and turned him round the black of his skin was bisected by white lines.

I thought he understood. I hit him again to make sure and walked away.

Now, sitting on the bed drinking another whisky while Sandy finished her eyelashes, I realised that it wasn't really that easy. For one thing I wasn't so young and I probably couldn't do it. For another it didn't work. Any more than the drink did. Any more—I thought, looking at the swell of Sandy's breasts as she raised her arm level with her face—than sex. At least, it only worked for a while.

She sipped at her drink and then ran her tongue along her lower lip. After that occasion when I had found her beaten up she had gone off the streets and gone back home; for a time. But like most girls who start and try to give it all up, she had come back. Older and wiser and less easy to boss around. She got work as hostess in one of the so-called drinking clubs where you got punters to drink coloured water and pay you large sums in return for a promise that you would meet them later round the corner and take them home for a nice time. Then Sandy had discovered that she could earn more as a stripper.

So she spent her days rushing from one tiny cellar to another, with her costume in a tiny leather case. At first she even used to remember which name she was dancing under and where. But then she had realised that it didn't matter. No one was buying her name: they were buying her body—across the haze of the floodlights and through the poorly recorded music. Which was as near to true contact as most of them wanted or dared.

Somewhere along the way we had slept together. After I had stopped being a legitimate cop and she no longer resented me expecting it as fair trade. And when she had lost any thought of charging me as just another customer.

It had been nothing to do with love, nothing to do with any ideas of romance: it was all to do with the needs of the body. And it had worked. We knew we did not have to be suspicious of each other; neither of us wanted more than the other. What we both wanted was pleasure—and relaxation afterwards without feeling soiled by guilt or money.

It had continued to work.

Sandy stood up. She was tall: five eight or nine. She had on a red and black patterned blouse in some see-through kind of silk, a short black skirt that stopped a couple of inches above black boots which came over her knees; her light reddish hair curled down to her breasts at the front and it hung down from below a wide-brimmed black hat which had a band of blue and white beads at the crown. More beads—blue, yellow and white—hung from her neck down her blouse.

I reached up a hand towards her. She smiled and took it in her own.

'Scott Mitchell! You just sat there and watched me taking great care about putting on my make-up. If you think I'm going to get it all messed up just because you decide to feel randy in the middle of the day then you've got another think coming.'

I reached up my other hand and pulled her down. 'That's not what I've got coming—not exactly.'

She kissed me gently at the base of the neck. 'Don't you ever think of anything else?'

I sat up and seriously considered the matter.

'Well, there was a half-hour last Thursday week, when I distinctly recall thinking about steak.'

She pulled the hat off her head and hit me with it. I aimed my mouth for the riot of red hair she had set free and held her fast. We rolled back across the bed and when I raised myself above her the buttons at the front of her blouse had worked themselves undone. I knew her breasts were beautiful but still I never tired of the first sight of them; swelling from lace that looked sizes too small or free and naked. I lowered my head, and ran my tongue between them, pushing the edges of the material away until I could tease her nipples. Tease and bite.

Sandy jumped and gave a small shriek. Then she reached her fingers down towards the swelling inside my trousers. As she began to pull at the top of my zip I looked into her eyes and thought of Vonnie's face that morning. Alternately smiling and pleading. Then I thought of Candi's face last night. Empty. Dead.

Sandy's eyes were green and alive and they didn't want anything more dangerous or confusing than this. I closed my own eyes and kissed her. Hard.

—5—

Like I said, it didn't work for long but at the moment I felt good. I could even take the fact that old bum-freezer was waiting for me round the corner, standing inside a call box holding a non-existent conversation. They were probably the kind he did best.

I could even take the fact that I should have reported in to West End Central and hadn't, which meant that by now the law would be getting a little anxious and starting to shift uneasily on its fat arse. I could take the fact that I found some drugs in Candi's flat and that someone beat the hell out of me to get them back. I could take the look of fear behind the puffed-up slits of Maxie's eyes when I mentioned his visit from Godzilla. Just at that moment I could take a heck of a lot. Some big feller!

The office building still hadn't quite fallen down when I got back to it and the paint was still flaking away. At least the phone had stopped ringing.

When I got into the room the blinds were pulled down and they were waiting. They looked like hoods everywhere. They had the same anonymous clothes, the same anonymous faces, the same anonymous minds. They were all spawned from the same gutter and they never lifted as much as a little toe out of it until the day they lay back down in it again and stopped moving. All they knew about was taking orders and taking what they could get. All they gave in return was a kind of dumb loyalty and a blind, stupid obedience. If they were told to work somebody over good they would do it, no matter what.

And here was I thinking I was ripe to conquer the world: I said the feeling didn't last long.

Then one of them surprised me. He spoke. They were really high class!

'We've got a word for you, Mitchell.'

'I bet it's the same one I've got for you.' I was still feeling pretty snappy, but the slight jolt in his glazed expression told me that was something I might live to regret. If I was lucky.

'You listen! The word is—take a holiday.'

I was going to inform him that was three words but what was the use of asking for trouble when it had already arrived—packaged by arrangement with crombie.

'Is that all? Maybe I'd like to know who's sending me get well messages before I'm ill.'

He moved around the desk. His friend, the strong silent type, stayed where he was—between me and the door. If they hadn't already taken it there was a gun in my desk drawer. Maybe if I waved that at them they would go away and play somewhere else. Though I doubted it; they would only come back later and wave some heat at me.

'Okay, Mitchell, remember what we said. Leave town. Do yourself a big favour. Blow.'

They talked in clichés; they looked like clichés; they hit like clichés. The same old punches to the same old, bruised places. The talkative one swung a fist at my head while his partner aimed another low into my kidneys. I rode the first with a duck of the head and turned towards the second. The fist was bunched like a pound of bananas but it wouldn't do me as much good. I caught at it with both hands and held fast; then I swung up my knee. It hit him full in the groin and he gasped and tried to pull away. I held on and was about to give him the treatment a second time when something like a ton weight descended on me from what seemed to be a great height.

One of them picked me up and sat me in my office chair; the other kicked the chair out from under me. The chair splintered against the wall and I fell to the worn carpet with a thump and a fast loss of breath. The boot struck me in the left shoulder at the right height to numb my arm. To make sure the feeling had gone, they hauled me up by it and threw me down on top of the chair.

This was getting a little too repetitive for comfort. When the kick came in again I grabbed underneath it and hoisted it on its way towards the ceiling. At the same moment I was off the floor and diving into the gut of the hood beside the desk. He caught at my head as it buried itself into the cloth of his overcoat, but couldn't stop the impact. We bounced across the room and I got up fast, trampling on him as many times as I could in the process. I needed to get back to my desk first: I damn near made it.

Maybe next time. Maybe if I can get in a little more practice. Maybe.

The one with chorus-boy ambitions was waiting and he had a nasty-looking piece of piping raised above his shoulder. The nearer it got to my head the nastier it looked. Then I stopped seeing it altogether.

There's this movie called 'The Big Sleep'. I thought about it now; thought about a little guy in the movie called Jones. Jones is little and weedy and looks like a born victim. He gets himself hired to tail the hero around but he isn't very good at it. He gets himself spotted but he sticks to it all the same. Perhaps he needed the money, perhaps it was his pride. Who knows? He stuck to it when he should have gone home to his wife and kids and read a good book—any kind of a book.

Jones got too close at the wrong time. He ended up getting too close to death. He ended up drinking from the wrong cup and getting himself poisoned and then he slept all right. For good.

He was a mug playing a mug's game but I felt sorry for him: like a child trying hard to be a man and not knowing it wasn't worth it.

*   *   *

Bum-freezer hadn't got himself poisoned but he had got himself killed. I found him half-way down the stairs leading out on to the street. He had either been on his way up or on his way out: either way it made no difference. He wasn't going anywhere now. Arms and legs were crumpled at all directions from the break in the stairway. His head couldn't be seen at first, but when I knelt down beside him I saw it tucked down into his body and towards the wall as though it did not want to be hit any more. It was bloody and pulped on one side as though whoever had hit him was in a bad mood and wanted to take it out on something. He just happened to choose bum-freezer's head.

I looked carefully and delicately in his pockets for anything that might be useful. The only thing I found was a card: it read—

James Cook
Car Hire
01.485.7684

I put it in my top pocket and let the corner of his leather jacket fall back into place. In my head I drank a toast to success.

Then I went back to my office to call the police. They beat me to it by three strides. It was Tom Gilmour and he was annoyed. He was even more annoyed when I told him about the body that was cluttering up the stairs in a fine neighbourhood like mine. He even told me that if I touched the body before he got there he would haul my arse into the cells quicker than forked lightning. They should never have sent him on a year's exchange to New York: it's done nothing for his language. Nothing at all.

There was nothing else on Cook to identify him; I guessed that the solitary card had been a mistake. Just one more in a lifetime of mistakes. A short lifetime and probably not a happy one. I wanted to keep that information to myself for a while. If I could find out who had hired him to follow me it might help. Whoever it had been it wasn't the same person who had me warned off, that was sure. He dealt in professionals.

I told Gilmour I had seen him earlier that day and that maybe he was a tail. I told him about my visitors. Not that I could have kept that a secret. The top of my head looked like a launching pad at Cape Canaveral.

'What do you think they wanted? I'm behind with the gas bill. It's a new way of collecting debts: they get these riggers fresh from working in the North Sea and set them to work on dry land. It's more effective than sending reminders printed in red.'

'Listen, stupid! Don't fill my ears full of that wise-cracking shit! Already I could book you for failing to report first thing this morning. You just happen to be a prime suspect on a murder charge or maybe you'd forgotten that sweet fact? Now you've got dead bodies crawling out of the woodwork as though they're going out of style and a lump on your head the size of one of Raquel Welch's tits. You're in no position to make jokes; even if they were funny.'

'Tom, go easy will you? I've had enough pounded out of me for one day without you as well. I thought British cops were always calm and thoughtful and gave out with cups of tea and cigarettes. That time in Manhattan South really stirred you up.'

He sat back in the one remaining intact chair in the office and looked up at me, perched precariously on the edge of the desk. Down on the stairway men were dusting the walls and bannisters for prints and drawing chalk marks around what had been James Cook of James Cook Car Hire. Limited. Very.

Since he had got back from the States, Tom even dressed differently. His suits were somehow fresher, sharper; he walked with a certain bounce which hadn't been there before; he flung words around with disregard for whom they hit and how. He had added to the basic training and experience that had made him a good cop a toughness which threatened to make him a great one. And here was I withholding information and trying to beat him to the punch.

'They were interested in my health. They told me to take a holiday. I tried to argue with them and they didn't like it. That's all.' I looked up at him and saw he was listening, just. 'I don't know where they came from or who sent them. As far as I know I've never seen either of them before. If you like I'll come down and look through some mug shots and see if I can pick them out. Otherwise . . .'

I let the sentence hang and looked at him, waiting for him to interrupt. He wasn't going to so I went on.

'The other guy I told you about. I saw him earlier today, once definitely, twice maybe. I thought he was following me, but I couldn't be sure. The first time I knew he was near the office was after I came round from my visit from the tourist agency. I found him on the stairs. Then I phoned you.'

'What did you take from the body?'

I looked him full in the eye. 'Not a thing.' I stayed looking at him until I thought my integrity was certain. Whatever else I could do, I could lie with the best of them.

Gilmour went to the head of the stairs and looked down. He shouted a couple of orders then came back. Lit a cigarette and sat down again.

'And last night . . . ?'

'Is that your case?'

'Don't give me is that my fucking case! I've gone out to bat for you more times than I can remember. So don't try to get official with me or you might get some of the same.'

I closed my eyes and concentrated for a moment on the dull pain inside my head. I knew that he was right. I said so. I also said, 'It was just like I told the cops in Nottingham, nothing left out. She phoned me the previous evening and asked me to go up. When I got there she was dead. As I came out of the flat I was jumped. It's this week's in thing: hit Mitchell and claim the jackpot.'

Something inside my lump throbbed in sympathy.

'You used to know her, didn't you? Know her well, I mean. Did you tell them that?'

'I told them I knew her: I guess I didn't go into details.'

He grinned. 'I bet you didn't or they would be having a field day. Ex-lover kills mistress in rage of jealousy. Boy, you would be good for a going-over on that one!'

'Tom, I hadn't seen her for what—three, maybe four years. Does it seem likely that I would get a sudden burning desire to go and put a bullet in her back because she was being unfaithful to me?'

'No. But when you're without a better lead that would do.'

'And are they stuck for leads?'

This time he smiled outright. 'How should I know? Like you said, it isn't my case.'

He got up and looked round the shambles of a room. 'Why you left the force for this I'll never know. You don't look as though you make enough to keep yourself in toilet paper. Are you working at the moment?'

The view from the window was one of a partly-demolished wall which had been decorated with technicoloured graffiti and admonitions to the developers to keep out. They needn't have worried: there was no sign of anyone developing anything in a hurry. I looked down at the wall and still wasn't sure if I should tell him. But I did.

'Sure I'm working. Since this morning. Someone paid me a nice retainer to investigate Miss Carter's murder.'

Gilmour let out a low whistle.

'You're really chasing your own tail this time, aren't you? You're going to investigate a murder for which you're your own suspect. Christ. Mitchell! You do things by your own rules and nobody else's, don't you?'

I shrugged my shoulders. I was beginning to think that it was time Tom went. I wanted to be alone with my own stupidity.

'How long do you think they're going to let you wander around free? You think you can solve a case from inside a jail?'

I looked at him and wondered how much he knew that I didn't. I guessed about as much as I had ahead of him. For now, anyway.

'Look. Clear up this mess here then come down to the station. Sign a statement and then get the hell out. But for Christ's sake go easy—or the next time I come to scrape somebody's head off the stairs it will be yours.'

* * *

With that encouraging thought he left. If that's the way your friends think about you maybe you didn't have much of a chance. I picked a piece of broken wall mirror up from the floor and surveyed my head. I wished I hadn't bothered. Then I knelt, down and looked at the pieces of my shattered chair to see if they could be stuck together. To do that would have been a gesture of hope too: and about as useful as writing on brick walls before they were pulled down.

I left the pieces and went out without bothering to lock the door behind me. The only thing worth taking was the gun and that was now in my pocket.

-6-

The street was a street in North London like any other. Two storey villa houses with small front gardens and stubby privet hedges. At intervals along the pavement there were plane trees, their broad, angular leaves spreading over your head as you walked. Outside number forty-seven was parked a black Humber Hawk, beside which a small girl was standing with a bucket almost as big as herself. She was about to wash down the car and it must have seemed to her like scaling Everest. Except that she was probably used to it.

Inside the windscreen a small card poked up with the same printing as the one I had found in bum-freezer's pocket. Now I knew his name I should get out of the habit of calling him that. Not that it mattered any more.

A woman who could have been any age between twenty-five and fifty came to the door in carpet slippers and with a tatty print dressing gown pulled round her. I guessed that under that she was dressed all right, but I didn't like to think about it for too long in case she wasn't. Her hair looked as if the closest it had got to a hairdresser's lately was on the other side of the road, walking fast and trying not to notice. I told her my name and she remembered it from my phone call. She asked me in and I walked past her into the hallway.

It was littered with children's toys and old pieces of newspaper. I followed the trail into the small living room at the end of the hallway. Pushed open a door and found myself staring at four kids, all younger than the one who was washing the damned car. The youngest of all was sitting strapped into a push chair, head forward, asleep with a grubby dummy clutched in his mouth. Two curly-headed little girls who looked as if they were twins were intent upon covering each other with jam from fingers of bread which were on a piece of old newspaper on the table. A boy sat on the floor, doing nothing but whimper.

The woman knocked a couple of magazines off of a chair and asked me to sit down.

She lit a cigarette, looked glad when I refused one, offered me a cup of tea and when I said no to that also, poured herself one from a brown china pot on the table. The tea looked strong and stewed and it was probably the only thing which kept her going. That and waiting for her old man to come home with some money.

'You said on the phone that you wanted to hire a car for a few days?' The voice was wheedling, servile.

'Yes, that's right, Mrs Cook. Three, maybe four days. Would that be all right?'

She coughed and sipped at the tea. 'Well, I suppose so. My husband's still not been back, you see. Not since you phoned, like. But there's nothing else down in the book.'

She opened a small red note book and put it back down again. Then another drink of tea, another drag at the cigarette.

'Your husband's out on a job, is he, Mrs Cook? A driving job, I suppose?'

'No, not driving. We've only got the one car, you see. No, he went up West early this morning. I don't know what for. Just said he had a job to do.'

'You don't know who gave him the job, Mrs Cook?'

'No, I . . . here, you're asking me a lot of questions. What do you want to know all that for? You said you wanted to hire a car.' She stood up and went to the door. 'I don't believe you want to hire our car at all. You're from the finance company, that's what you are. Always sending people round to check up they are. Well, Jimmy told them last time—they'll get all the payments that are owing at the end of the week. The man agreed, too. Now what are you here for? They can't change their mind like that.'

She was holding on to the door now and was on the verge of breaking into tears. She clung to that wood as though it was the only thing that would support her. At any moment I was afraid she would be in hysterics and what I needed I needed fast before the police found out who that battered head had belonged to.

I got up and moved towards her; she backed up against the wall. I knew that if I didn't move now I would get nothing from her at all. She would just close jam tight.

I caught hold of her by the shoulder. It was like catching hold of loosely covered bones. I felt her jump with fear and cower back even further.

'Look, Mrs Cook, I'm not from the finance company. That I promise you. I want a little help and I'm prepared to pay for it.' I let go of her shoulder and reached inside my coat for my wallet. At the sight of the notes I offered her she calmed and I went on.

'This job your husband is out on—did someone come round here or was it a phone call?'

She spoke quietly but definitely. 'Oh, no, no one came round. They phoned him up, whoever it was; course I don't know who it was. Jimmy doesn't bother me with the business side of things; I have the home and kids to look after, see.'

She looked past me round the little room as though all that justified her statement.

'But think, Mrs Cook, have you any idea where the call came from? Any name? Would your husband have written it down anywhere?'

For an instant I saw the eyes go past me again, then flicker back to my face quickly. I looked round to where she had been staring. There on the table lay the red book. She must have re-alised how much I wanted the information and thought she could bargain for more cash. I didn't have the time. I jumped for the table ahead of her bird-like hand.

There it was, entered neatly and carefully. Two-eighteen a.m. Nottingham. Howard. What could be more precise than that?

'You'd remember this, Mrs Cook. A phone call in the middle of the night. That's hardly normal for a car hire business, is it? Or were there often calls at that time about other kinds of business?'

I had hold of her arm again and this time I applied pressure; not too much, but just enough. I don't enjoy hurting people, especially skinny women whose eyes are already full of tears. But I often don't have the choice.

My fingers went harder into the edges of the bone.

'He . . . he said "Bloody Nottingham again", that was all. I don't know who it is, but I think it's someone Jimmy met when he was driving vans for some jazz band or other. That's all I know, honest.'

Her weight went out of her arm. She slumped back into her chair and the tears coursed down her lined cheeks. I took out another two notes and put them on the top of her dressing gown, near her hand.

'That's for keeping quiet about me being here and asking questions.'

I didn't know if it would buy her silence and I suppose that I didn't much care. I stood in the doorway and looked round the room: the two girls had given up smearing themselves with jam and were sucking on the fingers of bread; the baby was still asleep; the boy on the floor had started to whimper more loudly and was trying to catch hold of the bottom of his mother's dressing gown. I closed the door quietly and went out into the street.

The girl was wiping away at the side of the car nearest to the traffic, oblivious to any dangers. I gave her a quick smile and turned up the road: she didn't appear to notice and if she did she didn't smile back. Why should she?

*   *   *

I surfaced from the underground at Leicester Square and walked through into Wardour Street. I thought maybe I'd call in at the arcade and see if Maxie had anything for me yet. But he had said tomorrow, so I didn't bother.

The building I was looking for was encased in smoked glass for the first two floors and this was centred by a large embossed coloured dragon. The entrance was to one side. A uniformed commissionaire sat behind a desk in the foyer reading a newspaper. He didn't look up as I came in. To the left there was a smoked glass door, with a smaller dragon. I pushed it open and went through into a large carpeted room. Marooned in the middle of this, a blonde in a bright red dress was seated behind a white desk looking as though she were waiting for someone to throw her a lifebelt. I waded across the carpet.

'I'd like to see Candi's recording manager.' I paused, looked her full in her pretty blue eyes and smiled. 'Please.'

'You'd like to see Candi's recording manager?'

Why was it that everyone repeated my questions at me as though I asked the stupidest questions in the world? Perhaps it was because I asked the stupidest questions in the world. Perhaps I needed to go for diction lessons.

I smiled once again and said please. Once again.

This time she smiled back. It was a nice smile, showing nice white, even teeth and causing a dimple to appear beside her mouth at the right hand side. It said that she was really a nice young girl who came in to work every day from the suburbs; a girl who once upon a time had thought that being a receptionist for a record company was a big deal, but who now knew that it was not. But while they were paying her dress bills she would pretend it still was. Sort of. That was what her smile said to me, anyhow. I supposed it said different things to different people in different places. I was wondering what things it might say to me somewhere different.

'You're sure you don't want to see someone else?'

The smile was slightly coquettish now. I wished I had time, but I didn't.

'You have read the paper I suppose?'

I told her that I had but that I supposed Candi's manager would still exist. Someone had to push all that posthumous product on to the market.

'Then you want Patrick Gordon-Brown. I'll buzz him for you.'

She smiled again and crossed her legs underneath her red dress. I heard the slight swish of material as she did so. She followed my stare and grinned.

'That is Gordon-Brown with a hyphen?'

I didn't care if he spelt it with a semi-quaver in the middle but I felt that I needed to say something and right at that moment that was all I could think of. Well, almost all and the rest didn't bear saying. Not right there, anyway.

She went on looking efficient and happy: which I suppose she was. Someone had to be.

'There's no answer, I'm afraid. Perhaps he's not back from lunch yet.'

'Not back from lunch?' I looked at my watch. 'It's almost time for dinner.'

'Well, he did have a business lunch, I know, and sometimes these things just seem to go on and on.' She almost giggled. 'I don't know what they find to talk about.'

The giggle did it. There was something about a lovely blonde who spent her days giggling from the splendid isolation of a marooned desk that I could not resist.

'What time do you have lunch? That is if you don't mind having lunch with old men.'

'You're not old and I wonder why it took you so long to ask and usually from one to two but you'd better phone first. The number's here on the card.'

And she handed me a small orange card with a dragon logo and an address and phone number. I made my way towards the door.

'What's your name, by the way. I'd hate to get hold of the wrong person.'

'It's Jane. Look: its printed here on this badge on my dress. You'll never make a detective, that's for sure. As a matter of interest, what do you do?'

I let the door swing to behind me. Keep-'em-guessing-Mitchell, that's what they call me. Sometimes.

It was too late to go to the office and I didn't want to face the mess anyway. I went home instead.

I hadn't opened the bottle when the phone rang. It was Vonnie. She wanted to know what I'd been doing. I told her I had been having a lovely time being hit on the head. She asked if I had found out about her sister's murder. I told her that I hadn't. She said good-bye and rang off. Ten pounds down her particular drain.

No sooner had I put some scotch into the tumbler than the phone rang again. I let it ring and drank the whisky down. That was the way I was feeling.

It was a voice I didn't know; quiet and cultured and with a distinct sound of breeding and money. Not the kind of voice that I conferred with often.

'Mr Mitchell?'

I told him it was, indeed, Mr Mitchell's residence and that Mr Mitchell himself was speaking.

'I'm so glad. I telephoned your office and there was no reply. I did call several times actually, but there was no reply on any occasion. So I took the liberty of trying your home number. I hope that you don't consider, that to be an awful impertinence?'

His tone suggested that of course I would not. Well, I did. I didn't want to talk to anyone right now. At least not a stinking rich old Etonian who could buy me for the price of one of his pet dog's dinners. But I didn't say so. I didn't say anything. So he went on.

'I have a problem, Mr Mitchell. A personal problem and one which I believe you may be able to assist me to solve.'

'I'm not a social worker, or a psychologist, you know, I'm . . .'

'I know just what you are, Mr Mitchell. You are a private detective. And by repute a reliable one or I should not be calling you. Now do you think you can help me? You see, my daughter is missing.'

I thought for a moment.

'Well,' I hesitated, 'ordinarily that sounds the kind of case I like, but as of now, I'm rather busy.'

'Mr Mitchell, I will pay you two hundred pounds in advance, twenty pounds a day plus expenses and a bonus of another three hundred pounds when my daughter is found. Now I am sure that those fees are in excess of what you would normally expect and I am equally positive that you would be foolish to pass them by.'

I thought for another moment.

'Will you come into my office tomorrow, Mr . . . ?'

'It is Mr Thurley, with an "ey" at the end, and I would much rather that you came out tonight to see me. I'm frightfully tied up tomorrow and besides I would so much rather arrange the whole business as soon as possible.'

There was room for a slight questioning at the end of the phrase, but it was only slight. I asked for the address and got it. I said I would be there at nine. He said he would be delighted to see me. I was about to say 'Super!' when I heard the phone click.

The house was deep into the stockbroker belt and the cab drove slowly and almost reverentially over the semi-circular gravel drive. I paid him off and looked around. The house itself was bursting with black wooden beams which stood away from white plaster. Fake Tudor but expensively so. The windows were latticed and in several of them lights showed. The door was studded with the occasional knuckle of brass and sported a massive knocker in the shape of a dog's head.

On either side of the house there were bushes and shrubs which seemed to go back some way into the darkness. The space in front of the drive was grassed over with the casual precision of a billiard table. At its centre was a bird bath which would have housed a family of Orientals with comfort.

I knocked on the door with the dog's head. Melted down it would have fetched a good price at two or three scrap dealers I knew. I'd bear it in mind for leaner times.

The guy who answered the door wasn't in full butler rig-out which came as a terrible shock and surprise. I mean, what are things coming to?

Instead it was a young man wearing a check sports jacket, an open-neck white shirt which had a scarf loosely knotted inside it, beige trousers and tan desert boots. He had longish hair which sprayed out behind his head and the centre of his face was dominated by a thick moustache. Either hired help was even more difficult to come by than I had been led to believe in my chats with my neighbours in the local launderette, or Mr Thurley was keeping strange company.

On the way through the doorway I handed the young man my coat and contrived to push my hand against the outside of his jacket. What was Mr Thurley doing with a companion who sported a pistol in a shoulder holster?

'Mr Thurley said would you like to wait in the library? He'll be down in a minute.'

I said yes and followed him into the spacious tomb-like room across the polished wooden hallway. He closed the door silently behind him—very quiet and well-mannered, I thought, not your average, run-of-the-mill punk—and left me surrounded by shelves and shelves of books. From floor to ceiling they rose up all around me. Leather-bound for the most part, leather-bound and unread. Just part of the decor. Probably bought as a job-lot and by the shelf-length rather than the title.

I was browsing along the nearest line and being uncertain why they rang little bells deep inside my head when the door opened and the proud owner came in.

He was taller than I had imagined from his voice, taller and altogether stronger. Forty-five to fifty, six foot and pretty fit by the stance and the suggestion of muscles underneath his clothes.

'Mr Mitchell.' He stepped forward, hand outstretched. I took it and met his grasp. It was strong and firm, yet the hand itself was oddly smooth. He clapped me on the shoulder and offered me a drink.

A push into a section of the shelving sent back a number of false-fronted volumes and revealed a small but well-stocked bar. I chose a Bells and ice and we adjourned to the leather reading chairs in the centre of the room. They had the air of being little used and the leather seemed to sigh a slight cry of surprise and complaint when I slid down into it. I sipped at my large whisky and waited.

Thurley drank some of his gin and tonic then took a photograph from his pocket and passed it across to me. It was a polaroid picture of a girl of sixteen or seventeen: short dark hair, oval face with high cheekbones and rather strange, staring eyes which seemed to belong in another face. Perhaps when that photo was taken they did.

'That's my daughter. Buffy.'

I nodded. 'Is this the only photograph you have?'

'The only one that is in any way recent. That was taken a month or so ago at a party we had here for her sixteenth birthday. No, wait, it must have been longer than that. It was before she went back to school—she's at boarding school, you know. That is, she should be. I have no idea where she is. Except that I presume she's somewhere in London. That's where they usually go, isn't it?'

Again I nodded my head. The nice thing about people like Thurley was that they assumed no one else had the brains to hold a conversation except themselves. It made for a restful time.

'I got a letter from the school late in September saying that she had gone missing. Absconded. They wanted to know if she had come back here. Well, of course she hadn't. Not even to collect her clothes, though she would have had some with her at the school, naturally.'

Naturally. Unless it was a school for incipient nudists.

'Have you not heard from her at all, Mr Thurley?'

He shook his head.

'And you have no idea where she might be?'

'None at all.'

'You have reported it to the police?'

'Yes,' he said, 'that was the first thing I did. But they had little to go on and apparently if nothing turns up in the first week or so then it's pretty hopeless. It appears they haven't got the chaps to look. Well, stands to reason, I suppose.'

'Who did you talk to?'

'The Inspector at the local station, I know him personally of course, and some fellow in town. Gilmour, I think it was. He was the chappie who referred me to yourself, actually.'

Good old Tom. I wonder if he would do the same thing right now?

Thurley looked across at me in what I assumed was meant to be his most earnest manner.

'I want Buffy found, Mr Mitchell. As you know I am prepared to pay well. I think she is merely being silly and rebellious and that she will see the error of her ways and return. But there are some pretty unpleasant people about nowadays, so I believe, and I would hate for her to come into contact with any of them.'

There were more questions I wanted to ask, but he was standing up and offering me a large brown envelope.

'In there you will find names and addresses of her closest friends, though they all appear to be as mystified by it all as I am myself. We have never quarrelled in our lives, my daughter and I, never since the day her mother left us.' He flicked at a non-existent speck on his immaculate cuff. 'There is also a cheque for three hundred pounds made out to yourself: that is your retainer and a week's payment in advance. You will let me know about your expenses in due course. Thank you, Mr Mitchell, for being so prompt. I wish you every success in your enquiries, for both our sakes.'

I wondered if that was meant to sound as threatening as it did.

'I believe you came by taxi. If you wish, John will drive you to the station or else he will ring for a cab for you.'

I thanked him and accepted the offer of a taxi. Chauffeurs who toted .38s I could do without.

-7-

The sound of the disc jockey sniggering through his early morning chores gradually brought me to the surface. I lay there for what seemed a long time, trying to think about something concrete but ideas crumbled away from my mind like falling masonry. A girl in white with a neat bullet hole in her back; a girl with falling red hair and an open laugh; a girl in a photograph who looked as if she had lost part of her mind. Too many girls: too many questions.

Then came the voice—strong and clear and not quite as I had heard it last. Someone had cushioned it and fashioned it with strings and choir; the melody was followed by the piercing tone of an oboe which remained steady when her voice veered off the line.

I wanted to turn it off but could not. I could no more move than I could fly. Nothing could have shifted a muscle of my body. Nothing. I was like a rabbit being stared down by a stoat and there was not one thing I could do about it.

But the voice finished and faded as voices do and the d.j. was talking inanities again and I could reach out and press the square grey button which freed me.

I pushed off the cover and swung my legs on to the floor. Something warned me that if I stood up straight away I would fall back down. So for five minutes I sat on the edge of the bed while the song wound and rewound itself round inside my brain. Then I thought I could get up. I got up and went through to the kitchen.

After two glasses of orange juice and several cups of black coffee I thought I could stand to speak to people. Real people, not the shadows of my dreams.

I phoned Sandy: it rang a dozen times without response.

I phoned West End Central: Inspector Gilmour was off duty till eleven.

I phoned Dragon Records: a cleaner told me that no one would be in until ten o'clock. Civilised hours!

I phoned Sandy once more: after the seventh ring a sleepy voice said, 'Hello.' When I said it was me the phone went back down on the hook. But fast. I went and poured out another cup of coffee. By the time I was back sitting by my phone it had started to ring. I waited for the second ring: it didn't do to appear too anxious when dealing with women.

Sandy let me in wearing a yellow-towelling robe, last night's make-up and an expression of extreme annoyance. She opened the door and left me framed in the doorway. She turned round and walked back towards the bed, taking off the robe as she went. She got back under the duvet, with nothing on but the make-up and the expression. I closed the door and went over and sat beside her. Her hair lay across the pillow and I stroked it, gently with the tips of my fingers. After a while her own fingers sought mine and pressed them. I moved my hand to the back of her neck.

Inside the bed it was warm and firm. Gradually she stopped looking annoyed but I couldn't do much about the make-up. We lay there held close and I wanted to stay.

'Sandy?'

'Uum?'

'A favour or two?'

'Which?'

'Two.'

'Why should I?'

By way of an answer I pulled her even closer: a while longer wouldn't hurt. But nothing lasts for ever: not pain, not pleasure: nothing.

'Sandy?'

'Uum?'

'About these favours.'

'Sod you!'

She threw back the cover and jumped off the bed. Hands on hips she stood glaring down at me; she looked angry, stark nakedly angry. She was very beautiful.

'Who the hell do you think you are, Scott Mitchell? You wake me up at this god-forsaken hour of the morning when you know damn well that I've been grinding my arse off till past three in the morning. You expect to jump into my bed for free when any fifty other mugs would pay through the nose for the privilege. Then you have the bloody nerve to ask for favours. Huh! Favours! What the fuck do you think you've been getting for the last hour? There are times when you make me want to thump you right between your know-it-all eyes!'

By the time she had finished she was even more beautiful. Legs apart, weight rising up on to the front of her feet in her anger, muscles in her thighs tensed. Fire in her green eyes. Fire in her voice. Imagine her . . . or, better, don't. It might not be safe.

No reply was the easiest and best. Sandy grabbed her robe and stalked off to the bathroom. By the time she returned she was wearing new make-up and a new outfit and I was sitting waiting with two cups of coffee.

She sat and allowed herself to smile, almost.

'What do you want, Scott?'

Okay, I thought to myself, it was going to be all right.

'First, I'd like to borrow your car till the morning. I have to be in Nottingham later today and then back in London after midnight.'

Sandy nodded.

'Is it in the garage?'

'Yes,' she said, 'the keys are in the usual place. Just make sure you pay for the petrol this time.'

'Oh, Sandy, come on . . .'

'No, you come on!'

I made a move towards her and she pushed me away.

'That's not what I meant and you know it!'

I did, but I wanted to keep her in the right frame of mind for the second favour.

'What's the other thing?'

As answer I took the polaroid photo from my wallet and passed it across to her. She put it down beside her cup and looked at it with mild interest.

'Who is she?'

'I thought you might know.'

'You've got the picture.'

I reached for the photograph and propped it against the edge of the saucer.

'She's Buffy Thurley. She's sixteen and she's run away from boarding school to seek fame and fortune in the bright lights of the big city. At least, that's what her old man thinks. And he's prepared to pay a lot of money to prove that he's right. Then bring her back home to daddy.'

Sandy looked at the picture, then at me. 'Do you think daddy is right?'

'Could be. From the expression in her eyes in that picture I'd say she was stoned up to the top of her sixteen-year-old head when it was taken. But then maybe I'm old fashioned: maybe that's how all young girls celebrate their birthdays in stockbroker country. Invite round the huntin-shootin-and-fishin-set and break out the champers and offer vintage grass for chasers. How the hell should I know? The nearest I usually get is the tradesman's entrance and a bottle of light ale.'

Sandy held my hand and put on her best supercilious expression: 'Darling, you'll have me weeping if you don't stop.'

I had the urge to say something rude, but I checked it. Instead I asked if she had seen her around the clubs but she hadn't. I stood up and picked up the photo; then gave it back to Sandy.

'You could take this and keep your eyes open. Maybe ask a few questions: show the photograph around. If she is in town then someone must have seen her.'

Sandy hesitated, then agreed. I thanked her, kissed her on the cheek and took the keys from the small table beside the door.

Sandy kept her car in the basement of a large garage in Brewer Street. I had used it before and I liked it. It was a two-litre Saab in silver and black. The windows were in dark glass and the wheels shining aluminium. It was safe and fast and distinguished and she hadn't got it through good works but who the hell was I to moralise. It sat waiting at the far end of the garage and the man who sat waiting in the front seat was reading a newspaper as though it was the most natural thing in the world to be doing. Except that the light was bad and he hadn't bothered to switch on the interior lamp; except that it wasn't his car; except that he was one of the two guys who called on me yesterday. The one who said nothing and let a piece of piping do the talking for him. The one who probably smashed in Cookie's head with as little thought as a normal man would give to stepping on a bug and squashing it into the linoleum.

I would have turned round and walked back the way I had come: but I wanted to use the car.

I walked over to it and he wound down the window. I could see he was reading the sports page, but the gun he held across his lap didn't look very sporting. Just heavy and blunt and deadly. Not the kind of a gun you would use to make a small hole in a young lady's back; more the kind you would use to make a large hole in a private eye's head.

Underneath the gun was an envelope. The usual anonymous brown envelope: they must sell them by the thousands. He took it out from under the gun and handed it to me through the open window. I took it and stood looking at it as though it might go off.

'Open it, stupid.'

He spoke, too, though with difficulty. Two high-class boys.

I smiled down at him. I mean, why not be friendly? Was it his fault that he was a small-time hood and a murderer? Well, was it?

Okay, so I pass on that one too.

I said: 'It doesn't have my name on it.'

He offered to write it on by one of the more devious methods I have heard suggested and told me to get it open before he changed his mind.

Not wanting to be disobliging I pushed my finger under the flap and pulled it across. Then I shook the contents down into my waiting hand. A number of ten pound notes dropped with a substantial feeling to them.

'We told you yesterday you ought to take a holiday. But we thought you might not take the advice. This is to help you make up your mind. Call it expenses.'

It was quite a speech. I wondered how long it had taken him to rehearse it. I slid the money back into the envelope and passed it back through the window.

'I told you it didn't have my name on it. I couldn't take anybody else's money. Thanks all the same. Now if you could see your way to moving out of my car . . .'

He grabbed the envelope from my fingers and started pointing the gun at me. If there's one thing I can't take from cheap hoods then it's bad manners.

My hand was still just inside the car window from where he had taken back the envelope. I rammed it down on the gun and leant over and pushed. The butt ground down into his groin and he groaned and spat. As his head jerked towards me I punched for his face with my left hand, the knuckles outstretched. My fist caught him above the bridge of his nose and the far knuckles went hard into the corners of his eyes. He swore again and tried to lift up the hand with the gun. At the same time he clutched for the door handle. I let go of the gun and yanked on the door from my side. It sprang open and his own impetus threw him out and down on to the concrete.

He hadn't let go of the gun and as he tried to level it I kicked at his right arm. My foot struck the forearm just behind the wrist and the gun went spinning upwards. If this were a movie and I were the hero I would have caught it and had the drop on him. As it was I didn't think about catching it and anyway he dived right at me. I was off balance already and his weight sent me thudding into the side of the car. I cannoned off the edge of the door and rolled against the front wheel, with his weight on top of me. A fist found my stomach and fingers sought out my eyes: instinct, took my head to one side and brought my knees up fast. I was lucky to budge him at all, but shift him I did.

We were both on our feet: the gun was on the concrete underneath the Saab. The envelope of money was on the floor of the car. Of all the things, this stupid thought ran through my mind: in the middle of the morning in the West End why was there no one driving in or out of the garage? Then a more sensible thought: where was his partner from yesterday? All the while I was thinking I guess that he was thinking too, but I don't have an idea what about. He didn't say.

He took a step forward and jumped at me with his left arm swinging for my neck. He wanted to push me out of the way and get to the gun. I went with the blow and let him past. Then as he stooped to scoop it up I launched myself at his back. Elbows first, hard into the shoulder blades, knees next, into the base of the spine. His shout was muffled by the ground as he tried hard to bite a chunk out of the concrete.

I was off him and hauled him up by the collar, so that the force choked on his throat. My fist sank through the flaps of his coat into his belly. A shower of saliva flew from his mouth; his face was grazed deeply along one cheek and a flap of bloody flesh hung away from his lip so that his mouth resembled an old fish that had been gaffed too often. I went in and grabbed hold of the lapels of his coat and moved him back against the wall. Three times I hit his head back against the open brickwork; the third time there was no resistance and I let him slump slowly to the floor.

I picked the envelope up from the floor of the car and pushed it inside his torn shirt. Then I thought for a moment and pulled it back out. I took out two of the notes and transferred them to my wallet. Expenses for the time wasted. I gave him back the envelope. He didn't say thank you.

The gun was heavy and I removed the clip and put it in the glove compartment of the car. The gun I stuffed after the envelope.

Still no one had driven into the garage. Commiserating with the owner under my breath, I switched on the engine and let the Saab into gear.

The red dress had been replaced by a blue one, but the smile remained the same. Jane looked at me as though I had crawled in from the latest horror movie; I knew what she meant but I didn't have the time to do anything about it.

'You look as though you just lost a good fight.'

'Uh-huh. I just won a bad one. Is your Mr Hyphenated-Gordon-Brown in yet or is he still out to a business breakfast?'

She didn't laugh: she had taste. But she did get through on the intercom system. He was in. I turned away and headed for the second floor.

'You won't forget our lunch, will you?'

I wouldn't forget but I was rapidly losing my appetite.

The name above the obligatory dragon read 'Patrick Gordon-Brown—Recording Manager'. I knocked on the frosted glass and went in. A dark-haired version of Jane was sitting at the left of the room behind a large desk. She was looking longingly at an electric typewriter as though she was about to seduce it; she could have had on Jane's red dress from the day before but I doubted it. I just hoped they didn't turn up at the building with them on the same day. Businesses have been known to fail for less.

I asked for Mr Gordon-Brown and gave my name. She gave it back into a little speaker at the edge of her desk and pointed to the door opposite. I smiled a thank you and she smiled all right back but she wasn't as appealing as her colleague downstairs. It was when I was opening the door that I realised why: she hadn't giggled.

Your friendly neighbourhood recording manager didn't look as though he was going to giggle either. Thickly striped shirt open at the collar, black, tight trousers, tinted glasses without rims. He held out a well-manicured hand.

'It's lovely to meet you, Mr Mitchell. Janie said you wanted to talk to me about dear Candi, God rest her soul.' He offered me a seat, a cigarette and a drink in swift succession. 'You're a reporter, are you?'

I told him that I wasn't. A photograph of Candi looked at me from behind his desk; the same pose as in the one which had been in her flat. At the bottom corner she had signed it 'To Patrick, With All My Love'.

'Oh, I see, I understood from Janie in Reception that you were—a reporter, I mean.' He showed several expensively-filled teeth.

I told him I was just a friend. Had been a friend.

'I see. A terrible thing, naturally; terrible. To happen at such a time in her career makes it a true tragedy.'

'Why now in particular?'

'She had never really broken big on the American market. All over Europe and Scandinavia she was a big name—Australia, too. But in the States, nothing. Just a big zero. Till the last month or two, that is. One of her singles went to number two in the Billboard and Cashbox charts and the album rose to the mid-twenties. Oh, yes, she was about to take off there all right. We had a whole tour lined up: supper clubs, a few places like the Troubador for the hipper audience, television. And now . . . nothing.'

'Just money for her memories.'

He looked puzzled, slightly annoyed. 'I'm afraid I don't quite follow.'

'I heard it on the radio this morning. Her new record. Wouldn't you say that was cashing in?'

Now he did look hurt. What right had I to make remarks' about his integrity?

'That single would have been issued regardless, Mr Mitchell. As would the album it was pulled from. And we're putting that back till next month so that we can redesign the cover.'

'So you can put on a picture of her coffin,' I suggested. 'Just to pull in the necrophiliac end of the market.'

He stood up. 'So that we can call it a memorial album and use a simple picture of her with a black line round it, if you must know. It will all be very tasteful, I can assure you of that.' He felt that his dignity and that of his company was restored and he sat down again.

He even apologised: I had never realised what nice young men worked in the record business.

'Excuse me. I worked with Candi for a number of years and we were very close . . .'

I interrupted him and pointed at the inscription on the photograph behind his desk: Yes. I can see that.'

He turned and half-smiled: 'Oh that, that is merely show-business talk, Mr Mitchell. Our relationship was merely a working one, I assure you. A very close one, but a working one only.'

I tried to work out whether he was happy or sad about that fact but I couldn't.

I switched tack.

Did you look after all of Candi's affairs, or just the recording side of things?'

'Oh, no.' He took a long cigarette from the box on the desk, offered one to me and when I shook my head replaced the box on the desk. He lit the cigarette with a table lighter in the shape of a dragon: they weren't about to let anyone forget who was paying the bills. If anyone stepped out of line maybe they just burnt them up: instead of a retirement clock, a full-scale funeral pyre.

He inhaled deeply and let the smoke float out from slightly parted lips. 'Oh, no, that wasn't my job at all. In many ways I wish it had been. I might have made a better job of things for her.'

'I thought you said her career was largely successful?'

'So it was, but something funny was going on with the money side if you ask me.'

I leaned forward without trying to look too interested.

'And did she?'

'Ask me? No. But I loaned her money from time to time. Quite large sums, too. Not that I begrudge that, of course. Nor did I ask her what she wanted it for.'

'Why couldn't she ask her personal manager for money? Presumably she'd earned it?'

He blew a smoke ring thoughtfully towards the ceiling.

'I really haven't the slightest idea. I don't even know what sort of arrangement they had. She wouldn't discuss it with me: not that I tried very hard. She had the same manager as when she started working solo, as far as I know. Some chappie in the provinces somewhere. Had to do almost all the business by telephone, or letter. Inconvenient at times.'

Something was becoming clearer. 'Nottingham?' I asked.

'Yes, that's right. Do you know him then?'

Try it, Mitchell. Play your hunch. 'Howard, you mean?'

'Yes, that's the name.'

I sat back in my chair. 'No. No, I don't know him.'

Patrick Gordon-Brown looked bemused. I stood up and held out my hand. He shook it automatically.

'Thank you, you've been very helpful. I may drop in on you again some time. Perhaps we could have lunch.'

I left his office and was half-way through the outer door when he called after me.

'I say! Look! I don't really know what it was that you wanted.'

Nor did I when I arrived, but I thought that maybe I did now. I thought of winking at the secretary but decided against it: I would save it for Jane on the way out. You do it too often and it makes you blind: or so my old granny used to say.

– 8 –

The motorway was crammed full with lorries and idiots who thought they were driving in the Grand Prix but who would never have got round the first hairpin. Show them a length of straight road and they'll race along it, no matter what. I stopped at the service station for a cup of coffee that tasted as plastic as the cup in which it was served. I left the doughnuts on the counter, begging for a home like fat boys in an orphanage.

On the last stage of the journey it began to snow. That was almost all I needed. I huddled down into the expensive-feeling seat, plugged John Stewart into the eight-track and got on with the driving. The only trouble with motorways was that you never got slim girls with suitcases and names like July standing by the side of the road hitching lifts. Hell, where did I think I was going anyway? Seattle?

In real terms it wasn't long before I hit the Nottingham turn-off, but it seemed like a snowy eternity. Now I knew why I didn't run a car of my own: I just hated driving. Even one like this.

I parked the Saab in the multi-storey and crossed the road into the Victoria Centre. Howard was in the phone book, with about twenty-five variations of initial. I cross-checked in the yellow pages and found one under 'Clubs and Entertainment'. There were two numbers: one for the 250 Club and one which I thought might be a home number. I dialled the latter and there was no reply. I tried the 250 without much hope of success. While it was ringing I wondered whether the number was to do with the location or was the price of fresh air: whatever, no one at the other end of the phone was about to tell me.

I walked out of the centre and went into a little Turkish restaurant beside the car park. They gave me a fine helping of lunchtime's moussaka and a local paper to read with my tiny cup of sweet coffee and pieces of turkish delight. I ate the delight, left the coffee and used the wooden stick to pick the remnants of minced lamb from between my teeth.

The murder was still front page news and there was a picture of the man in charge of the case, a Superintendent Leake. He was standing next to the inspector who had questioned me and taken my statement. Neither of them looked particularly happy, though Leake seemed to have more about him. From the picture he was about fifty and surprisingly short. I wondered how he had got into the police in the first place. I figured if he could make superintendent with his height then he could solve murders. I thought I would go and pay him a visit.

On the way to the station I called Tom Gilmour. He was in and he was up to his mothering arse in paperwork. His words, not mine. He told me he had found out who the corpse on my stairs belonged to and I tried hard to sound interested. He didn't say anything more, so maybe the money I had given to Mrs Cook had bought her silence. For a while, anyway. Or perhaps she had been in no fit state to tell them anything very much.

He asked me where I was and I said that I was in Nottingham and that I was about to go to talk to the officer in charge of the case. He said something not clearly audible at the other end of the phone. I thought about asking him to repeat it, but decided against it. Instead I told him about my morning visit from the hood with the gun. He told me to watch my mothering arse and I told him to look after his own—all that paperwork must be bad for it.

Superintendent Leake didn't look as if he used such coarse expressions. He was indeed a smaller man than you might expect in the tallest force in the country, but I guessed he must have compensatory factors. Like, maybe he had a brain that worked. After talking to him for a quarter of an hour I knew that he had and that it worked well. I always knew there must be civilised and intelligent cops somewhere and here was one.

I showed him my card and licence and he didn't look at me as though I was a traitor or a fool. He asked me what I knew and I said that it was precious little. I told him about the pressure to keep my nose out and about my conversation with Candi's recording manager. I said I was going to call on Howard and he raised an eyebrow. He had spoken to him yesterday and got nothing: no facts, no suggestions, not even an impression as to the man's feelings.

I asked if anything was known about him. He had no form, but the police had watched his club from time to time. Mainly because they suspected dope was being passed there. So far, though, they had come up with nothing. I promised that if I found out anything useful I would let him know.

Leake gave me what information he had in return: either he had unearthed very little or he wasn't being as straight as he appeared. The only prints in the flat had been mine. There were none of Candi's either, which suggested that whoever had been there before me had wiped the place clean. It also made things look better for me. The bullet was a .32: a small calibre and an unusual one for a professional to use. He asked me if I carried a gun and I looked shocked and said I didn't but that if I did it certainly wouldn't be a .32.

They had got some incomplete prints from the hallway and the stairs, but so far they hadn't been able to match them with anything. They were now in London at C11 being checked through the system.

There was nothing more. The interview was over. I thanked him for his time and for being so open.

'There is just one thing which bothers me, Mr Mitchell,' he said as I stood up.

I looked at him enquiringly.

'If a man beat you up on the stairs outside the building which housed Miss Carter's flat and if we presume not too long a gap between that happening and yourself coming round, why did no one see him? My men in the car were outside the flat nearby for a while before they saw you coming out. They say that they saw no one. Certainly, after the murder was discovered by us there were policemen all over the building.' He took a lengthy pause. 'It certainly makes you think, Mr Mitchell, doesn't it?'

I was out in the street again with nothing much to do. I tried both of Howard's numbers without any more luck. So I did what I usually do when I have time to kill. I went to see a movie. It was a re-run of Hawks's 'Rio Bravo' and by the time it was over and I had managed to get past admiring Angie Dickenson's legs, I had picked up a lot of respect for old John Wayne. No matter what difficulties they threw at him he didn't back down. Of course, he did have a few people helping him. They might only have been a drunk, a cripple and a singing cowboy who looked as though he was only just weaned, but they were there. All I had was a scarred stripper with red hair, a worn out hunch that probably wouldn't lead me anywhere at all and a thirst. But like I said before, this isn't a movie.

It was time to try out the thirst and the hunch on the 250 Club. Like a lot of similar places it was over the top of a large tailor's. There were posters on the stairs and at the landing a mean-looking brunette took a couple of pounds off me with the expertise of Arnold Bennett skimming the skin from a rice pudding. If you see what I mean.

A red velvet curtain pushed aside into a small room with a bar at one side. Behind this room was another, about the same size and with a small bandstand at the far end. There were one or two fellers at the bar, chatting to the usual brass barmaid. They must all come from the same mould straight to places like this. A small guy in a dark suit was taking drums from their leather cases and setting them up on the stand. Nobody took much notice of me. I bought a pint of bitter for my thirst and a scotch for myself and went and sat in the inner room and watched the drummer putting his kit together. From a speaker over the door came the music of someone who might almost have been Charlie Parker but wasn't. Just like I might have been John Wayne! I called it as Sonny Stitt left it at that.

It was quite a bit later that the man I guessed to be Howard came in. There were more paying customers by now, including one or two part-time prostitutes and someone I figured to be a plain-clothes man Leake had sent down to see how I got along. The only thing was, I couldn't be sure if he was there to watch me or Howard. Both, I supposed.

Howard was a big man, a fat man. He had his arm round the shoulders of a thin guy carrying a saxophone case and was laughing from underneath dark glasses. It was a sound I didn't like: slightly unearthly, unnatural. He clapped the sax player on the back a few times, went round behind the bar, goosed the barmaid—or so I assumed from her practised reaction and the customers' snorts of delight—and poured out a couple of liberal scotches. Then he and Mr Sax disappeared into a room beside the bar which could have been the gents but which was probably the band room.

I looked round. The drummer had finished setting up and was sitting on his stool reading the *Melody Maker*. A double bass had been laid on its side in front of the upright piano. Most of the people round the bar seemed involved in a fairly noisy conversation. The guy I figured for a cop was sitting on the edge of the group drinking beer and doing a good job of listening. Above the increased sound the tape had changed to Monk playing Ellington. I waited until he had played the riff at the opening of 'Sophisticated Lady' that takes him into the melody, then I got up and headed for the door beside the bar. I hoped that if I moved not too fast and not too slow no one would notice: except for the copper, in case I needed him.

I mean, any stranger could mistake it for the gents.

Not once you got inside you couldn't.

It was a small room, no bigger than a large cupboard. A naked light bulb hung dimly from the ceiling. The sax man was sitting on a wooden chair, slumped down and with his jacket on the floor by his feet. His left shirt sleeve was rolled up and in his right hand he was holding a plastic syringe. The needle had pierced the vein just below the centre of his arm.

He had his eyes shut tight and was biting deep into his lower lip. He didn't open his eyes when I came into the room and shut the door quickly behind me. There was a key on the inside and I turned it damned fast. I had the key in my pocket and my gun nestling in my hand before fat-boy knew what had hit him. I tell you, there are times when I'm good and when I'm good you had better watch out!

Howard didn't speak but the front of his gut began to tremble slightly, like a gigantic jelly. Maybe it didn't like the fact that a Smith and Wesson .38 was pointing straight at it from a distance of less than two feet.

I looked for the expression behind his glasses but could see nothing there. There was no sound for several minutes except for an intake of breath from the guy who was shooting up. I saw his finger ease on the end of the syringe and his head lowered; his eyes blinked, then opened. And he found himself looking at me standing there with a gun. Strange trip.

He looked as though he was going to speak; at least his mouth opened and closed a few times. In case he was I told him to shut up. It was Howard I wanted to talk to.

'Okay, we've only a little time before someone comes and knocks on this door and wants to know why you're taking so long getting fixed. So listen hard and answer fast if I ask you a question. Got it?'

He nodded and looked across at the junkie in the chair. I eased his face round gently with the barrel of my .38.

I was beginning to enjoy this more and more.

'I'm the guy who found Candi's body. That wasn't all that I found. I also found a few things in a shoe-box that whoever had cleared out had carelessly left behind: and they sure weren't shoes. As I was leaving someone slugged me and took the things back. Maybe you know what was in that box. Maybe it even found its way back to you. Am I getting warm?'

Whether I was or not, Howard certainly was. The sweat quietly ran down his forehead and behind his glasses; it ran down his sideboards into his neck; it sprang out in the palms of his podgy hands.

'Now all that means Candi was hooked. Whether she was mainlining or not I don't know because I didn't have the sense to look for the marks at the time. But a quick check with the path. lab report will turn that up. But perhaps she was still taking orally, I don't know. It doesn't matter.'

I paused for breath and pushed his stomach with the end of the gun. The vein to the right of his forehead leapt out into sharp relief. The sweat flowed more freely. He was surely as scared as all hell and it wasn't for no reason.

'Okay. I'll tell you my version of the story. You were Candi's manager. She trusted you and you got her hooked on dope. Then you sold it to her. The deeper she got hooked the more you sold. You were taking a percentage off her earnings for managing her and then another percentage after that for feeding her habit. She was getting so little herself she borrowed money from her recording manager and from Christ knows who else besides.'

I grinned at him and waved the gun in his face.

'How does that grab you so far? Shall I go on? 'Cause now we come to the part where it becomes a little less clear and this is where I want your help. Several things could have happened at this point; things that could have caused someone to get so annoyed with Candi they wanted to put her out of the way. She might have been into someone for a lot of money and not look as though she was going to pay it back. She might have tried to turn her back on the whole thing—the singing, the dope, everything. She might have been trying to get back at you in some way; maybe even blackmail.

'Now, which of those ideas do you like?'

I fanned him with my gun again but it didn't seem to cool him down. The sax player was still sitting on his chair, as though he didn't believe it was all happening. I let the barrel come to rest alongside the fat man's temple.

'There isn't much time but don't think you can stall me for long. Which of my little ideas do you like best? Tell!' The gun was making a dent in the skin and I knew that he was going to call my bluff. Despite all that shaking blubber and all that sweat, he knew that I wasn't going to use a .38 in there with a crowd of people outside and no other way out.

But I had hit more home chords than were comfortable and he knew it. I was thinking what the hell to do next when there was a bang on the door from the outside. A voice shouting above the music and the chatter to find out if Howard was all right.

For the first time he spoke: 'Sure. We're on our way out now.'

I looked at his glasses and wished I could see behind them. Next time I would.

'All right. I'm going out of here behind you and I'm leaving the club. But I'll be back to see you again and you won't know when it's going to be. If anyone tries to follow me tonight or to get to me in any way then I'll use this. I'm fed up with being pushed around and taken for a patsy. Okay?'

He nodded. I turned to the guy on the chair.

'You'd better put that thing away and roll your sleeve back down. There's a law against that sort of thing, you know.'

I walked past the copper at the bar without a glance. I waited outside to see if he was going to follow me: or if anyone else was. When nobody emerged in five minutes I called down a taxi and went to collect my car from the car park. I had an appointment with Maxie.

−9−

Rain had filled the air and washed the streets. There was a newness, a freshness that had no place where I was walking. My feet carried me along a path that could only lead to death: my own and how many others I could not reckon. It was an inescapable path yet a bitter one—bitter with the reek of cordite and the sharpness of broken promises. A street lined with nightmares and tainted with death. This rain was a liar and a cheat and I cursed it as I turned the corner towards the arcade.

It was nearly three and I was late: the lights inside the arcade were dimmed; the place was deserted except for a grey tabby rubbing its leg against the leg of one of the pin tables. I bent to stroke it and its back reared as it jerked its head away and spat. I moved past it and on towards the door.

The light showed dimly over the woodwork. I knocked twice and the sound was lost in the blankness of the moment. After a few seconds waiting I tried again: this time I thought there was a faint scuffling sound from the other side of the door. The handle refused to turn to my grip.

Time to use a little force, I said to myself and then the scuffling grew louder and began to scratch at the wood. I stood quite still: my hand was on the butt of my .38 and I watched as something applied pressure to the handle of the door. A long pause followed by a faint but distinct click and then the handle itself began to turn.

My gun in my right hand, I stepped across the face of the door and yanked it open—fast. Falling from the dying light of the room, something collapsed into the space directly in front of my feet. Something large, something that might have been a bundle of old clothes and sacking: but for the remains of a human head which landed nearest to my toe. Something that was Maxie—or what was left of Maxie.

I knelt among the unswept grime and cradled that mewling thing in my arms. The already swollen leprous face was now a morass of congealed blood and opened flesh. I knelt and held him because he was still human and because that made him more important to me than the cat which moved silently behind me.

Maybe.

Or maybe it was because there was life somewhere within his beaten form and I wanted to get the information that I needed as long as there was the slightest chance.

I lifted the body and carried it into the room, banging the door closed with my foot. I laid him on the table and fetched water from the filthy sink in the corner: I took out my handkerchief and began to clean away his face.

When I had done what I could I went out of the arcade and walked back to the car. From the compartment under the dashboard I took the half-bottle of scotch I had bought to keep me company on the cold journey home. There was enough left—I hoped. I took the bottle back and started to force the contents down Maxie's throat through the torn purse of his lips. After a while he began to cough and splutter and hold his body against the racking pain.

I leant my head close to his face and had to inwardly clench myself to keep it there.

'Maxie. Can you hear what I'm saying? Can you see who it is?'

His eyes showed nothing at the back of their slits but he managed to nod his head. I went on.

'You had something for me. Tell me what it was?'

No movement of the head this time: no acknowledgement.

I shook him not too roughly by the shoulder nearest to me.

'Maxie! The information! I need to know. Now.'

His head rolled away from mine and I pulled it round again to face me. There was a cut below his left eye which was like an over-ripe plum that has been bitten into by the sharp beak of a bird. I closed my eyes for a second and put my mouth closer to his ear.

'Look, Maxie. The drugs. Where would I get a nice steady supply of drugs; all clean and without danger? Where, Maxie? Come on, you know where, Maxie.'

Once more the rolling away of the head: once more the pulling back. Each time more desperate: each time fiercer. Knowing that time was running out—Maxie's time. My time. Time.

'Maxie! For Christ's sake!'

I raised him from the surface of the table and supported him with one arm, while I tried to get more whisky into him. He gulped and choked and most of it slobbered back down his face, stinging him as it ran through his sores.

Then the puffed balls that were his eyes seemed to grow more aware. The hold I had on him tightened; the hole beneath his nose tried desperately to form words. I put the side of my head to his face and listened.

'Scott . . . you . . . you've got to get me to . . . doctor . . . too late oth . . . erwise . . . there's no ch—' He broke off as a pain cut through the length of his body: his hands went to his chest and the hole that was his mouth opened wide. I held him to me: I was sure he was dying and so was he.

But it passed this time and he made another effort to speak.

'Doctor . . . now . . . now Scott . . . dying.'

'Okay, Maxie, I'll take you to the doctor. But first tell me about the drugs. The drugs, Maxie! You just tell me and then I'll put you in the motor and we'll go to the doctor.'

He said nothing, whispered nothing. I just prayed he was still listening.

'You said it was getting more difficult. You said that someone else was moving in. Someone big. Who, Maxie, who?'

'East End . . . running stuff for some—uh! my chest! like a strap across me! . . . I don't know who . . . they use the muscle . . . knocking small boys out . . .'

I shook him hard.

'I know that, Maxie, I know all that. You gave me that before. What I want now is names. Names, Maxie! If you want to get to that doctor give me some names!'

He spoke again but the sound was getting more and more feeble every time.

'Don't . . . know . . . names . . . young feller . . . moustache long hair . . . a nigger . . . big as houses . . . big as—ooh! pain! it was him as done . . . as done me . . .'

The sound trickled off into a constant moaning.

I lifted his head and held it in front of mine.

'You must know more than that, Maxie. More than if you want help.'

He slumped back and I felt as though he was slipping away from me. I looked at the whisky bottle—it was empty.

'Maxie!'

I pulled back my hand and slapped him hard across the face. Twice: across and back. The mouth-thing opened slightly. I bent my ear to it.

'Don't need . . . no help . . . no doctor . . . now.'

I shook him. I pulled him upright. Shook him again. Laid him back on the table. Listened for a pulse that no longer beat.

I went over to the sink and washed my hands; took up the whisky bottle and put it in my pocket; used the handkerchief smeared with his blood to wipe any of my prints from the tap, the table and the door. From the dirt and grease of his clothing they would learn nothing. Using the handkerchief, I closed the door on Maxie's body.

The cat was still in the arcade. It sniffed its nose up in the air as I came out of the room. Slowly, gracefully, it walked towards me and went to rub itself against my leg. I swung back my foot and kicked at it, kicked at it as hard as I could. Then went out into the wet streets.

By the time I got home it was too late to go to bed, too early to do anything else. I made coffee and couldn't drink it. Everything I touched or tasted had the feel, the stench of decay. I ran a bath and lay in it and tried to think.

Candi was hooked on something: from the things I found in her flat it was probably something like amphetamines or barbiturates. She was hooked and she was broke, probably from having to pay for whatever she was hooked on. Then somebody killed her. It could have been because she was refusing to pay up any more; it could have been because she was threatening to bite back on her source of supply and whoever that was got scared. It could have been something else altogether. But suppose it was something to do with the drugs. What then?

I knew that Howard was involved with drugs in some way, but if he was pushing then he had to get his supply from somewhere. And if someone was moving in on the market and trying to get it sewn-up, they wouldn't stick to London. They would move out into the provinces as well. Which made it very likely that Howard had been squeezed out. Besides, I couldn't see him killing anyone himself and if Cook was typical of the kind of no-hope help he hired then he wouldn't get anyone to do it for him. No. It was far more likely to be someone from outside. Someone from this mob. Maxie had said an oversize Negro and a young moustache. The Negro I had certainly seen and from his looks and from the way he had dealt with Maxie, I couldn't imagine him using a little .32 on Candi. He wouldn't even have been able to hold it between his fingers.

But a young, long-haired moustache. There were hundreds and hundreds of them and they all looked alike. How could you tell one from the other? Until you knew one, of course.

I thought about dear John, opening the door with a servile smile and a gun bulging through his jacket. John with the trust of Mr Thurley with an 'ey'.

Altogether too smooth, Mr Thurley with his Eton and Guards airs and graces and his library full of unread leather-bound books. Bought by the yard. Bought from where? What had Vonnie said about Martin's little business venture?

I had to talk to Vonnie again. And to Thurley.

But before I talked to either of them I wanted to speak to Tom Gilmour. There was some more information I could do with and which he might have.

The water in the bath was growing steadily colder and a light scum had formed across its surface. It was time to get out: I should have got out sooner.

-10-

Tom Gilmour's office had the air of a room where things happened: I didn't think it would be wise to query what too many of them were. When you spent your life dealing with petty hoods and larger villains, it didn't pay to be over-gentle. So if the blinds were pulled down once in a while and the door was locked, what did it matter what went on inside? As long as the course of justice was being pursued.

It mattered if you were the one sitting on this side of the desk. It mattered if you were the one they suspected, the one they needed to talk, the one they thought was withholding information.

'You had no idea who that mother with his skull bashed in on your stairs was?'

Gilmour looked sharp even at this hour of the morning, when I am usually only working on half-cylinders. He looked sharp in his American-style suit and with his eyes cutting the space between us. Not a man to treat without caution; not a man to lie to.

'No idea,' I lied.

He rolled a pencil around the blotter on his desk. A new blotter, virgin white: perhaps he didn't write much; perhaps it was stationery day. Perhaps he was a very particular man. He spoke carefully. I listened the same way.

'He was a man called Cook. A small-time guy, a grafter with not much sense and very little in the way of know-how. But he might have had something in the way of guts.

'You were right when you said you had seen him around. He was tailing you all right. We don't know who put him on to you, but we do know it started straight after the papers leaked it that you found Candi Carter's body. Or maybe before that—maybe it was after the murder but before the news hit the streets. Now that's a whole new ball game.

'If Cook was put on to you before the morning that means whoever hired him knew you were there because they were there themselves. Or they knew someone who was—someone who would want to tell them about your being there. If that was so, it makes it look good for you as far as the murder is concerned, but it leaves us wanting very much to find out who hired Mr Cook.'

Gilmour got fed up with rolling the pencil; he pushed his chair back against the wall and stuck his feet out on to the desk. He crossed them on top of his nice new blotter. This morning he just didn't care.

'Who hired him to tail you, Mitchell?'

I continued to look at the soles of his shoes. At times like that anything was better than having to stare continually at his face.

When I didn't bite he went on, 'Oh, but then you didn't know anything about him, did you. I forgot.'

He swung his feet down suddenly and stood up. He moved round from behind the desk and the muscles in my body tensed. His hand came to rest alongside my shoulder at the back of my chair.

'I'll tell you something interesting, Mitchell. Cook was only a little man, a small man in many ways. He ran his business from a Victorian terraced house—car-hire with a single car and a little snooping on the side. Not an especially careful man by all accounts: if he had been careful he wouldn't have got his head smashed in, would he? Not careful and yet you would have thought there would have been some record of business, even if only for tax.

'Do you know—and this is going to take you by storm, pal—do you know there was nothing there.'

The hand moved a fraction closer to my back: I was aware of it tensing, then it moved away and he was back in his chair at the far side of the desk.

'One of his kids—there were a whole mess of those—said her dad used to have a little red book in which he wrote down all his jobs. She looked for it and couldn't find it. We looked and we couldn't find it either.'

I had to ask. There was no way I couldn't—not for my own peace of mind.

'Was there no one else you could ask? Didn't he have a wife or anything?'

Nothing for what seemed a long time. Gilmour went back to his pencil and began to doodle with it around the heel mark left on his blotter.

'Interesting question, Mitchell. Interesting.'

The point of the pencil dug hard into the white paper; dug through it and snapped.

'Sure he had a wife. When we went over to see her, after a constable had gone round with the news, this little girl came running up the road. Running and screaming. Ran right into us. Smack dab in the middle of us. She was crying and shouting and she didn't make sense so we took her back with us to the house.

'It was an old-fashioned house, with a bathroom added on at the back, out beyond the kitchen. The girl took us to the door and pointed: then she ran away.

'The door was ajar. You could just see a shape, a shape hanging. When we opened the door we found Mrs Cook all right; hanging from the light flex in the centre of the room. One leg trailed over the bath, the other over the floor. The floor was wet: the front of her dress was stained.

'When we found the rest of the kids in the upstairs part of the house they were sitting playing with some crayons. There was crayon everywhere—all over the floor, the wall, all over their hands and faces, in their mouths.

'Two women pc's came and cleaned them up and took them away. Now they're in a home. Until they're eighteen they'll be in care.'

He shrugged his shoulders. 'In care. Maybe they'll be better off. It didn't look as though they were getting too much care where they were.'

Tom Gilmour stood up and stared out of the window, down on to the street. My mind left the building, the country; settled in a camp for itinerant workers in California. I saw the faces and bellies of kids who hadn't eaten a good meal for weeks. Saw the faces, the eyes, staring widely, wildly. Staring at a large pot full of stew made from bones of meat. Children fed on the Grapes of Wrath.

But fuck it! Children in another country, in another age, in a fucking movie! Why couldn't I think of what was real, what was here and now. Why couldn't I think of kids smearing each other with jam, kids asleep with foul dummies in their mouths, children who did nothing but whimper and cry?

What about a little reality, Mitchell? Too strong for you to take, huh? Too much for a big private eye with a Smith and Wesson under one arm and a hole where his heart should be?

Then Gilmour was asking me a question and I didn't know how many times he had asked it before.

'I said you wouldn't know anything about an old guy called Maxie being killed some time late last night? An old guy who ran an amusement arcade?'

'Sorry, Tom. I drove straight back from Nottingham and went to bed. As soon as I woke up I came round here. Why, anyway? Is there any reason why I should know him?'

'Easy,' Gilmour said. 'Stay cool. I thought you claimed to work as a private investigator. I thought it was your job to know things like that.'

I smiled. He was the only English police inspector I knew who would tell anyone to stay cool and meant it seriously.

I followed up the smile with a question or two of my own.

'I could do with some help, Tom. Nothing much, just a little information. About a man called Thurley, for instance. You know him?'

Gilmour thought for a moment.

'Sure. He lost his kid. Girl of about sixteen. She went on the run from school and he thought she might be in the golden mile. I had some people look around, ask a few questions. We didn't come up with anything. In cases like that we rarely do—unless we happen to strike lucky quick. I suggested he try you. I thought you might fancy a few days sleazing around the porn shops and strip clubs: besides, he looked as if he'd pay well. And you look as though you could use the money.'

I thanked him for the hand-out. Then asked if he knew anything else about Thurley.

'Nothing. Seems he used to work in merchant banking and moved from there into various directorships. I don't know any more than that. Why? Have you got any reason to suspect there's any more?'

I showed him two empty hands: 'Nothing. Except a feeling that he wasn't all he seemed under the veneer. Could you run a check on him?'

Gilmour stood up. He had work to do, but I wasn't quite ready to go.

'And there's a youngish feller who works for him. About twenty-five, long hair and moustache. Unless I'm mistaken he carries a gun in the holster under his jacket. Either that or he's got a strange growth.'

Tom Gilmour was looking more interested now, though I didn't get the impression I had rung any bells inside his head.

'Thanks, Scott, I'll ask around. Get someone to keep an eye open.'

I was on my way through the door when I let him have the last question.

'A big black Negro—strictly maxi-size. How about him?'

This time the bell rang and the coins came rolling out for free.

'Wilson Marley. Six eight. Over two hundred pounds and every one of them weighs killer. He's working as muscle for a guy called Jupp, Frankie Jupp.

'For years Jupp worked strictly around the East End—gambling, girls on the game, robbery with violence. Big in his way but limited. Now suddenly he's putting feelers into the West End—and out of London altogether. The Drug Squad have been getting rumours for some time about Frankie moving some really hard stuff around. Hard and expensive. If he can do it, then it makes sense from his point of view.

'If he can shut up the small guys dealing in cannabis and LSD and push stuff like cocaine, amphetamines and barbiturates then he stands to make a lot more money. But it's a strange move for him and my guess is that there's New York money behind it. Whatever he is up to, Marley is doing most of the footwork and most of the fistwork, too.

'Anything you turn up about those boys, Scott, you'll be doing me more than a favour. What I wouldn't give to nail those mothers! But—Scott—take care. That Marley will take your head off as soon as spit in your eye.'

When I got across town to my office I had visitors again. Or rather a visitor. And she was prettier by far than on the last occasion.

Her hair was pulled down and back so that it just framed her face, which was pale and without an apparent trace of make-up. She wore a pale blue dress that clung to her above the waist and fell away loosely below it. The neckline and the hem were ornamented with soft brown patterned leaves. She stood outside my door, looking very demure except for one thing: or two. Where the material clung to her breasts the nipples stood out as firm as stones. I wondered how precious they were. I wondered who she was out to tease—or make. I wondered if that someone were me, and if it was then I wondered why.

I pulled my keys from my pocket and went to unlock it; then I remembered that I didn't need to do that. I had never locked it.

'You could have come in,' I said when we were inside.

She smiled faintly: 'I did try the handle . . . but then I didn't like to go in. I mean, it would have been prying, wouldn't it?'

And again I caught myself wondering.

'Have you found out anything, Scott?'

'Very little, Vonnie, but I'll tell you what I know.'

I told her about Howard and about her sister's involvement in drugs. She didn't seem in the least surprised at that; thought it only to be natural for the kind of life she was leading. And I supposed that she was right. I added that the murderer might be whoever had been supplying her with the dope. She nodded her head and said it sounded likely. What did I think I was going to do next.

I said that I wasn't sure.

It seemed that she had ideas of her own.

She came and stood beside my chair so that her dress was close to my face. I had only to push out my tongue . . .

She eased her hand on to the shoulder of my jacket.

'It must have been a shock for you, Scott, finding Ann like that. Alone in that room with just her picture on the wall for company.'

For the second time that morning I was aware of a hand moving close by my head. Only this time it began to stroke my neck, finger by delicate finger.

'You were very fond of her, weren't you, Scott. I can remember seeing you together when you brought her home to the house after taking her out. I can remember seeing you kiss her: I was only young at the time, really.'

The pressure from the fingers was stronger, their message more insistent. The phone rang. I leaned forward across the desk and lifted the receiver. When I spoke into it, Vonnie was standing away from the desk, taking a sudden interest in the faded carpet.

'Scott Mitchell. Who is this?'

The voice at the other end of the line was educated, well-oiled and well-fed.

'Ah, Mr Mitchell. I tried to contact you earlier, but no doubt you were out working.'

I coughed something down the phone which he could take for whatever he wanted to take it for.

'I merely wondered whether you had come up with anything yet, Mr Mitchell. I do realise that you have had very little time . . .'

I interrupted: 'You're right, Mr Thurley, I have had very little time and every time something starts to happen I get interrupted.'

I sensed him bristle, but he covered well.

'I'm terribly sorry, Mr Mitchell. It was merely a parent's anxiety, you know. I hope you didn't mind my calling?'

'Not at all, Mr Thurley. You do that anytime. Now if you will excuse me?'

He did so in a most polite fashion. I have rarely heard a telephone receiver put down with such good breeding.

Vonnie was sitting across from me, on top of the low filing cabinet. I couldn't be sure how angry she was, but the paleness of her face was highlighted by two red spots by her cheekbones.

'What did you say Martin was doing on the side?'

'Scott! On the side makes it sound unpleasant, almost illegal.'

I gave her one of my best smiles. She returned with one of hers. Anyone watching from the centre of the room would have thought they were at Wimbledon.

'He's buying and selling books, Scott. Rare books, leatherbound ones—heavens, I don't really know much about it.'

'And whatever it is is keeping him pretty busy?'

'Why, yes, he's often late home, but what with his work in the library and this new thing . . .'

'How long has it been going on?'

'What do you mean?'

She looked alarmed and stood off the cabinet: her nipples were firm once more and she seemed to be breathing more strongly.

I stood up and faced her: I felt safer that way.

'Come on, Vonnie, calm down. I mean Martin having to stay out working late for his new job?'

She relaxed a little: 'Oh, I don't know, Scott. Several months. But why do you ask?'

'I just wondered how long a pretty girl like you had been on her own at nights. You could have called me, Vonnie. I would have kept you company—unless someone else was doing that job?'

The colour returned to her cheeks.

'Scott, that's not a very nice thing to suggest. Besides,' she came and stood so close that if I breathed outwards a little harder I would have pushed her backwards, 'you know that I was always the little stay-at-home. You can remember that, Scott, surely?'

I could but I didn't want to remember it; not then with her that close to me. With the memory of her sister so close too. Memories of Ann—of Candi.

'What about Martin, Vonnie?'

'What do you mean?'

'Are you sure it is always work that keeps him out late? Not somebody else?'

She was not quite so close to me now, but still close enough. She laughed up into my face and her breath was sweet and warm.

'But Martin's a librarian!'

She said it as though being a librarian shrouded him in a cloak of purity. She and I had obviously known different librarians: but that's another story.

I looked at my watch. I said, 'It's nearly lunchtime, Vonnie.'

She reached out and took my arm in hers.

'Does that mean you're offering to buy me lunch, Scott Mitchell?'

I gave her arm a squeeze with mine. It was slender and small within my grip.

'I'd love to, but I already have a date for lunch. Maybe some other time.' I bent down and kissed the top of her head lightly. 'Maybe the next time you're checking on my progress.'

-11-

Today she was wearing a pink velour top and a brown skirt; a beautifully open smile and the badge that said 'Jane'. I waited a while and she finished putting photographs and duplicated biographies into brown envelopes. She stood up and a large brunette came and took her place: strictly second division.

I held back the dragon and we walked out on to the busy street. It was good to pace alongside her as we cut through the crowds and made for lunch and an hour of getting to know each other. Something in the youth and vigour of her stride got through to me, something in the way she smiled at those who jostled past her. My blood pressure quickened, my ego jumped, my whole body felt as though it was fresh back from the health farm.

She took my arm as we turned the corner into Greek Street and as she did so the car swung hard towards us. I saw its sudden movement from the edge of one eye; I had probably heard its engine a second sooner. Whatever it was that warned me, I acted, and fast.

Jane I pushed into the doorway of a café; I pushed her and leapt backwards away from the spot the driver had calculated. The front slid across the pavement and the nearside bumper rammed itself into the wall. It dragged plaster for ten or fifteen yards, then pulled back and on to the road. The car accelerated and was gone into the lunchtime traffic.

I looked up from where I was sprawled on the pavement: a crowd had already begun to gather round me. It was incredible that no one else had been hurt: incredible that someone would try to make a hit at that time of day and in that way.

Somebody, somewhere must be getting very scared.

I allowed myself to be helped up and muttering thanks and platitudes about stupid, drunken drivers went into the café to find Jane. She was sitting at a table, with the Italian waiter doing a great job of restoring her confidence. She didn't look any the worse for wear.

I went over and sat down beside her. The waiter hovered for a moment longer then went away. I held her hand and gave it a squeeze; I tried my drunken driver routine but it wouldn't work on her.

'Listen, someone was driving that car with a purpose so don't try to tell me that it was an accident. Somebody wanted to hurt you badly . . . to kill you.' She held my hand more tightly and looked hard at my face. 'Just what sort of a man have I agreed to come out to lunch with, anyhow?'

I took one of my cards from my wallet and gave it to her; she didn't exactly look impressed.

'And I said you'd never make a detective! I thought your reactions back there on the pavement were pretty quick. Were you expecting that?'

'At that particular moment in time, nothing was further from my mind. I was an ordinary guy taking an extraordinarily attractive girl out to lunch and feeling pretty pleased with himself into the bargain. I must have moved out of instinct.'

She gave my hand another squeeze: 'Most people's instincts are so slow that they would be on the way to the hospital by now. And so might I.'

She leaned across and kissed me. It sure was my day for getting a lot of attention, one way and another. The waiter was back by the table and for a moment I thought he was going to break into a bit of an old Italian love song. Instead he thrust a menu into my unoccupied hand and asked if we would like to see the wine list. I said no, ordered a carafe of red and freed my other hand for the important business of choosing a meal. Two meals. She was still there, after all. Many a young girl who had been pushed into the restaurant that way would have got up on her high horse and ridden out. Or would still be too nervous to order Uova Tonnate, followed by Vitello alia Genovese. I hoped my Lasagne would be as good as usual.

When we were drinking our coffee I asked her what she knew about Candi.

'You were the man who found the body, weren't you?'

I was getting so famous I could become the next Burke or Hare—or both rolled into one.

'I realised as soon as you showed me the card,' she went on. 'I hadn't connected you before. Though we've all talked about it a lot at the office, of course.'

Of course. But had she heard anything that sounded interesting, anything that anyone wouldn't have read in the papers?

'No-o, although a few people did say she might have been asking for it.'

'What did they mean by that?' I asked.

She thought about it while she was taking her next sip at the coffee. It didn't look as if she was in any hurry to get back to work.

'Well, you must realise that I didn't have much to do with her. She usually went straight past my office and up to see Patrick. But you get to hear things, you know.'

'What sort of things?'

She was obviously unsure of how much she should say.

I assured her that it would be all right so she went on.

'There was a tour all set up, for the States, I don't know if you knew anything about that?'

I nodded.

'Well, I heard Patrick saying to somebody that he doubted it would ever go ahead. He doubted if she would be able to make it.'

'Drugs?'

'I don't know. It may have been that. Patrick didn't say; but he did say she had been acting very strangely. Very difficult, apparently, whenever it came to doing recordings or getting anything together at all. I think he had a soft spot for her and that's why he put up with it. But it sounded dreadful: as though she were throwing sudden fits in the studios and shouting out that everyone was trying to ruin her career. Just horrible things she would say sometimes. Then the next minute, almost, she would apparently forget about it all.'

I asked: 'Do you think she would have made any serious enemies doing that?'

Jane thought for a moment. 'No, I don't think so. I mean, it wouldn't have made her many friends. But we're used to pretty crazy people in this business. No one would have hated her for what she did, not enough to want to kill her, if that's what you're thinking.'

I paid the bill and offered her a brandy to compensate for the shock. I looked very carefully both ways, crossed the road with her and went into the pub opposite.

'I imagine that if she did want to get hold of some dope of one form or another—more than just grass, say—it wouldn't be too difficult for her to do so?'

Jane swirled her brandy round at the bottom of her glass.

I don't know how but she managed to make that quite innocent gesture into something that was very sensuous. Or maybe that was a reflection of what was going on inside my head.

'Some of the musicians who come in are on junk—I think—but she probably wouldn't be able to get hold of it as easily. Though there are always people willing—aren't there?'

She looked at me with hesitation, as though afraid of showing that she knew more than perhaps at her age I would have thought she should.

I shrugged my shoulders and she went on.

'There are always big parties at weekends. Well, not so much big as strong . . .' She faltered.

'Strong?'

'Yes . . . well, they have quite a sex scene going, so I'm told, and there's blue movies and that sort of thing. There must be a lot of stuff pushed there . . . I suppose?'

She looked oddly innocent, as if the things she was talking about were things she knew of but didn't know. It was as if the world that surrounded her had just bounced off her so far: or was that what I wanted to think?

'You said, "so I'm told". You've, never been then?'

'Certainly not! Though it's not for want of being asked. Patrick is always on at me to go. He gets on to all the girls who work there to go—to fill out the numbers, not to get involved. Although no one would complain if you did.' She laughed. 'This girl Susan who works in the imports office, she went to one and she looks the least likely girl to want to join in with anything like that. Apparently it took three of them to keep her quiet! Normally they pay girls from outside to do that sort of thing.'

I was very interested but I didn't want her to think it was for the wrong reasons. Though had she known my real reasons she might have preferred good old-fashioned lust.

'What sort of people go to these parties?'

'Music people. Disc jockeys, singers, producers—anyone who Patrick wants to keep on the right side of, anyone he wants to sweeten up.'

'With a spoonful of sex all provided free,' I suggested.

Jane nodded. Her brandy glass was empty. I offered her another but she said she had to be back at work.

'How often are these parties held, Jane?'

'Almost every weekend, as far as I know. I've been taken off the invitation list, I think.'

'Could you get back on to it again?'

I wasn't sure of what was going on inside her head and I wasn't clear what the change in expression in her eyes meant, though change it certainly did. It probably read: Oh, Christ, not another one!

'I expect I could. But why?'

'Because I'd like to go with you.'

'Look,' she said, 'if they ask me along it's because they want another free girl. I can't get invited, if I say I'm bringing a man with me.'

'Then don't tell them I'm going with you until we arrive on the doorstep. Then you can tell them you had misunderstood. They won't keep us out once we've got that far.'

Or so I hoped.

I took Jane back to the offices of Dragon Records. She promised she would do her best for the coming weekend and then call me: and she thanked me for a nice lunch. She didn't say anything about the hit-and-run, though. Perhaps it had gone clean out of her mind.

I had to make two phone calls: the first was to Sandy. She was in and in a good mood. I made pleasant noises for a few minutes and then got down to business.

'Anything about the Thurley girl?'

'Something, but not much that's any use. She tried to get a job in one or two strip clubs but no one would take her on. She looked young and one place thought she looked pretty high. But nothing else. Do you want me to keep trying?'

'Uh-huh. Listen, Sandy, if she couldn't get a job anywhere dancing what might she have to do?'

'Well, she could go on the game, if she could get the connections—not that that would be difficult. They're out waiting for kids like her. Or she could model. At least that's what they call it. Dirty pictures—stills, movies, anything like that.'

'Can you ask around then, Sandy? It might be important.'

Her voice was getting less good-humoured by the minute.

'That's what you always say . . . and have you still got my car in one piece?'

'Sure. Can I borrow it for another day?'

I said good-bye before she could change her mind. Then I hung up and dialled the number of the Holborn Library. I asked to speak to Martin.

When he came on the phone he sounded the busiest man in the bibliographical world. When I told him who it was he slowed down and sounded surprised and a little intrigued. When I said I wanted his advice about a book he sounded amazed. I don't think that his picture of a private investigator included the reading of books. He probably put me down as a sub-species that couldn't read at all.

When I asked him to recommend me a good general work on drug abuse he was stopped short in his tracks. I heard a sharp intake of breath at the other end of the line and when his voice came back on it sounded strangely high and almost quavery. But the professional in him won out. He named a couple of books and I asked if either was in stock. One was and he promised to leave it at the check-out point with a note saying it was all right for me to take it. I thanked him, asked him to remember me to Vonnie, and put down the phone.

I could picture him taking off his spectacles and wiping the mist clear. I bet that put his cataloguing back a little.

I pulled in at the motorway service station but didn't bother to try the coffee any more: it might prove to be addictive. Instead I opened the book on drugs and turned to the section on major stimulants.

Amphetamines stimulate the central nervous system. They cause mental and physical activity at an increased rate, including a marked increase in the rate of the heart; they depress the appetite and keep tiredness at bay. Prolonged use, though, causes mental depression or fatigue. Use of amphetamines may often result in a feeling very like paranoia, with visual illusions and ideas of persecution.

They are usually taken orally, though they can be injected. Severe reactions can occur after taking thirty milligrammes, but some addicted users have been known to need regular doses of as much as four to five hundred milligrammes.

I shut the book. That could be a hell of a lot of dope. And it could cost a hell of a lot of money. Martin had given me a lot of what I wanted. I hoped my return visit to Howard would give me some more.

*   *   *

The house was on one of the roads leading out of the city. It was large and stood in its own grounds, though a coat of paint would have done it no harm. It was not late but there were no lights to be seen from the windows. Yet I understood that Howard was at home; that when the club was closed he was always at home. I drove past the house and parked the car. With a torch in my pocket I walked back.

The back door was easy. I pushed it shut behind me and tried the torch. A small rear hallway with a pantry down some stone steps to the left. I went on and tried the handle of the door at the far side of the hall. It turned quietly and a quick flash of the torch told me I was in the main entrance hall. More stairs, carpeted and to my right. Closed doors to left and right. No sign of any other light.

Then my ears grew accustomed to a dull thump, a rhythmic bass that moved my foot slightly in time as I stood waiting. Waiting for what to happen? Christ knows!

I tried the stairs: slow and easy does it. As I climbed the sounds grew more distinct. The first pulse was joined by the distant noise of a voice. Male, wiry, strong yet mournful; muffled by the doors and walls, by whatever was keeping it in. Slowly from door to door, listening. Then, with no light still from under or round it, I found the right one. And now I could hear the song. A black man singing the blues.

'I walked all night long, with my 32-20 in my hand,
I walked all night long, with my 32-20 in my hand,
Lookin' for my woman, well, I found her with another man.'

The classic blues, the all-time statement of human jealousy aroused to the pitch of murder. It wasn't only the eeriness of that disembodied Negro voice coming through the door into that black space in which I stood; it wasn't only the edge to the voice as it sang of death which reminded me of Candi's voice on her last recording; it was a pricking at the base of my skull, a crackling of the hairs along the back of my hands, a tightening of the skin across my forehead.

For the time it took the singer to finish his statement I was held at that door. Then I moved away. If Howard was in there, listening in the dark, he was unlikely to hear me taking a look around.

I searched and found nothing: nothing that I wanted. Whatever Howard was going to give he was going to give in person. Or not at all.

I went back to the room. The piano began its introduction to another blues. I held the handle, thought for a split second, then went in—fast. I slammed the door shut behind me and its sound echoed dully in the darkness of the room. No other movement as the echo died on the air. Just the crackling surface of an old recording sending out a woman's voice: rich, powerful, filled with scorn and knowledge.

'I've had a man for fifteen years, given him his room and
    board;
Once he was like a Cadillac, now's he like an old, worn
    Ford;'

Gradually my eyes were getting used to the light and I made out a shape away across the room. Not tall, not small. My hand was tight on the grip of my gun and now I raised it and aimed it at this shape.

'I'm tired of buyin' porkchops to grease his fat lips,
    And he has to find another place to park his old hips,'

'Howard!' My voice cut across the record and it sounded wrong in that room, intrusive and somehow out of time.

'Howard! I said I'd be back to talk to you. Find the light switch.'

No movement.

'The light switch! If I fire this gun in this light I may only wound you in a very nasty place.'

Slowly the shape started to move, away from me, towards the wall.

'The groundhog even brings it and puts it in his hole,
So my man's got to bring it to satisfy my soul,'

The light came on and I was ready for it with one hand up to shield my eyes. But Howard didn't try anything. Just stood over by the wall. Even in the total blackness of that room he was wearing his dark glasses. A short, fat man with dark glasses and short, balding hair; plimsolls on his feet and fear in his hands as they moved up from his sides then fell back again, hopelessly.

'You got to get it, bring it, and put it right here,
Or else you can keep it out there.'

The voice rose to a climax: the needle hissed off the record. I looked around the room. It was partly sound-proofed and the walls were covered in black fabric. To my right there was a huge record player, amplifier and a cabinet full of what looked like old 78's. High on the wall at either side were two speakers. There was nothing else in the room.

Except for Howard and myself—and I had a gun.

When he spoke he didn't say any of the things that I expected him to say.

'That was Bessie Smith. Do you like Bessie? She was the greatest of them all of course. A fine singer. Fine singer.'

I couldn't tell if he was talking out of nervousness or if he was stalling for time. It didn't occur to me at the time, but now I guess it could have been that at that moment Bessie's voice was the most important thing to him. Even if I had thought it then, it wouldn't have mattered.

'I'll tell you something, Howard, then you tell me something.

A few hours after Candi Carter was killed you made a phone call to London. You called a creep called Cook and told him you'd make it worth his while to tail me. Well, he believed you and he tried his best and now he's been paid off all right but not by you. Now for you to call him then means one of two things. Either you murdered Candi, or you've got a good idea who did. Whichever it is, I want to know and I want to know fast.'

He didn't move. I did. I went over to the cabinet and picked out a record. Heavy black shellac. It broke easily when it hit the floor. So did the next. Howard still hadn't moved, hadn't spoken.

The next few records I smashed across my knee, the ones after that I threw at the wall above his head.

In 'Kiss Me Deadly' the records belonged to Fortunio Bonanova and they were grand opera. Arias for a failed wop singer to sing along to. Now it was different. I might have liked to listen to a lot of these records. Instead I broke them into little pieces.

But still Howard had not moved or spoken.

'Tell me, Howard. Tell me before your collection gets down to zero.'

I took one in my hand and went over to him. I looked at his face: from under his dark glasses the lines of his tears ran silently.

I dropped the record and brought my hand back across his face; the glasses flew off and skidded over the floor. The eyes that had sheltered underneath them were white at the rims, pink at the centre. I slapped him again then punched him in his fat gut. He folded over and went down on to his knees.

I dropped down beside him and the .38 was so close that even with his eyes he couldn't miss it.

'You've got five seconds and then I'm going to start taking you to pieces like I've taken your precious records to pieces. Only you'll feel it more. You might not believe that now, but once I start in on you then you will. Now! How did you find out I was at the flat when she was killed?'

I hit him with the barrel of the gun and he flinched away and grasped his chest. But he started to talk.

'I didn't know what was happening. I didn't know until he came, John came. He had been to see her. She owed money, a lot of money. He had been here first but I was fed up with paying her bills and getting the kind of treatment from her that I had been getting. So he went to see her himself.

'When he came back he said that she was dead. Said that he heard someone inside the flat and waited. You came out and he knocked you down. He took some pills you were carrying and saw your name from your wallet. Then he went inside and found Candi. He came straight out and left you there. He went out of the building by the fire escape and came here. He said it didn't look like the work of a private eye but I didn't know. Cook had done some jobs for me before so I phoned him. I thought if he watched you for a few days he might pick up something I could use. I don't really know why I did it. It was stupid. Stupid.'

I put my gun away in its holster.

Howard was still kneeling in the middle of the floor of his blacked-out room surrounded by broken pieces of rare recordings, spread like crazy paving over everywhere.

He picked up the nearest section. He said: 'This was Bessie Smith's last ever Columbia recording. "Safety Mama". November, 20th, 1931.'

But I was no longer listening. I went out and shut the door behind me.

–12–

Patrick lived in a large block of flats near Regent's Park. Lots of white paint everywhere and bushes in tubs outside, from behind which doormen in braid and peaked caps suddenly appeared to whisk open car doors.

I left the keys to the Saab with a superannuated juvenile lead from the days of Ginger Rogers and Fred Astaire and allowed myself to be ushered through the revolving doors. Jane went just ahead of me, turned in the foyer and waited. There was enough snob and chic in there to sink the QE2. She was wearing a short fur over a plain black dress with a neckline that did things to my blood pressure that sent it strictly over the limit. I asked one of the waxworks the way to Patrick Gordon-Brown's flat and hated the sound of my voice as I did so. It was one of those scenes that tricked you into behaving as though you had manners. In the lift Jane stood close to me and squeezed my arm. She reached up her mouth and kissed me on the point of the chin. I was thinking that it was a long while since anybody kissed me there; the only contact that usually came the way of my jaw was in the manner of right hooks. I was still thinking that when the lift stopped and the door opened out on to a corridor with a few hundred yards of red carpet. They must have known we were on the way after all.

The face at the door didn't like the look of a guy standing in the shadow of the young lady in the dark fur. When it saw me at closer quarters, it liked me even less. We were told to wait. The next face was even less impressed and distinctly rude. Until Jane tried some of her girlish charm: he didn't say anything nice, but at least he stopped being nasty and went away.

The face which appeared next belonged to Patrick. Although he recognised me, he wasn't any too pleased to see me there. Perhaps I should have said because he recognised me. But this time Jane's smiles were more successful. The door opened and we stepped over the threshold.

Patrick led us to the bar, excused himself and left for what were obviously more important matters. I got Jane a gin and tonic and myself a double whisky—all courtesy of Dragon Records, no doubt—and took a careful look around. Most people were standing in little knots, drinking and waiting for something to happen. They mostly looked Kings Road trendy—which made me look like an exhibit from a V and A retrospective. I suggested to Jane that we wander around to see what we could see. Or who.

The next room looked more promising. For a start there was hardly any light, though when your eyes became accustomed to it you could see a little more than shapes. A stereo played a watered down version of black soul and the atmosphere was sweet with the scent of cannabis. A few couples were dancing in the middle of the room; or they were holding each other and checking out all the vital parts were present. I stared harder at one of these groping couples: a disc jockey of supposedly virile appetites was fondling the tight little arse of a fair-haired boy in baby blue denim. No one seemed to think it extraordinary, least of all Jane, who pointed to a gap in the floor cushions and suggested that we went over and sat down.

We sat for a while and drank and she began to tickle the edge of my ear with the tip of her tongue. Every now and then people would get up from the floor and head in the direction of the door at the other side of the room from where we were. I guessed it was the bedroom, though it could have been the communal bathroom. The end of Jane's tongue had now begun to explore the inner reaches of my ear and I shivered with what I could only suppose was pleasure. I sure wasn't cold.

I was on the point of suggesting that we go across the room and take a look at what lay beyond the door when Patrick came up and started talking to us. Not that he had anything special to say, but he was very interested in what I was doing there. I mumbled something about being curious about how the other half lived but it didn't go down too well. So I left him with Jane and went looking for a little more scotch. Hell! I needed a lot more scotch!

There were more people milling around now and more faces that I half-recognised. Maybe if you were good enough or big enough to be known straight-off you didn't need to hustle your business with a load of free booze and sex. Not that there had been much of the latter yet. Though I was still to penetrate beyond that much used door.

When I got back to Jane and Patrick, two other guys had joined them and Patrick was busy selling product as though his life depended on it. Which in a way I suppose it did. Just a little more air-play, sweetie, and it's bound to break big.

I pulled Jane to her feet and as I did so I wondered why I had never kissed her. When I had, I wondered why I had waited so long. I kissed her again and took hold of her hand, firmly. We went over towards the famous door.

On the other side it was darker still and I had the sense of having stepped into a Chinese puzzle and hoped that I had the key. I nudged down with the inside of my left arm against the weight of my .38.

There appeared to be a large bed in the centre of the room and a lot of writhing around going on top of it. More movement was evident around the sides of the room, along the floor. Just down by Jane's foot I could see fairly clearly a figure half out of a dress, whom I guessed was a woman, though who was I to make such rash assumptions, being serviced—I can think of no better word—by two other figures which were quite evidently male.

On one wall someone had erected a screen and the flickering light from this lit up forms and faces for seconds at a time. One epic had obviously just finished and the coloured titles advertised the start of another. It was called 'Hot Pussy' but it was not about to appeal to cat-lovers everywhere: not even roast cat with orange sauce.

The scene opened with a white girl in a short polka dot dress going to the front door and gasping with surprise at seeing her coloured friend standing at the other side. At least, I assume she was her friend as she kissed her full on the mouth for some time and in close-up; she certainly wasn't the milk-lady as she wasn't carrying any bottles.

In the next scene they were in the bedroom and whitey was showing her friend the contents of her wardrobe. Then—what do you know!—her friend started to try on some of the clothes. Whoever scripted this should get a Nobel Prize for originality above and beyond the call of duty.

She took off her white blouse to reveal a hefty pair of tits bulging out of a little coffee-coloured bra. She took off the bra and they sagged down a couple of inches; this must have worried the hostess as she spent the next few minutes trying to revive them with various manipulations of her hands and lickings with her tongue. I'll say this for her—she tried hard. But it didn't seem to work. So they forgot about the new blouse and lay down on the bed.

The coloured girl began to unbutton the top of the other's dress. Well, fair's fair. They played with each other's tits for a while and just as this was getting pretty boring—for us as well as for them, our hostess sneaked her hand under the hem of her friend's skirt. And would you believe it? She wasn't wearing any knickers. This was soon reciprocated and they lay back along the bed kissing each other and pushing their fingers inside each other with practised ease.

I tried to catch a look at Jane's face in the flashes of light, but I couldn't tell if she was aroused or embarrassed. Whatever effect it was having on her, it was working on the others all right.

The figures on the bed were moving around as though they had suddenly found a nest of fleas. The lady to our left was now less in her dress than out of it and the two young studs were working hard.

All the while I was looking around me I was trying to imagine how Candi would have reacted to the situation. It's difficult to imagine someone with whom you have experienced sex in the most private and personal of ways indulging themselves in public in a place like this. But when she got high perhaps she hadn't cared. Still it wasn't a thought I liked: orgies were okay as long as you didn't get your emotions messed up in them, I guessed. So what was I doing here with Jane?

I must have missed the end of the movie, because when I looked at the screen again the film was in black and white and it looked as if whoever had made it had switched on the camera and fallen asleep. No movement from that area at all; but plenty on the single bed against the wall. They hadn't even bothered with the excuse of a plot—just three people screwing and sucking.

A girl lay on her back, buttocks slightly raised. A man lay half over her, penetrating her from above. Alongside the girl, whose face I could see, lay another girl, incongruously wearing stockings and a suspender belt. The two girls had their mouths open and were touching tongues. The girl whose face I could see had her eyes shut and was smiling.

There was a blundering cut in the film. Now the man was lying on his side and I could see that he still had his socks on. The girl in suspenders was lying behind him, leaning over his body and kissing his side. The other girl was lying on her back, with her left arm holding her left leg in the air so that the man could find his way inside her. Her leg was thin and covered up to the top of the knee by a shiny plastic black boot; the other leg hung over the edge of the bed. Her vacant eyes were staring straight at the camera as if she were lying there taking a rest before dying. The eyes of Buffy Thurley.

I grabbed hold of Jane's arm and pulled her out of the room. I wanted to find Patrick and fast. He was leaning against the bar looking as if cold cream wouldn't stain his nylon sheets. I tried hard to look a little excited but basically unconcerned.

'Great stuff, Patrick. The films, I mean. Really good—better than the usual run-of-the-mill thing.'

I leaned over away from Jane and tried the old man-to-man bit.

'I'd like to get hold of something like that for a little home consumption. Where do you pick them up from? Or does somebody bring them along?'

He looked at me as if I were proving to be an even greater embarrassment than he had feared. I asked him again, pretending to be rather drunk and getting louder by the minute. I hoped he would say something if only to shut me up. He did.

'They're brought along, old man, I just ask for a fresh supply each time. They seem to keep some people happy.'

He looked at me with something near contempt, and then behind me to where Jane stood, wondering what the hell was going on and wishing she had never come in the first place—had never brought me.

'Look, there's the chappie over there. Standing with his back to us talking to that girl in blue.'

I thanked Patrick and told Jane to go and powder her nose. She didn't like it, but she went all the same.

I walked over and stood behind him. Put my hand firmly on his arm, just by the elbow. Excused him from the conversation. Led him to a corner.

He was wide-eyed with a mixture of astonishment and fear and I could see the expression magnified through his glasses. I wondered what classification this little experience was classified under.

'Well, Martin. I didn't expect to speak to you again so soon. Or did I?'

He was looking wildly around himself now, looking for someone who would come and get him off the hook. But I was hoping that everyone else would be too concerned with their own peculiar reasons for being there to worry about us.

'Do you come here often? Or is that too corny a question?'

He spluttered and stumbled over his words: it was really his first time. I tightened my grip on his elbow and smiled into his glasses in case anyone was looking.

'You liar! You're often here, Martin. You often come here because you've got business here. And the sort of business you've got involved in brings all kinds of pleasures on the side. Doesn't it?' My grip was stronger still and the sweat was starting to run down his face; his mouth was twisting into a grimace of pain.

'It must have been very different from all those dry and dusty volumes, Martin. Very different. Lots of willing girls only too anxious to drop their knickers for some of that extra cash you found yourself with. Not just any old girl, either. Some important ladies, Martin, some important people. Stars, even, stars, Martin. You creep! I bet that really turned you on—the idea of getting inside the knickers of somebody famous. Like Candi, Martin. Like Candi. She was good, Martin, wasn't she? You don't have to tell me though, Martin. I know how good she could be!'

I let go of his arm and pushed the flat of my hand into his stomach. I began to increase the pressure and I held him as I did so. I didn't want him going down yet.

'You weren't only into leather-bound classics, Martin, your export business brought you in touch with more than that. Like some nice pornography. That's where the big money was, wasn't it? A little filth for the expense account taste. A little sex for those who can't get it straight.

'What happened once you'd started, Martin? Found you'd taken a liking to it, did you? Well, they say a man should be interested in his work, don't they? Maybe someone thought you would be a good front man for posh set-ups like this one. Perhaps they looked a bit rough—your contacts over here—for this sort of trade. So they thought you would make a nice smart messenger for them. Here, Martin, just drop these films round to the party tonight, will you? Collect the cash while you're there and grab yourself anything that's going while you're there.'

My voice was louder now and I was conscious that people

were listening. Patrick called across and started to come over towards us. Martin shook free of my grip and began to run across the room, heading for the door. He made three paces before my foot tripped him and sent him sprawling. I reached down and yanked him to his feet. I wanted something in return. I wanted to hear him shout with pain. Now. Here. Here where he and Candi had . . .

My fist smashed into his face and his nose poured red blood out on to the carpet. He went back against a trolley of glasses and sent it flying. I dived down among the broken fragments and held him by the throat; then I shook him and drove my knee hard between his legs as he threshed on the floor. Hands pulled me up and I took Martin with me. I jerked free and lashed out at him again, splitting his mouth at its edge. We were both splotched with his blood.

I wasn't sure why but I wanted to hit him again and again. Then something made me stop hitting him and I looked round and Jane was standing to one side. She looked as though she did not believe what was happening. I looked down at my fists, clenched hard. Looked at Martin's shattered face: the terror in his eyes. The fear of someone who thinks he is about to be killed. All around us was silence, stillness. A crowd of people watching. For some perhaps it was another part of the entertainment

Martin's glasses were on the floor. I reached down and picked them up. I handed them to him and his hand took them but it didn't put them to his face. Just held them in front of him like some strange gift.

-13-

My dream was all glasses and eyes, moving, interchanging, slipping in and out of focus. Pink eyes, white eyes, eyes staring with fear at their centre. The cracked lenses and twisted rims of a pair of spectacles. Lying in the middle of an all-black room. Dangling from the hand of a corpse. Looking. Looking into me. Jane's eyes looking at me. Not knowing what she saw. Not knowing if she saw. Hating what she saw. Closing, moving away. Blind.

A smash of glass and I thought it was in my dream. But then I sensed that it was not. I opened my eyes and looked at the digital clock. Five-ten. The glass must have been the small window downstairs near the door. I jumped out of bed fast and grabbed for my pants; then for my gun.

I pulled open the bedroom door and they were half-way up the stairs. This time they too had guns and they were pointing straight at me. I stood poised with one hand on the bannister rail and the other holding the Smith and Wesson.

'Put your gun away and get dressed, Mitchell. You'll catch a cold.'

It was the chatty one; back in command. His friend wore a plaster across his nose and a nasty expression all over his face. I turned around and went back into the bedroom.

One of them took my gun and I let them take it and pulled on my trousers and a sweater. I didn't like what was happening: not one little bit.

'We warned you.'

'Yes, we even offered you money.'

'But you wouldn't listen.'

'You just kept getting your nose in the way.'

'Where it didn't belong.'

'And now we're going to have to put it out.'

'Permanently.'

Oh boy, now when they both talked they were something else. If only they had had the build for it, these two guys would have made the next Laurel and Hardy—or was it Old Mother Riley and Kitty MacShane?

'Did you know she was a man?' I asked them.

They exchanged blank looks: something else they had a talent for.

The one with the plaster said: 'What the fuck are you talking about?'

'The lady in the picture, of course.' I pointed at the wall behind them. They fell for it; only the slightest of movements towards the wall away from me, but I hoped it was enough. It had to be.

I kicked at one and chopped down on the gun arm of the other. The gun fell to the floor but the man still stood in my way. My kick had landed high on his partner, but he was holding himself as though winded and his gun was against his chest. As I kicked again I wondered if it was free of the safety catch. The explosion told me it had been. He had tried to bring it back round to face me but the underneath of my foot pressed it back into his body as his finger squeezed down on the trigger. He fell back with a scream.

His friend grabbed my arms from behind and I butted back hard with my head. It must have caught him on the forehead as that was where he was holding when I turned. I punched him twice in the belly and dropped to one knee to grab his gun.

He was game. He didn't give up. He lashed out and booted me over against the bed, then jumped for me. I rolled aside and raised the gun high and fast. Then brought it down. The noise as it struck the back of his skull was as empty as a hollow drum. I did it again to make sure.

Then I looked at the boy with the plaster and the new gunshot wound. The bullet seemed to have gone into the meat of his shoulder and there was quite a lot of blood. He looked at me and spat in my face: I let him have it with the barrel of the gun and it raked away the plaster and gave him a new cut to add to his collection. I took his gun off the floor and gave him a lecture about safety. Then I went downstairs and phoned the law.

Tom Gilmour sat in the back with me and he kept the journey pretty functional. We were going to take them in and get them booked and then he and I were going to go back to his office and have a nice little talk. Maybe. Or maybe we wouldn't be in his office. It could be the blank, anonymous room downstairs which they kept for questioning their prime suspects. Far enough away from the enquiry desk to ensure that old ladies who came in to enquire about their missing tabbies didn't lose all their respect for our wonderful British police.

I didn't know and looking across at Gilmour's face sure didn't help any. Mostly it was stony, impassive—except when it was creased by a heavy scowl. But that was okay.

If you had seen what his face had seen then you would be stony too.

He spent seven hours on a ledge in Upper Brooklyn. The ledge was twelve storeys up and no more than a foot wide. All Tom had to hold on to was the sill of an open window and a few remaining hopes. The girl had no window and no hopes. She stood jammed back against the brickwork of the building, arms spread out wide as though she were waiting to be crucified. It was early evening; it was gathering dark and it was raining. A dull, insistent rain which beat down and down and down. Not that the rain mattered. It wouldn't have altered things if there had been a heat-wave.

Tom Gilmour squatted on that ledge until he had lost all feeling in his legs; until the arm which held fast to the wood of the ledge was an unmoving thing which he had long forgotten as a part of his body. And all this while he talked and tried to get the girl to talk. Most of the time it was just his voice and the beat of the rain, against the wall and up from the ledge.

Occasionally she would say something: and it wasn't very nice. It was not very encouraging. She swore at her father, whoever and wherever the bastard was; she swore at her mother, for having opened her legs on that fatal occasion and for opening them at every opportunity ever since; she swore at the son-of-a-bitch who had got her pregnant then gone off and left her, too late to have an abortion, with a life inside that she neither wanted nor needed.

Tom had said what about the child, the child who is alive inside you. And she had said it is for the sake of the child that I am doing this. And she had pushed back with her hands against the wetness of the wall and had simply dived out into the greying air.

She hadn't waited for them to come for her with the nails.

Tom watched the first fluent movement outwards, then turned his head away before the fall turned into a tumble, a vain flapping; he covered his ears from the scream, pushing his head down against the arm which held his own life fast. Even through the muffle of hand and shoulder he could hear the sickening thump.

That was just one thing: one event in the year Tom Gilmour had spent with the police force in New York. He learned a whole lot and he saw a whole lot. He came home a different man: something was missing from the centre of his body and its place had been taken by something new inside his brain. Something shining, efficient and metallic. Deadly. Maybe in a way Gilmour himself had died out on those streets.

Now he was a faster cop, a harder cop, a cop who carried his gun whenever he could squeeze the authority and who loved to feel the strength of its handle between his two hands. He had seen in New York what a city could become and now he saw in London what a city was becoming. And he didn't like it. Now he was a better cop.

A stony one. As stony as a dirty, rain-streaked ledge a foot wide and twelve storeys up.

The car pulled in outside West End Central Station and we went inside.

Gilmour took me up the stairs to his office and shut the door behind me. He went over and pulled down the blinds. Then he offered me a seat and when I sat down he kicked it away from under me. I hit the floor with a thump that must have told the guys in the office downstairs to put the earplugs in again. But Tom just stood there looking at me with an expression that was a mixture of contempt and pity.

'Christ! Mitchell, you are one hell of a creep! When are you going to realise that there isn't always going to be someone like me around who is going to leap around in the early hours of every goddamn morning bailing you out of the shitty messes you keep falling arse over end straight into?'

He spat into the wastepaper bin. He missed and he rubbed his shoe over the offending phlegm.

Then turned back to me: 'You see that yellow mess that just coughed out of my gut? Well, that's you. And you see what I did to that mess? Well, that's what I'm just liable to do to you.'

I was on the point of asking him what for, but I stopped myself. I thought that given time he would tell me anyway. He did and he didn't need much time.

'All the way along you've been withholding enough evidence to fill a paper sack and then some. You said that you had no idea who that little creep was whose head was bashed in on your stairs. Well, you knew, Mitchell. You knew and as sure as all hell you went round to his house and you found out what you could—and you got hold of his little red book into the bargain.'

I must have looked surprised for he sat hard on the front of his desk and eased the toe of his shoe into my shoulder. It sure wasn't comfortable on the floor but I wasn't about to try to get up and get pushed down by a foot in my face. That wasn't my kind of luxury.

'You're thinking how do I know. I know, Mitchell, because although it had obviously escaped your notice there is a whole goddamn police force in this city and there are more of them than there are of you. So when the police woman was talking to the little girl, after she had gained her confidence with a few sweets and a good heart-to-heart about girlish matters, she found out about the visit. The visit some man had made when she was cleaning her daddy's car the day her daddy didn't come home. And when she started to remember, boy, did she remember you good. She could describe you as well as if she'd been your own kid, not that of some dead jerk lying in the mortuary with his head staved in.

'So that's how we know for one. For two, we found this in the desk in your office.'

This time I did get up—or try to. Why didn't I listen to my own warnings just one time? The flat underside of a size ten struck along the side of my face and I hit the filing cabinet hard. Hands dragged me up and when I moved my arm so as to rub my back, one of them hit me across the cheek so that it stung, then went numb.

I was always getting hit, and this day had started off worse than most. First two heavies break into my quiet little residence and try to take me to the cemetery. Then along comes the big bold copper to the rescue and proceeds to take over where they left off. One of these fine days I was going to start hitting back and when I did . . .

'Stop feeling sorry for yourself, Mitchell.'

I rubbed my face, trying to encourage a little feeling back into it.

'Did you have a little thing like a warrant to go looking round my office for little red books?'

'Don't crap around with me, Mitchell, and don't waste my time belly-aching about your legal rights because you forfeited those a long time ago. You forfeited those the first time you put one tiny toe outside the law yourself.'

He looked at me and something rose up in his throat again and this time he hit the bin. It was getting later and he was getting more control over his faculties. I hoped like hell that he didn't feel impelled to hit me again.

But instead he turned round and went behind his desk. He sat down and took out a half-bottle of scotch and a couple of glasses. Carefully, he poured two small measures: it was still early.

He passed one over to me. I pulled the chair up from the floor and sat down. I took the scotch and it felt good and warm as it went down. He reached over with the bottle and poured me another. That felt good too.

He shrugged: 'Besides, your office lock was still busted. We just went in and looked around.'

He put the bottle back in the drawer and took out the red notebook. He turned to the page with Howard's name on it and reversed it; he pushed it across the desk so that I could see it. I sensed I was supposed to say something but I didn't. So he did.

'We knew already, I guess. When you went up to Nottingham and saw Leake and told him you were off to see Candi Carter's manager.' He paused and sipped at his own drink. 'Funny man, that Leake. Seems he took a liking to you, said you seemed all right. Liked the fact that you went and told him what you were going to do.'

He stared at me over the desk.

'Of course, that's what you're supposed to do anyway. You might try doing it with me a bit more often.'

I nodded and asked, 'Did Leake say any more?'

Gilmour shook his head, 'Not much that was of any use. They're checking out all known acquaintances of Candi Carter's and hoping for a lead that way. The flat brought them nothing at all: whoever went through that and cleaned it up would make a good housewife. Spring cleaning wasn't in it! But he didn't go much on you in that role.'

I asked, 'What about Howard?'

'They busted a couple of musicians on the night you went there first. There was a guy in plain clothes watching you watching Howard.'

I said that I had known that.

'After that it seems that Howard had another visit and Leake guesses it was from you. Whoever it was scared the shit out of him. I guess it was you, too. What did he tell you?'

I hesitated but the numbness in my cheek was only now disappearing and besides I preferred Gilmour when he was handing out scotch rather than punishment. Not that Howard had told me very much that was positive. Just eliminated a few possibilities.

'Howard didn't help much, except he convinced me that it wasn't him that finished Candi. He was fed up with the way she had been using him all right, but he wouldn't kill her. I got the impression that he was stuck on her.'

Gilmour asked, 'Did he have any idea who had done it?'

I didn't want to tell him about John until later that morning: I hoped I would be able to see that person first myself. My questions were more urgent. Then Tom could have him. So I told him part of the truth—which is all most people ever get anyway.

'She was into drugs pretty heavily and . . .'

He interrupted: 'We knew that from the autopsy. Boy, she was so high inside that the doctor nearly went on a trip from just sniffing the samples.'

'Amphetamines?'

He nodded again. 'Mostly. How did you know?'

I put it down to intelligent guesswork and went on.

'Howard said she owed and owed big. He wasn't prepared to cover for her any more. If you talk again to her recording manager at Dragon he'll tell you the same story. All the fall guys she had been leaning on and putting the bite into were moving out of the way and letting her do her own falling. And she didn't like it: she was used to softer landings. She grew to think that was all other people were for: catching her when she fell.'

Neither of us spoke for several minutes. In the smallness of that office we were both left with our own thoughts of girls falling.

Then Tom said: 'You knew her pretty well.'

I looked back at him and he understood the look. I carried on with my story.

'Howard reckoned that whoever had sold her the stuff was moving in to take payment. Or else to snuff her out as a warning.'

'He wasn't supplying her himself, then?'

I shook my head: it still hurt. 'Not by the end.' She wanted more stuff than he could get. Besides . . .' I couldn't stop myself breaking into a yawn. I had forgotten that it was still early and I hadn't exactly had a restful night's sleep. I tried again. 'Besides, he was being edged out of the market.'

Gilmour looked more interested.

'You told me before about a guy called Jupp who you thought was trying to pull the dope market together and get the really heavy, expensive stuff into the business. Do you think it might have been from one of his contacts that Candi was buying?'

He thought about it but not for very long.

'Yes, that's very possible.'

'Would Leake have had this information, about Jupp and what he was up to?'

Gilmour wasn't sure and he said so.

I said: 'Then you might pass it on to him with my compliments. Tell him that it may be that if he finds out who Candi was buying from then he might find a murderer.'

Personally I wasn't too certain about that, but it sounded convincing. At least Tom said he would pass on the information. But his face didn't show how convinced he was either.

He said: 'You'd better go out and get something to eat. You don't look any too good.'

I didn't feel it: but the thought of food made me feel a lot worse. But there were things I wanted to do and it was time to do them now. And quickly, before I was beaten to it.

I stood up and thanked Tom for the help and the drink.

As I was on my way through the door he called me back.

'Scott, I said before that if you can get anything on Jupp or any of his boys we'll be grateful. But don't let us know when it's too late: or it may be too late for you too. You best remember you won't be playing with punks when you tackle them. That Winston, for instance. He sure is one big black mother!'

I thanked him for the advice and shut the door behind me, I guessed that now he would let up the blinds and let in the light of day.

When I got on to the street the light of day didn't look too appealing to me. There were places I would rather be than walking the streets at this hour. I would rather be in the warm, in the dark.

I found myself thinking about Jane.

I found myself thinking about Sandy.

I found myself thinking about Vonnie.

I found myself thinking about Candi.

It wasn't any use: my thoughts were getting colder all the time.

I went home and started my daily round of coffee. When I thought it was a respectable hour for making calls and I guessed that the kidneys would be warming on their silver tray, I phoned Thurley.

I told him I had definite information about his daughter's whereabouts. There was a long silence in which he must have thought I was speaking from the grave. Then I asked if he had the three hundred there and ready. He said no but he would send John to the bank for it.

His voice was still emptier than usual: he was losing a little of his command, a little of his cool.

'Are . . . are you sure you have seen Buffy?'

'Sure I'm sure.'

'But where? Is she all right? Can't you tell me over the phone? Then I can send John round to fetch her.'

Yes, I bet you could, I thought.

I said: 'Never mind where for now. I'll tell you all of that when I get there. But take it from me, when I saw her she looked to be in pretty fine shape. And mixing with some very friendly people: very loving.'

I could sense that Thurley didn't understand what the hell I was rambling on about. Which was just fine. I wanted him to stay as confused as he could. And I wanted him to think that I knew a lot more that he didn't feel safe about my knowing.

But I thought I had better suggest I wasn't the only one in the know. I didn't want to arrive at the Thurley residence and find a repetition of the earlier attempt to gun me down.

So I said, 'You remember Tom Gilmour at West End Central? Well, I've just been taking an early breakfast with him. I told him I was on the way round to see you. He said to be sure to pass on his regards.'

I hung up and got over there as fast as I could.

When I got there the door was open and there was no John to usher me in. Maybe he was still at the bank. Maybe. I found his master out on the terrace.

Thurley was wearing a hacking jacket and a pair of jodphurs. I didn't know if he had been riding or was about to. Perhaps he rode into town as shotgun when John fetched the money from the bank. Or perhaps he liked the image. I didn't like his image: I thought his image stank.

It stank of privilege and hunting foxes so that your dogs could tear their bellies open with their bare teeth—dogs you had kept starved so that the lust for meat drove them to any lengths for their kill. Well, Thurley had a pretty pack of hounds and I thought I had just dealt with two. And dear John, hovering behind the coffee pot, was a third.

But what Thurley really killed with was something much less obvious and more appealing than men with guns. It came in the shape of cylindrical or spheroid pills, or it came as pure white powder. It killed through the mouth or through the vein. And every time it began to kill it brought in money. And if the money stopped coming before the kill had happened then John or someone like him would go round with their gun bulging inside their jacket.

For Thurley did none of this. He never touched the stuff, never even saw it. He just arranged that such and such a shipment be made, met and paid for. Then he sent it to someone like Jupp who sold it on the ready-made market. Except for a small amount that was kept back for special customers. Customers almost as special as Thurley himself. And someone with rather more style took that to its destination. Possibly someone presentable like John. Or more possibly someone respectable like Martin, someone with the ability to move without suspicion.

'You seem strangely preoccupied this morning, Mr Mitchell.' Thurley was standing in front of me, offering me a cup of coffee.

I took it and nodded.

'But you have found Buffy?'

I nodded again, 'Yes, I've seen her. I can tell you where. Do you have the three hundred?'

'Really, Mr Mitchell, you do seem rather unnaturally concerned about your fee. I thought such matters were normally settled up at the conclusion of a case. In retrospect as it were.'

I looked at him and still didn't like what I saw; not one inch of fatted flesh, a laundered and scrubbed surface.

'We're at the conclusion of the case, all right, Mr Thurley. Don't you worry about that.'

He was uncertain. He hadn't even expected to see me again—at least, not alive. As a mention in the newspaper of passing interest, maybe. Something inconvenient to be swept out of the way like an offending piece of dirt that had no rights to life.

He couldn't understand what had gone wrong with the two hoods he had sent round to get rid of me for good. But the fact remained he was playing it well: no chips in the veneer as yet. Perhaps it was time to make some.

This I was about to enjoy;

'Tell me, Mr Mitchell, only the other day you said you had not achieved anything. Now you say you know where dear Buffy is. How did you manage to move so smartly?'

I sat down. I was going to relax for this one.

'In my job you have to move smartly. Take this morning for instance. You'll never guess what happened to me at ten minutes past five this morning . . . ?'

I let it hang on the morning air, but that was so flat the water in the ornamental pond didn't crack its face into a smile.

He asked, 'At ten past five this morning?'

'At ten past five my house was broken into by two guys with guns who wanted to choke me off. They'd tried before but their arguments weren't persuasive enough, so this time they were told to finish me off period.' I paused long enough for his eyes to drop away from mine and flicker back. 'That was what you told them, Mr Thurley?'

He looked as if he had been hit full in the face and when he had wiped away the shock he protested.

'You are either joking in rather poor taste, or else there is something more sinister behind that absurd accusation.'

'Cut the crap, Thurley. You wanted my nose out of things all along and when I turned up at the scene of one of your prize drops last night that was more than you could take.'

'Really, Mr Mitchell, I have no idea what would constitute a prize drop as you term it and have no idea where you might have been last night. Nor would I be interested to know. My sole concern with you is that you find my daughter—which you claim to have done. If I wanted you "out of the way", then why, pray, would I hire you in the first place?'

I stood up. I sensed that we were getting near the climax. And I didn't want to miss the best view.

'Okay, Thurley. Just listen. You hired me because you half-realised that you wouldn't be able to scare or buy me off, though you kept trying that too. But you thought that if I was working for you that would give you a reason to be near me, so that if I found anything out that looked as if it might endanger your operation you would be in a good position to shut me up. Fast.'

I looked at him. Still not a hair out of place. He stood there looking for all the world like an advertisement for England in an American magazine.

'You said something about an operation, Mr Mitchell?'

'A nice clean line in drug peddling, Mr Thurley.'

He was still smiling. He still looked unruffled. The gun that nestled in his hand was small but deadly enough from that range: it was a shiny .32.

I stared down the end of it.

'I always thought of them as ladies' guns—or are you just being genteel?'

'Under the new set of circumstances, Mr Mitchell, I think we can dispense with the witty remarks, don't you? Now, before we do anything about your absurd allegations I believe that you have some information about my daughter. I think you should let me have that now.'

I started, my eyes on the finger that rested against the trigger.

'I saw her last night. You know that I was at a certain party, of course. Well, she was there.'

He didn't believe me and he said so. I told him that I had proof. I reached in my pocket and handed him a number of frames from the film I had taken with me when I left.

He took them and held them up to the morning light. There he was in the garden of his country house, surrounded by all that natural life, staring at tiny pictures of his sixteen-year-old daughter in a blue movie.

His chin drooped, the hand holding the frames faltered, that with the gun moved slightly away from its target. I jumped and the gun went off. I don't know where the bullet went but it didn't hit me. I wrenched the little gun from his grasp and he hardly struggled at all: he was numbed by the images he held in his hand.

'You asked me if I had found her. Well, there she is. Served up as dessert for the jaded sexual appetites of a group of people half out of their minds on the dope that they got from you in the first place.

'And why do you think she ended up in that film? I'll tell you why. Because you drove her there. Because you knew she was smoking dope when she was still at home but you thought it was smart not to bother about such trivialities. And when she got on to bigger things she left home and looked for ways of paying for it. She found them all right. Thanks to you. You really were a provident father, weren't you?'

Thurley was a different man; all the starch had wilted, had been washed out of him.

'Mitchell, you can't believe that I . . .'

'That you knew she was making movies for people to jerk off to? No. I don't think you knew that. But it was the market you were into and it was probably peddled by the same organisation. You were in dirt up to your arsehole, Thurley, and you know it.'

'What are you going to do?'

'I'm going to get the money that's coming to me, then I'm going to have a word with your friend, John. Then I'll see.'

He called John from the house, where of course he had been listening all along. I couldn't figure out why he hadn't interfered before, but I guess he was well house-trained. He came out on to the terrace.

'John, fetch Mr Mitchell the money.'

He disappeared and we stood there, two men with nothing between them but a few torn dreams and a little .32 with a silvery barrel and a pearl handle. While we were waiting for John to return I thought a lot of things about the gun. From the looks on his face, Thurley was thinking about less pleasant things than even I was.

The moustache reappeared with a package wrapped in plain white paper and tied neatly with string. He had been busy!

I told him to open it on the table and count it. It was all there. Now all I had to do was get out—after I had asked friend John some questions. He was standing across the table and he still hadn't made a move. The .32 was still in my hand and now I pointed it at him.

'The gun. Take it out nice and slow.'

What happened next was fast enough to deceive the eye so I'll take it gently.

While I had been so intent on watching the one I knew had the gun I lost track of Thurley; I thought he was too wrapped up in his own worries, anyway. It goes to show that you should never underestimate the ruling classes. He had got round behind me and moved up on me quietly enough to grab me by the gun arm at just the right moment.

As he did that John went for the gun: like I had told him. The only difference was that he drew it and fired . . .

I had begun to swing round towards Thurley as he pulled at my arm. It was enough. The bullet that was meant for me caught Thurley low in the neck and flung him back across the lawn and into the pond.

With my free arm I brought up the .32 and fired before John could get off another shot. I hit him in the right shoulder and he dropped his own weapon on to the terrace. I picked it up, but quickly.

'Right, now talk fast. You slugged me outside Candi's flat. Is that right?'

He winced with pain but nodded, agreement.

'But you hadn't been in there before that evening?'

I took hold of his injured arm and gave it a little twist, just to make sure he couldn't concentrate on lying.

'You don't know, who was in there before me?'

He moaned but didn't answer. I twisted the arm a little further back. The moan became a shriek of pain, but at least he nodded his head. We were getting somewhere.

'Don't nod. That could mean anything. I want words, nice clear words and lots of them. Now!' The arm went back one more time. 'Who was in there?'

'I don't know! Honest I don't! I went along there from that fat sod, Howard. They were getting fed up with the way she was holding out on payments, making excuses all the time. So they said would I go over and see what I could do to frighten her into finding some money fast. Maybe rough her up a little, but that was all. Honest. That was all. Then when I got there, the light was on so I waited outside. Then I guess you come out. I let you have it and then took a look to see who you were.'

I interrupted. He was talking well now but I wanted to stay in charge of the direction.

'Who did you tell you'd left me there?'

'I told Thurley when I got back, and . . . oh, Jesus, can't you do something about this arm . . . and I told Howard that night. After I left the girl's place.'

I asked if there were any bandages around. He said there were so I told him to get some. I pulled away the sleeve of his shirt and helped him to patch up the wound enough to stop the bleeding for a while longer. By then I would be finished and he would be able to phone a doctor or take his chances as he wished.

'Neither of them knew that I was going to be there?'

'Of course not, or else what would have been the point in letting me go for barging in?'

I set to thinking fast. That meant that neither Thurley nor Howard had tipped off the cops it might be worth hanging around and turning me over when I emerged. But someone had to know that I was going to be there that evening; and it had to be someone who knew that I would have a better than average motive for killing Candi myself.

If you were down—nearly all the way down and all of your usual friends had turned their backs, then who did you turn to? Candi had tried me that previous evening when she had sounded near to despair. I wondered who else she might have spoken to, and whether in her conversation she had mentioned that I was going up to see her and when?

My thoughts were interrupted by another moan from John. The blood was rapidly draining from his face, and it was also starting to seep through the bandage round his arm.

I left him and walked outside to the back of the house. I took a few steps towards the pond. The body was floating upside down and the little eddies of blood were moving out slowly over the still water.

I went back into the house and made sure I had my money and my gun. John had disappeared and I didn't particularly care where.

-14-

There was a weak sun in the sky for a change and I thought at last we were in for something better. The wind had disappeared and the stillness of the air made it seem like walking behind glass. The law had taken Moustache back to the station and were holding him for Candi's murder. They weren't certain but at least he was a better suspect than I had ever been. He was loudly shouting his innocence and when Leake got down to talk to him I thought he might be believed. But in the process they would find enough on him to put him away for a good long stretch.

As for me, I believed him too. At least, I believed that he hadn't finished Candi with a .32 in the centre of her back. It didn't seem like his style. At the moment I had one or two ideas whose style it might have suited better.

I thought I would walk back to the office, so I left the car parked outside the flat and did a little thinking on the way. But the ideas wouldn't go straight: they were as stubborn as pigs when you try to drive them through a gate. After a while I stopped trying to organise them and watched them snuffling and snorting around inside my head.

The man I had called to fix the door and the lock had evidently been for the office was shut up tight and he had left a nice neat bill tucked inside the letter flap.

I tossed it on to the desk, unopened, and put my feet up. I didn't have to wait long for the phone to ring. I picked it up and it wasn't the voice I was expecting. Instead it was Sandy's and her normal throaty tone was choked and shredded with pain. She didn't have the strength to say much but before she was finished I was on my feet and the phone was lying on the desk croaking away to an empty office.

I ran the length of three blocks before I found an empty cab and shouted the directions in the driver's startled ear. But speed he did and I paid him well and took the stairs three at a time.

When Sandy opened the door, though, I was stopped dead in my tracks.

She was standing in her robe and her face was drained of every sign of life. Her eyes were dead, flat: the eyes of a fish that had lost its fight for survival. For a split second I thought of the faces of women I had seen in photographs of the last war. Then I reached out gently and slid away the brown towel she was holding round her head.

The scalp had been savaged, brutalised: where there had been a luxuriance of red life there was now nothing but a stubble. A stubble that had been hacked and torn as the hair had been cut and pulled from its roots. Blisters of blood rose up in between the jagged ends of hair.

I wanted to speak but no words would come. I wanted to take her in my arms but her deadness forbade it. So I stood there. I stood there and she raised her hand and slapped me across the face with what strength she had left. Then she slapped me again and again, the blows staggering on and on, becoming less and less powerful until finally they were the merest caresses of my cheeks. Then when she could lift her arm no longer the tears welled up in her eyes and broke down her face.

And still I wanted to hold her and still something held me back. 'Who?'

One word and in that room I did not recognise my own voice.

In response she found the strength to hit me again and to scream.

'That's it, isn't it? Who? That's always the question from you. That's why I ended up like this, because I asked too many questions on your behalf. Too many questions of the wrong people. There are places where it doesn't pay to be nosey. Oh, but you know that. You know it even though you say, "It will be all right, all you need to do is to show a photograph, ask around. It will be all right!"

'Well this time it wasn't all right, was it. And I'm not going to tell you one thing more. I'm not even going to tell you who it was that did this. Because if I do and they find out—and they will find out, then they'll come back and next time they'll kill me.' Her voice was like broken glass and what it was saying rubbed against the inside of my brain.

'I've said my last thing to you, Scott Mitchell. I've run my last errand, done the last dirty job for you I'm going to!'

I couldn't just stand there. I had to say something or turn round and walk away. I tried. I said: 'Sandy, your hair will grow. It will grow and you will be all right . . .'

The look in her eyes stopped my voice like a stopper shut tight.

'Yes, Scott, the hair will grow. And I could wear a wig until it does and carry on making a living. My living. Making it the only way I know how. But what people pay for is my body, Scott. My body. That's what they pay for—to see it or to sleep with it. And who's going to pay for this?'

She pulled aside the edges of her robe, then let it fall around her feet. She stood there in the middle of that room quite naked and with two giant lines carved down her body, from the space between her breasts to the bottom of her stomach. She looked as though someone had ridden a tractor across her and ploughed out a bloody furrow. Not deep enough to raise too much blood, but deep enough to turn aside the edges of the skin, deep enough to scar. To scar so well that make-up would not cover its effects.

'Who's going to pay for this body now!'

She screamed it in my face with her last available burst of energy.

I didn't need to ask who any more: I knew.

I could do nothing else. Maybe somebody else could have done, but that somebody else was not there. I was. Scott Mitchell.

I turned around and walked away, the lines through her body etched behind my eyes.

I asked Gilmour one question. When he gave me the answer I checked my gun and got the keys to the Saab.

The approach was flat, the narrow road leading through a waste-land of rubble and brick. The houses had been pulled down and a new industrial area was going up. Across the emptiness of the landscape I could see the cranes reaching up off the river to a sky that still held a watery sun.

I drove past a collection of smashed and rusting cars and thought I was getting nowhere. Then, suddenly, I swung round a corner behind a corrugated building and there it was. The words 'Billiards and Snooker' showed on a sign at the side, although the glass had been smashed and the light was not working. I drove the car round the gravel area that was used as a car park, trying to avoid the holes full with water. There were seven other cars there already. I put the Saab at the end of the park, beside the edge of the building and facing back the way I had come. Also blocking the exit of anyone else.

I slid out to the gravel and walked round the building. The main door was on the far side; I ignored this and went on round. There was a small window quite high off the ground. I pulled my-self up and looked inside. It was dimly lit except for where lights were switched on over tables in play. Four of them. At the far side of the hall, facing the entrance, sat a man in a wooden arm-chair. He was holding something across his knees, but I couldn't make out what it was. I looked from table to table and saw what I was looking for at last. On a table in the centre, just breaking off into the reds, a massive Negro leaned over a cue that looked like a toy in his grip. I dropped down to the ground and continued to walk round the building.

There was another door. Of course, there had to be. I was slowly easing it open, unsure of what was behind it, when a voice spoke quietly into my ear.

'Oh, no, sweetheart. Let's go in the right way, shall we?'

I turned slowly and looked down the barrel of a Luger: it looked old and nasty and as though it might go off at any minute. On the other end of it was a grinning guy of about twenty with the two front teeth clean out of his head. That's what you get for smiling so much—sooner or later someone takes it the wrong way and punches your face in. Not that that was one of my problems: smiling, I mean.

I allowed myself to be pushed back the way I had come, still, nervous about the Luger and wondering whether he was going to search me for my own gun now or later. He was pretty good. He stopped me by the door and told me to put my hands high against the wall and my feet apart. Then he frisked me as if he was enjoying it. He found the gun and eased it out of its holster.

'Nice one,' he chuckled, 'police issue, is it?' He chuckled again. He really was a happy little soul. 'All right, sweetheart, open the door and through you go.'

When we entered the hall all but the most serious game stopped and looked round at us. The Luger prodded me over towards the man in the chair.

He was small and he looked old and tired. Perhaps he had taken so long to build everything up that he had lost interest by the time it had happened. It's that way sometimes. Whatever he looked like he didn't look like the boss of a crime organisation. If anything he looked like a retired docker. His neck had started to go straggly and the hands with which he nursed the thing on his lap were boney and veined. The thing was a bayonet.

He saw me looking at it and spoke: 'My boy was in the Korean War. Brought this back as a souvenir. While he's inside I have it as a kind of keepsake. Company till he comes home. Nothing like your own flesh and blood. I never trust anyone else.'

I wasn't sure if this last remark was meant for me or for those clustered round.

The one who had brought me in showed Jupp the gun he had taken from me.

'He had this on him, boss. He was trying to slope in the back way. Sneaky, like. Weren't you, sweetheart?' He accompanied this with a poke in the back with the Luger. I was still afraid it might go off. Maybe Jupp was too, for he told him to put it away. Then he asked me who I was and what I wanted.

I told him my name and then I turned and pointed to the Negro, who was still chasing the very last red around the cushions.

'I want him.'

Jupp laughed—a dry crackle of a laugh, a memory of a laugh that sounded as real as ashes of roses.

'What do you think you're going to do with him, son?'

I looked back into the old man's face: 'I'm going to kill him.'

For a moment something flickered in the tired eyes then lay to rest.

'I doubt it, son. Even if I was to let you try, I doubt if you could do it. But suppose you did, would you try to kill all the rest of us? Would you try to kill me? 'Cause what he did, son, he did because I told him to.'

He fingered the edge of the bayonet without looking at it, almost unconsciously.

'I told him to, boy.'

There was no answer. I knew that I had no right being there: not if I had any sense of respect for my own life. But there I was and I wasn't expecting to get out alive. I just wanted that big spade first.

I turned my back on Jupp. I took off my jacket and holster and stood there watching the big man pot the yellow ball with a long shot down the table, then curl the cue ball back for the next colour. He was good.

'Cut that fucking crap and come where I can take your head off your shoulders!'

It was loud, loud enough for him to hear and for him not to be able to ignore. Not in front of all these people. Not in front of Jupp. Not that he wanted to.

He turned from the table and came towards me; he hadn't put down the cue but held it in front of him, slightly raised. I began to move to my right, not too quickly. I didn't want to startle him into a move just yet. He kept coming at me and I watched as the cue got higher. Then I reached fast to the side of the nearest table and grabbed up the rest that was hooked there. I grabbed it and brought it up as the cue in the Negro's hand swung down for my head. The rest was longer and it struck him alongside his head, causing his own blow to fall short. But it didn't stop him coming. He lifted the cue again, with two hands, and brought it down on top of me. I tried to parry it with the rest, held across the path of his swing. The cue snapped through the wood of the rest and thumped down into my leg above the knee. I was aware of a blinding pain as I jumped to one side and rolled over the top of the nearest table. He followed me with another swing which broke his cue against the slate bed.

Then I jumped for him and aimed my fist at the side of his head, and in my fist was a billiard ball and the crack as it landed on his jaw bone cut clear across the room. He shrugged his head and looked at me in disbelief. I aimed up at his face a second time but got nowhere near it. His arm wiped mine aside and something equivalent to a power-shovel drove into my face and sent me into a stack of cues on the wall.

I went down hard and came up spitting out blood and bits of broken tooth. I also came up with a cue and lifted it off the floor, aiming it for his groin as he followed in his punch. I hit him full on and he let out a piercing yell and clutched at his balls. I brought back the cue fast and caught him one high on his undefended temple.

For a moment he stood there, perplexed, swaying. I was sure he must go down. Instead he reached inside my next swing and grabbed me off the ground. He hauled me high into the air, swung me once in a full circle and threw me across the room. I landed in a sprawling heap across Jupp's chair.

My fall sent the old man tumbling and when I got back up as far as my hands and knees the bayonet was close to my grasp. My

fingers clutched at the end of it; I looked at the Negro. He was
standing a little unsure of himself: the blow to the temple must
have shaken him after all and he was confused about knocking his
boss to the ground.

There wouldn't be a second chance. I pulled back the bayonet into a swing and went for his right arm. The old man must
have kept the blade well-honed for it cut through his sweater
right into the flesh of the upper arm. As I pulled it away and
as the blood followed, he let out a high scream of wonder and
grabbed at the wound. I lifted the bayonet high and aimed for
the area just above the bone of his right hip. Once more the
steel bit home and the giant staggered to his knees. That was
where I wanted him: the bayonet was right back over my head
at the beginning of an arc. My eyes were fixed on the top of his
shining skull.

'Freeze!'

The Negro's eyes clung to the blade above his head.

I stood balanced and in mid-swing: my own eyes were still
sharp on their target.

'Everyone back to the far wall. And keep your hands high,
high, high.'

Tom Gilmour stood at the doorway. His feet placed slightly
apart, both hands tight round the Magnum that was aiming behind me, aiming at Jupp who was holding the boy's Luger in his
skinny hand. He had been about to shoot me in the back of the
head. Then the room was full of cops.

Tom came over and lowered my arms from the position in
which they had stuck. He lowered them and took the bayonet
from my grasp. Took it and dropped it to the floor with a clatter.
Then he turned to the Negro who had not moved, except to attempt to stem the flow of blood.

Gilmour looked at the cut in his right hip and kicked him in
the leg just below it.

'All right, you black mother-fucker, shift your arse over to that
wall!'

– 15 –

Vonnie was wearing a white blouse that buttoned up to the neck and ended in a cute little frilly collar. She had on a plain black skirt and she was sitting beside me changing the plaster on my cheekbone.

Her hands were small and cool and I liked the feel of them on my face. Still I flinched when the plaster came away from the bruised skin and she tutted at my babyishness. She leaned her head over towards me and put her lips alongside the centre of the bruise; she ran her kiss down the cut. It was good to close my eyes and concentrate on that. On that and nothing else.

I needed to forget a lot of things: I needed to forget whose mouth was moving over me like warm silk.

'Do the police think it was this John who killed Candi, or do they think it was Thurley?' She was whispering in my ear. 'After all, didn't you say that Thurley's gun was the one which shot her?'

I moved my head an inch away. Her mouth came after it. I tried again.

'The same kind.'

'What do you mean? I thought you said it was the same gun.'

I kept my eyes away from her face.

'I said the same calibre gun. That doesn't make it the same weapon.'

She slid her hand over my arm and began to nestle up to me. She said: 'So they don't know for sure who did it yet?'

I said: 'You're showing a lot of concern.'

She said: 'Well, I did pay you to find out, or had you forgotten that?'

I stood up and walked a few paces away. I felt safer out there.

'No, Vonnie, I hadn't forgotten that. In fact, that was one thing that made me uncertain for longer than perhaps I should have been.'

Those clear innocent schoolgirl eyes were looking straight at me.

'Uncertain about what, Scott?'

'That you killed your own sister.'

The room was suddenly very cold: a shiver swept through me and the hair at the back of my hands began to crackle slightly. The smile moved off her face to be replaced by something that was a mixture of fear and hate. Then these, too, disappeared and the winning smile returned. She got up and came towards me; put her hands on my arms and raised herself to her toes. One of her hands crept up behind my neck and pulled my face down on to hers. She kissed me for a long time, her tongue hotly probing my mouth as though she were trying to get inside my mind. I let myself go limp and she was kissing nothing and she let go of me and stepped half a pace away.

Her face crumpled and the tears came; she wiped at her cheeks with the back of one of her smooth little hands.

Through her tears she said: 'Oh, why do you accuse me of such a . . .' and then the tears returned and stopped her saying more.

I didn't know whether she was playing at being Mary Astor on purpose, or whether she had seen 'The Maltese Falcon' so many times that she said the words unconsciously.

But I had seen it too.

'This isn't the time for that schoolgirl act!' I replied. 'You've been trying that on ever since I first saw you and it just won't work on me any more. So don't stand there forcing tears out of your face and looking like a virgin martyr!

'At first I couldn't work out why, Vonnie, until I remembered seeing your face a long time ago. It was at a party at your house and I was there with Candi and I was kissing her and I opened one eye and caught sight of you watching us. I knew that if you could look at us with such hatred in your eyes, such jealous hatred, then you were not the sweet unspoilt little thing you were busy making out to be.

'Jealousy like that doesn't vanish, Vonnie, along with childhood games and comics: it stays, it germinates, it grows inside until it swamps the person it's thriving in.'

The tears had stopped now and she was just standing there, listening and looking up into my face and I didn't have any idea at all what she might be thinking.

'You must have got to thinking about what Martin was doing those nights he came home late from meetings about his new business. And, besides, a woman can tell when her husband is having another woman.

'So you made it your business to find out. And you found out that he had been seeing your sister. And the jealousy you would have felt about anyone else was compounded inside your heart until there was only one way of letting it all out.

'And that way was through a .32 calibre hole into the middle of Candi's back.'

The look in her eyes was changing now: I thought it might have been like this when she had called on Candi.

'Candi rang me as she was afraid of getting a nasty visit from one of Jupp's boys, then how pleasantly surprised she must have been to see her sister on the doorstep. Only she didn't know that you had a gun in your handbag.'

Vonnie said, 'Scott, you don't have to . . .'

She reached up for me and kissed me again, but my mouth was closed and my face was like stone. She pulled her face away and looked at me with hatred in her schoolgirl eyes.

I knew the script. I knew there should be a knock on the door and I would say, 'Come in', and then the door should open and a cop would be standing there and I would say, 'Hello, Tom'.

But I hadn't said anything to Tom. Or to anyone else. Yet.

Vonnie was sitting on the settee, staring at her handbag. I went forward and picked it up by the handles and held it out in front of me.

'Is it still there, Vonnie? The little gun you killed her with—Candi—Ann—whatever you called her when you did it. Is it still there?'

I dropped the bag down on to the settee in front of her, without opening it.

I didn't look at her face again: I didn't want to see what was in her eyes.

I turned and walked to the door. Opened it. Walked out into the street. The wind was still cold and once again I pulled my overcoat collar up round my neck and hunched down my head. Looking for the warmth that was so difficult to find.

THE
GERANIUM
KISS

For Julie: forever

-1-

It was nine minutes after eleven and I was lying in a bath tub of water, that was gradually becoming the same depressing shade of grey as the sky outside. Or my last memory of it. But then, most of my memories were that colour.

It was early December and after pretending for a long time that it wasn't going to happen, it was winter. Summer had been hot and long; Autumn had produced reds and golds the brightness of kids' picture books. Just when everything had conspired to lull folk into a false sense of security—wham!

The thing that annoyed me most was that I had been surprised. I shouldn't have been. I'd been around long enough to know that life worked like that. Maybe I'd been around too long. Thirty-six years too long.

No. It hadn't all been like that. There was a time back there, somewhere. Four years less than four days. . . .

Something cut in on my self-pity. Downstairs the phone was ringing. Another thing I should have known. No-one would call for days. Then when I took a bath there would be enough bells ringing to make me think I was the Hunchback of Notre Dame. Not that I'd ever worked out whether the best thing to do was to jump out of the bath, grab a towel and run down the stairs or wait until they phoned again later.

If it was important they'd call again.

Maybe.

Maybe they'd just move on through yellow pages to the next private investigator in the book.

I stayed where I was. There's something about your own warm dirt which is eternally consoling. I guess in the end it has to be.

The phone stopped ringing. I began to apply my mind to the great human problem of how the hell I was going to pass the time until there was a reasonable chance of getting to sleep for the night.

I could walk down to the coffee shop and indulge myself in blueberry shortcake; stay home with my stereo and a book of bridge problems; wait in the bath until my skin began to flake off into the water . . .

The phone cut across my thoughts again.

Okay, I said to myself, let's go.

I splashed a good quantity of murky water on to the floor; pulled at a towel and secured it around myself at the third attempt; collided with the edge of the bath; half-ran, half-hopped down the stairs, almost slipping three steps from the bottom; grabbed at the receiver; in time to hear the phone cut off at the other end of the line.

I told the telephone exactly what it could do with itself and sat down on the stairs, drawing breath. Then I padded through into the kitchen and put water in the kettle, switched it on. Took down the glass jar of Columbian coffee beans and shook some into the electric grinder. Ground the beans, warmed the enamel pot. I measured the amount of coffee that went into the pot and the amount of water that followed it. Stirred everything up and set the pot on the cooker.

Now I could go upstairs and get dressed. It was five minutes off twelve o'clock.

At three minutes past midday the phone went again. Don't ask me why I noticed the time. Occasionally I get obsessive about little things like that. Once I swore to myself that I wouldn't be able to live unless I had scrambled eggs for breakfast every day. I had sworn I wouldn't be able to live without a whole lot of things.

But here I still was and it was a hell of a long time since I'd had scrambled eggs.

I took the phone off the hook.

'Hello,' I said, 'this is Scott Mitchell.'

'Well, hello,' said someone somewhere, 'I'm glad you're finally up.'

The speaker was female with the kind of voice that goes with all those ads for Martini and Bacardi and the other drinks I'd never really got around to. I wondered what she wanted from me.

'What do you mean?' I asked.

'Well, Mr Mitchell, you have been proving rather difficult to get hold of.'

'I've been taking a bath,' I explained.

'Oh,' she said with a slight smirk in her voice, 'then that would make you even more difficult to get hold of.'

'That depends where you had in mind getting a grip,' I said.

'That depends what you've got that's worth the effort.'

She was rising in my estimation with every minute and that wasn't the only thing that was rising. It wasn't every woman who could make me feel randy over the telephone in the middle of the day. But perhaps I'd been taking calls from all the wrong people.

'Are you still there, Mr Mitchell,' the voice said, 'or have you slipped away for a quick rub down?'

'A quick what?'

'A quick . . . oh, forget it!'

'I'm trying to,' I said, 'but it's hard. There's this image in my mind that's most disturbing.'

'The only thing I can suggest, Mr Mitchell, is that you take yourself in hand. There's nothing else I can do in the circumstances.'

There was a pause during which I was conscious of the sound of her breathing, then she added, 'Unfortunately.'

'There is one thing you could do,' I told her.

'What's that?'

'You could tell me why you phoned. I'm sure it wasn't only to brush up on your telephone technique.'

'Are you telling me that my technique needs improving?' She managed to sound almost hurt.

'Not at all,' I replied, 'but I'll withhold my written reference until I've experienced it in person.'

'Now, Mr Mitchell, you're bragging! Don't tell me that you can write. I thought you were a big dumb private detective.'

'I am. But I'm one of the newer kind. Got smart and went to evening classes: reading, writing and elocution.'

'What happened to the elocution?' she asked.

'I dropped out of that one. The teacher would keep coming up behind me with a long, pointed stick. Something to do with my diphthongs.'

'Your what?'

'Forget it,' I said, 'I haven't used them in a long time. And you still didn't tell me why you called.'

'You know a policeman called Gilmour,' she said.

I didn't know if it was a statement or a question, so I didn't reply. Just waited.

Finally, she carried on. 'He suggested that you might be the man to get in touch with. There's a little difficulty and we need some help.'

'We?'

'Yes.'

'Meaning you and your husband?'

'Meaning my employer and myself, Mr Mitchell. I no longer have a husband.'

'You make it sound as though you lost him in a waiting room at Victoria Station.'

'Actually, it was room 101 of the Royal Hotel. Now can we get on with business?'

'By all means. What kind of difficulty do you happen to be in?'

She hesitated, then said, 'I don't think I can discuss it on the phone, Mr Mitchell. Couldn't we meet?'

'I'm sure we could. But if you didn't want to talk about it on the phone, why didn't you go straight into my office?'

'I don't believe in trusting other people's recommendations too fully. I wanted to make my own assessment before arranging any kind of meeting. This is a very delicate affair, Mr Mitchell.'

'In that case,' I said, 'maybe you'd better try someone else. I'm about as delicate as King Kong.'

'But look how gentle he was with Fay Wray,' she replied.

I liked that. I liked a woman who'd seen a movie or two.

'So what's your assessment?' I asked.

'Where's your office?'

I gave her the address in Covent Garden and told her I'd meet her there in an hour and a half. She said it sounded a long time, but I figured that didn't matter.

Hard-to-get Mitchell, that's me.

'One last thing,' I said.

'It's Stephanie,' she said, 'Stephanie Miller.'

'How did you know that was what I wanted?' I asked.

'It wasn't,' she replied and hung up.

I poured myself some coffee and sat in the armchair. Yes, that's right, the armchair. I had visitors like starving people had food.

The coffee was a little strong by now, but that didn't matter. I sat there trying to picture what she might be like. Finally figured that she'd be above medium height, longish dark hair, strong face; good clothes over a better shape.

I considered calling Tom Gilmour at West End Central and asking him what it was all about. For no good reason, I decided against it. I could wait. I was the kind of guy who just thrived on surprises.

Why, I was already getting worked up about Christmas.

This year I might even get a present from someone other than myself.

After another cup of coffee, I got the car out of the garage and drove into town.

*   *   *

Since the vegetable traders had moved away from Covent Garden and the developers had threatened to move in, it was like walking around in some kind of ghost town. The painted iron work of the original market still survived and where properties had been demolished, kids had used the walls that surrounded the empty sites for a series of highly-coloured murals. Yet, despite all this, there was a deadness, a lack of reality about the place.

Maybe that was why I stayed there; why I still liked it. Or maybe that was because I couldn't afford an office anywhere else.

I pushed open the side door next to what had been a jewelry showroom and was now an empty space and another plate glass window waiting to be broken.

The stairs that led up to the first floor were dirty and looked as if they'd hadn't been swept in a long time. It was dark on the landing and I felt for the light switch. Nothing happened. I should have known.

The sign that had been painted on the frosted glass of the outer office door read, 'Scott Mitchell—Private Investigator'. The capital letters had all begun to flake away slightly, as though they thought they were giving the place too good a name.

I pushed the key into the lock and let myself in. Three paces took me over to the inner door and I unlocked this as well. Both locks.

Nobody could say that I wasn't a careful man. Sometimes. Usually when it didn't matter.

I pulled up the shade at the window and looked down into the street below. No-one walked the pavements. No-one drove along the street. I turned away and sat down behind my desk, wondered if I could take yet another cup of coffee. Decided that I could. After all, I hadn't had lunch.

The water boiled just as I heard a car draw up outside. When I looked out of the window, I was staring down on to the top of a neat little sports job in two-tone blue. After a few moments, I got a second mug from the cupboard and set it alongside the first.

Then I sat back behind the desk and tried to look the way I guessed she'd want me to look.

She didn't look too surprised when she came round the door and saw me sitting there. But then, maybe her expectations hadn't been too high.

My own had and she came up to them in every way. Not only that, but I'd managed to get the description right in most details—only the hair was fair rather than dark. She wore a mid-length dark purple skirt under a dark fur coat that certainly hadn't come from any jumble sale. She smiled and came towards me holding out her hand.

I stood up and accepted it, being a gentleman underneath all the tough, wise-cracking exterior. Her fingers were cool, her grip firm and confident. Her eyes were a kind of greeny-blue and they never left mine until we had both sat down.

'Coffee?' I asked, nodding my head in the direction of the percolator in the corner.

She made a face, as though anticipating some kind of gritty brown mixture, but said yes anyway.

Then she said, 'You live a long way from your office, Mr Mitchell.'

'I like to leave work far behind me,' I said, 'the only thing is that it has ways of chasing after me.' I tried my second-best smile. 'Oh, and won't you make that Scott. Mr Mitchell sounds too formal.'

'If you don't want your work to follow you home,' she said, 'why have your home number in the book as well as this one?'

'I guess, Stephanie, that I can't afford to turn down the possibility of being hired. If you see what I mean.'

'I see what you mean,' she replied. 'Oh, and won't you call me Miss Miller?'

I blinked and got up to pour out the coffee. By the time I had brought it back to the desk, she had lit up a cigarette. I hesitated a moment, waiting for her to offer me one so that I could refuse, but she didn't give me the opportunity.

I looked down at the way she had hitched the hem of her skirt above her knees and wondered what kind of opportunities she might give me. If any.

'That's not bad,' she said after sipping from the edge of the cup as though it might turn the tables and bite her. 'Not bad at all. Maybe you ought to be in the restaurant business?'

'Sorry,' I said, 'I already have a good business.'

She looked around the office. 'Where do you keep it?' she asked. 'This really is a good front.'

I laughed a little and drank some of the coffee. She was right. It was good and business wasn't. I tried to picture myself in a white apron pouring morning coffee and calling out for some more slices of home-made apple pie at the same time. I didn't like what I saw.

I said, 'Maybe what you've brought will help things along a little. Do you think we can talk about it now . . . or are you frightened that the place is bugged?'

Ostentatiously, I looked under the desk for a hidden recording device. As I did so, she crossed her legs easily and pleasantly.

'Are you really feeling for something under there?' she asked. 'Or is that just an excuse to look up my skirt?'

I grinned. 'It could be both.'

She said, 'Look, do you want me to tell you why I'm here or not?'

I shrugged my shoulders. 'It'll do. For now.'

She picked up her coffee cup and held it in both hands in front of her, not drinking from it, simply holding it. I wondered what it was about the things she had to say that made her need that kind of support, that kind of comfort.

'For the last three years I've worked for a man called Crosby Blake. Have you heard of him?'

I shook my head from side to side. I was still watching the way in which her fingers curled around the cup, holding it tight.

'Well, he's a rich man, Mr Mitchell. He made a lot of money from chartered aircraft and invested that in a great many things. He also owns a large taxi fleet and several firms which hire out vans and lorries.'

I interrupted. 'You mean he's nationalised the transport industry all by himself.'

'In a way. Except that he runs his business efficiently.'

'And takes all the profit.'

She leaned forward in her chair and stubbed out her cigarette in the ash tray.

'All that is merely background and largely beside the point.'

'Which is what?' I asked.

She looked up at him sharply and her voice was as cold as iced water. 'For a man who obviously isn't overburdened with work, you are very impatient. I can always take this somewhere else.'

I stood up and began to move around the desk.

'I hope you're going to get me some more coffee,' she said quickly, 'and not do anything petty and dramatic like opening the door and showing me the way out.'

I turned right and went for the percolator. As if I had been going to do any such thing as offer her the door. As if!

After I had sat down again, she continued.

'Mr Blake has no immediate family of his own. He has never married. He lives with his sister and her daughter—her husband was killed in a road accident sixteen years ago. A year after the daughter was born.'

'Which makes her seventeen,' I offered. I'd forgotten to tell her that I did arithmetic at night school as well.

She looked directly at me again. 'Which makes her seventeen and missing.'

I drank a little of the coffee. It had a sharp tang to it that tried to take my palate by surprise.

'Lots of girls go missing at seventeen. Including some from the finest homes.'

'I know that, Mr Mitchell,' she said, 'but Cathy isn't simply missing. She's been kidnapped.'

That took me by surprise as well. I looked at her and tried to see something in those green-blue eyes. But I didn't know what I was looking for. So I asked a question instead.

'When did this happen?'

'Two days ago.'

I whistled softly. 'You've told the police, of course.'

'Of course.'

'Then why . . . ?'

'Why come to you?'

I nodded.

'There's been a ransom demand. Crosby wants to pay it.'

I noted the switch from Mr Blake to Crosby and nodded for her to carry on. Maybe it would be three years before she got to call me Scott.

'The police are keeping well out of things. Maintaining a low profile, I think they called it. After one or two other cases recently, they've decided to handle things rather differently.'

'Which is why there's been nothing about this in the press,' I suggested.

She had finally felt able to put down the cup. But only to reach for the security of another cigarette. There was something strangely interesting about a confident woman coping with a situation that she found in some way upsetting.

Yet she did it well. I wondered if she even knew what she found disturbing and why. Wondered whether she realised the way she had been making use of her cup and now her cigarette.

'The police had some difficulty achieving it, apparently, but all of the media have agreed to give no coverage to the kidnapping whatsoever. For the time being. I don't know how long they will wait.'

She blew a gentle wreath of smoke in my direction.

'I hope it's long enough,' she said.

I asked, 'Where exactly do I come in?'

'Crosby was terribly uncertain about how to deal with the paying of the ransom, the whole business of making the arrangements. This thing has affected him really badly. I've never known him like it.'

The fingers that held the cigarette trembled very slightly.

'He wanted someone who would help him with those kinds of things. Obviously, the police themselves were out of the question. He asked the officer in charge of the case and you were suggested.'

I made a mental note to buy Tom Gilmour a bottle of scotch for Christmas, then remembered that since his trip to the States he drank bourbon. It wasn't the only habit he'd picked up over there; neither the worst nor the best. Just one of many.

And now someone had saddled him with a nice quiet case of kidnapping which he was having to handle as though wearing velvet gloves.

I wondered what he thought about that. Then I stopped wondering. I thought I knew.

'Okay,' I said, 'do I get the details from you, or from Blake himself?

'Mr Blake will see you this evening, if that's satisfactory.'

'This evening? What's wrong with this afternoon? Or isn't his niece a matter of urgency to him?'

She flashed me a look I didn't understand and said, 'Oh, yes, Mr Mitchell, I think I would say she was that.'

She was half-way to the door when I called her back.

'There's the little matter of my fee.'

She shrugged her shoulders. 'I don't suppose that it will worry Mr Blake, whatever it is.'

I stood up. I didn't suppose it would worry him either. No more than a fly walking up an elephant's back would worry the elephant. But I wasn't the elephant—not in this or any other story. And being a fly was getting frustrating.

'Seeing as Crosby Blake's a friend of yours, my fee is twenty pounds a day, plus expenses. All right?'

'You mean seeing that he's rich you'll put the screws on him and what you normally charge is fifteen. I thought I was going to like you, Mr Mitchell, but now I'm not so sure. I'm in danger of going off you before I got on.'

She turned round and walked smartly out of the office, leaving me staring at the swivel of her behind under the hem of her fur coat. I knew what she meant though. It was the way I normally affected people: especially myself.

And usually I charged ten pounds a day.

My call to Tom Gilmour seemed to be transferred through several dozen switchboards and exchanges, but finally I got through to him, sounding harrassed and as usual hanging on to as much of his American accent as he could.

It was like wearing an especially garish tie.

'What is it, Scott? I'm up to my mothering arse in work!'

I grinned down the phone at him. 'I know. I've just had a visitor. I gather you sent her this way.'

'You mean the Miller woman?'

'That's who. She's some lady.'

Tom grunted at the other end of the line. 'She's okay.'

'Look, Tom, the guy she works for, the one whose niece has been pinched. He wants me to go out there tonight and find out what's happened from him. I'd rather find out from you first. I don't want to meet him without an idea in my head.'

There was a silence and I could sense that Tom was weighing up the possibilities.

Finally he said, 'Get here in half an hour and I'll fill you in. But it will have to be quick. I've got so many bastards breathing down my neck, my collar's curling up with the heat.'

I said I'd be there and hung up.

What would I do without the telephone, I wondered. I didn't know. I took the cups over to the sink and ran the tap. Such a clean, methodical guy!

Tom Gilmour had been sitting in an office surrounded by maps, plans of a house which I took to be Blake's, piles of typed reports and four telephones. He couldn't do without them either but from the way they kept ringing when we were trying to talk, it was clear that he wished he could.

But I did get the basic facts, as far as they were known.

Three nights ago, Cathy Skelton had disappeared from Crosby Blake's Finchley home. She had been out that evening, had gone to a friend's house to play records and talk. She'd got home at around ten-thirty, made herself a hot drink, said goodnight to her mother and to Blake, then gone to bed.

Blake had looked in on her room at somewhere close to mid-night on his way to bed—something he apparently always did—and she had been sleeping peacefully. The light had been left on and there was a book lying open beside the bed. He had closed the book, put out the light and gone on to his room.

Her mother had already been in bed for half an hour.

In the morning, when Cathy's mother woke up, she went down to the kitchen in her dressing gown and made a pot of tea. She took a cup up to Blake's bedroom and left it outside the door. She did this at a little after seven every morning. Then she poured a cup for herself and made instant coffee for Cathy.

She took this up to her room. When she took the cup into the room, the bed was empty.

At first, she thought that Cathy had got up and gone to the bathroom or something like that. Nothing about the bed or the room suggested anything different. It was only when she had searched the house thoroughly that she became alarmed and knocked on Blake's bedroom door.

Neither of them could understand what had happened. There were no signs that the house had been broken into, so everything suggested that Cathy had left of her own free will.

The trouble with that theory was that she hadn't apparently taken any clothes, neither had she touched the money that she kept in a white glass jar on her dressing table. And there was no note.

So all through that first day, her mother sat at home and fret-ted and Crosby Blake phoned her every half hour to see if there was any news. Each time the mother's heart jumped with a mix-ture of joy and fear; each time she was let down; each time there was nothing to report.

That night the two of them spent awake downstairs. At first they called all of the friends listed in Cathy's phone book. None of them had seen her since she had disappeared. The girl she had spent the previous evening with said that Cathy had seemed the same as usual and hadn't said anything about going off anywhere.

When they had exhausted all the numbers in the book, they

had simply sat and stared at the walls and the blank television screen.

At a quarter to seven the following morning, Blake finally broke down and phoned the police.

Cathy Skelton had already been missing for a day and a half.

The police took careful details and said they would send someone round to the house as soon as possible. They gave instructions that as far as possible nothing was to be touched or moved. It was rather late for that.

At seven precisely the telephone rang: it was the first ransom demand.

-2-

When I was a kid there had been days when the sun had shone so strongly that the thought of cooping myself up in school for yet another day had been impossible. So instead of getting off the bus at the school stop, I had stayed on until we had arrived in the greener suburbs of the city.

Just by cutting across a few roads, it was possible to spend the whole day walking from park to wood and back to park once more. In those days some instinct had told me that was a better thing to do with a sunny day.

Who knows if I was right?

I thought of those times now, as the car entered Finchley, the starting point for all those journeys.

One of the roads I'd never walked down was the one known to us kids as Millionaires' Row. We'd walked hastily past the end of it, peering down in spite of ourselves, like looking into the top of a Christmas stocking you knew was never going to hang at the end of your own bed.

It was into this road that I now turned the car.

The houses were set well back from the pavement; well enough to provide room for a couple of Rovers, a quantity of gravel drive, some lawn, a few stone gnomes and a simple little water fountain.

Nothing elaborate, you understand. For these are basically simple people that live here.

I thought about parking in the driveway, but something wouldn't allow it. Instead, I drew in to the kerb—but not so close that I didn't have to put one foot in the gutter when I got out.

No-one was going to say that Mitchell didn't know his place.

As I walked towards the front door, I gave the house a, looking-over. For all the money that it must have cost, it was comparatively tasteful. If you liked creeping ivy and those stupid little square windows that were nearly impossible to clean. But then, people who bought places like this never worried about how the windows were going to be cleaned. They sure as hell weren't going to do it themselves.

I knocked on the door with a knocker that would have made an elegant nose ring for one of the wild bulls of Marathon.

After a couple of diplomatic minutes, the door opened wide and I was face to face with the lovely Miss Miller. Perhaps it was going to be a better evening than I had thought.

I slipped into the hall and she pushed the door to behind me.

'Working late?' I murmured.

She made a nasty face—something difficult enough when you looked as naturally beautiful as she did—and pointed to a walnut hatstand in the corner.

'Yes,' she said quickly, 'but not for you.'

I hung up my coat and hat and followed her through the door she had opened. It was a good pastime. I thought that I could get used to it. Following her, I mean.

I was wondering whether I would ever catch her up, when some guy thrust his hand at me and I found myself shaking it and looking up into a handsome enough face. Handsome enough for a fiftyish man who's allowed himself to go soft and who has lines and dark patches under his eyes from missing too much sleep.

'I am Crosby Blake, Mr Mitchell.'

I felt like telling him that I didn't think he was Santa Claus, but somehow I didn't figure my sense of humour would be appreciated.

'Would you like a drink, Mr Mitchell? It's a cold evening.'

It was and I accepted a large scotch. Stephanie poured it and she made her move towards the drinks trolley a shade before he asked her if she would mind. Obviously a girl with a good knowledge of her own duties.

I sat down in an armchair that sank so low I had the feeling I was about to pass through space. I sipped at the scotch and looked across the room at my new employer.

Crosby Blake was around fifty years old right enough, but maybe I'd misjudged the softness. There was something about the set of his body that suggested a time in his life when he had to fight for what he had got.

He was a little under six foot in height, with a head of dark hair allowed to grow fashionably long so that it brushed against the edge of his collar. His mouth was the only really troubling feature about him. Somehow the lips were too thin, the tightness too controlled. I wasn't sure what it made me think, but whatever it was I didn't like it.

'Miss Miller will not have told you of the events the night that Cathy disappeared. I had better begin there.'

He waited to see if I was going to say anything. I wasn't.

He carried on. The story he gave was basically the same as that I had got from Gilmour. I said so.

'You mean you went to the police before coming to me?' he asked, affronted.

'Sure,' I replied.

'Do you think that was necessary?' he asked.

'If I hadn't thought that, Mr Blake, I wouldn't have wasted my time doing it.' I put down my glass and leaned forward. 'I'm a professional and what you're buying when you buy me is my professional ability. Which means that I use my own judgment and do things in my way. Or I don't do them at all.'

I looked hard at those tired eyes and saw something begin to flicker deep within them.

'Just so long as that's clear,' I said.

I allowed myself to sink back in my chair. I felt better for that. Crosby Blake obviously didn't. He wasn't used to being spoken to in that tone of voice and right now he was trying to work out whether he should snap back at me or sit there and take it.

He finally decided that he was going to take it—for now.

From the corner of my eye I could see that Stephanie was looking at us with some interest. She wasn't used to seeing anyone talk to him like that, either. What I couldn't tell was whether she approved or not.

'May I ask you, then, Mr Mitchell, why you allowed me to go through the story once again?' The voice was calm, easy—restrained.

'I would have thought the reason was fairly obvious,' I told him. I was beginning to. enjoy this.

He looked at me and the thing that had shown in his eyes was more obvious now. It was temper. Pure temper. I wondered how long he would be able to keep himself under wraps if I kept needling him. But maybe now wasn't the best of times to find out.

'You wanted to see if there was any interesting discrepancy between my version to you and the one you got from the police.'

Smart boy, I thought.

'Right,' I said. There wasn't much point in pushing my luck right now.

'And are you satisfied?' he asked.

I nodded my head. 'Perhaps you could tell me about the ransom demand?' I asked.

He said he would.

'And could I refill my glass,' I said, holding it up.

Stephanie Miller was quick on her feet. She took the glass from my hand, giving me a strange half-smile.

'Let me, Mr Mitchell. We don't want you overusing your professional abilities, do we?'

'The phone went at exactly seven in the morning,' Blake began, 'and I went to answer it. I was anxious, naturally. I thought it might be Cathy. It wasn't, of course.

'At first I didn't think it was anybody. There was this silence that I thought would break when the person at the other end put the phone down. A wrong number or something like that.

'But nothing happened. I became conscious of someone breathing. It was really most unpleasant. Then he spoke. It was an odd voice, rather muffled and unclear—afterwards I realised that the person was probably talking through a handkerchief or something like that in order to disguise his voice.'

I thought he could leave the detective work to me. I said, 'What did he say?'

Crosby Blake blinked across the room, glanced at Stephanie for a moment, then went on.

'He said that he had Cathy. That she was all right. That she would stay that way as long as I did what he said.'

'Which was what?'

'I was not to talk to anyone about Cathy's disappearance. If he saw anything about it in the papers or on television then . . . then . . .'

He had stopped and a slight tick was bouncing along merrily above his right eye. He shifted his position in the chair, as though he had become suddenly aware that he was sitting in the middle of some wet and nasty mess.

'And then?' I prompted him.

'Then I would never see her alive again. No-one would ever see her alive again.'

The voice had broken into an odd tremble and the nerve above the eye was working overtime. If he kept stopping like this I'd never get to hear all of the story.

Stephanie got up and went over to him.

'Would you like a drink, Crosby?' she asked quietly.

Her fingers brushed his shoulder only for a moment, but brush it they did.

I took another dip into my scotch and let the thoughts that were running after one another round my brain have their head. They were sure having fun in there.

Blake took the glass and drained it in one swallow.

'I'm sorry, Mr Mitchell. This has all been rather a strain for me, I'm afraid. You see, I don't have any children of my own and Cathy has always been like a . . . like a daughter to me.' He paused and looked at me. Suddenly the temper was rising up behind his eyes once more. 'I feel so helpless, Mr Mitchell, so stupid and helpless. It's not a feeling I am used to.'

I allowed myself to sink a few more feet down into the chair.

'Apart from telling no-one, Mr Blake, what other conditions did the man make?'

'I had to get twenty thousand pounds in used five and one pound notes and have them ready at the house. He would get in touch with me and arrange where I was to leave the money.'

Blake looked up and his face was clearer.

'That was all?' I asked.

'That was all.'

'But you have seen the police?'

'That first time, yes. They arrived almost as soon as I had put the phone down from talking to him. There was nothing I could do to stop that happening. But since then, I have only spoken here to the man in charge of the case. Gilmour. I went to the station that is directing the enquiry, but it seemed unlikely that he could be both watching me and the house as well.'

'If either,' I said.

'But he said he would know if I got in touch with the police. That he would kill Cathy if . . .'

'He tried to frighten you,' I interrupted. 'I would doubt very much if he stuck around here to keep an eye on what was going on. No, he'd bank on the media getting hold of it.'

'Are you certain?' he asked anxiously.

I stared at him. 'No.' I said flatly. 'In things like this there's not much you can be certain about. In fact there's only one certainty when it all comes down to it.'

'What's that?' It was Stephanie's voice. I had almost managed to forget that she was there. Almost.

I turned to face her. 'The certainty is death. She could be dead already. She could have already been several hours dead when that man phoned.'

She put her face in her hands. Blake jumped up from his chair and slammed the empty glass down hard on the nearby table. Then he walked over to the corner of the room and busied himself with examining the pattern that was embossed on the wallpaper.

It didn't occupy his attentions for long.

'How can you sit there and say that?' he almost screamed at me.

'Look, I can say it because I'm talking about a girl whom I've never seen and that I don't know, don't have any feelings for. I can say it because it's a possibility, always has been ever since she left this house. I can say it because none of us must allow ourselves to become deluded by the prospect of ever seeing her alive again. I can say it because I can't afford to have you breaking down at the crucial moment. So you've got to face it now and get it over with.'

I stood in the centre of the room and he lifted his face to look at me.

I said: 'Your niece, Cathy, could well be dead. You have to know that. Know it and, acknowledge it.'

The head was lowered slowly; the voice was no longer either bossy or agitated; it barely travelled the distance between us.

'I know it.'

We were standing there like that when the door opened and a woman appeared in the doorway. A small woman, rather round, rather dull, rather bewildered. She looked up at me. Her mouth opened, stayed open, then closed without having uttered a sound.

The door closed and she was no longer to be seen. At no time had she looked either at Blake or beyond me to Stephanie.

'That was Cathy's mother,' Blake explained.

I nodded my head. I had known. I was thinking that there were a hell of a lot of things that I didn't know. And wondering whether I wanted to know them.

Blake walked back to his chair.

'Shall we sit down again, Mr Mitchell? This must be very wearing for you, walking in upon us while we are all in such a state. Although I imagine you must be used to it in your business?'

In a pig's eye I was!

I sat down anyway.

'He's been in touch with you again?' I asked.

'Once. At seven the following day.'

'That's today,' I confirmed.

He looked as though time had lost much meaning for him.

'Of course,' he said after a little thought. 'I've been so preoccupied with this business every normal consideration has gone through the window.'

Then what were you doing this afternoon that was so all-fired important that you couldn't meet me till tonight? I didn't say it, just thought it. I carried on listening.

Blake carried on talking.

'He asked whether I had got the money. I told him that I couldn't lay my hands on that amount so easily. He told me that I had to have it ready by tomorrow.'

'And can you?' I shot at him.

'Yes. I think so. He's going to call tomorrow with instructions. That's all I know.'

'Did he say when he'd call?'

'No, but up to now it's been at the same time.'

'So the police will be waiting to run a trace on him at seven.'

Blake looked confused for a moment. 'I don't . . . I mean, they didn't say anything to me.'

'No,' I said, 'they wouldn't. They probably didn't bother to tell you that the house was being watched either.'

This time he really looked rattled. Even Stephanie looked as though she would have dropped a stitch if she'd been knitting. Not that I could easily envisage her knitting; not for a good few years yet.

'But that will throw everything away if the kidnapper finds out.'

'Relax, Blake, that's one hell of a big if.'

He got up and walked over to the curtains.

'You're sure?' he said.

'I'm positive. And don't start twitching with those curtains. If our man is around he'll probably think you're making signals. Why don't you sit down and tell me what you want me to do? I still don't know.'

'When the man phones again and tells me what to do . . . I just thought it would be a good idea if there was somebody here who knows more about this sort of thing . . . than I do.'

I was one step ahead of him.

'And if I know the arrangements, I just might be able to think up some way in which you can get back your niece as well as the money. I mean, it's not that you mind paying it out, but if you could get it back again real quick that would be better.'

Having almost regained his poise, he jumped up again. This guy had enough inner spring to double for Zebedee.

'That remark makes, me sound a remarkably mean man, Mr Mitchell.'

I stood up, too. It was the growing thing.

'Not remarkable mean. Ordinary. This place didn't come from throwing your pennies around. Don't worry, Mr Blake, nobody's going to criticise you for trying to hang on to what's your's. However you got it.'

I let the last remark drop into the conversation as easily as a final raindrop into a pool. No-one said anything but the looks that passed between Blake and his secretary sure counted for a lot of ripples.

Stephanie stood up as well. Fine. Now we could all practise baton changing or something.

'All right, Mr Blake, I'm sure Miss Miller made you acquainted with my terms. I'll be here early in the morning.'

I turned and looked at Stephanie: 'A couple of slices of brown bread lightly toasted, orange juice and strong coffee. I presume that in these troubled times you stay at the house. In one of the guest rooms, naturally.'

If looks had the power to maim, I would have spent the rest of my life walking around sporting a particularly ugly wound—like a hole in the head. But they didn't, so I smiled back and headed for the door.

'Mr Mitchell,' said Blake, 'naturally I had assumed that you would stay the night yourself. So as to be here early in the morning.'

I held the handle of the now open door.

'Don't worry, sleeping isn't one of my problems. And thanks for the invitation, but too long in this kind of atmosphere gives me an acute sense of financial claustrophobia.'

As I was saying this, Cathy's mother appeared in the hall. I said goodbye to Blake and Stephanie and smiled at the worried-looking woman.

'Hello,' I said, 'Mr Blake has just hired me to help with things. I wonder if you could spare me a minute or two of your time?'

She looked confused, as though the last thing she expected was that someone would want to ask her about anything—except where the dinner was.

When it had finally sunk in, she glanced nervously over her shoulder. I could imagine Blake standing behind me in the doorway; I couldn't quite picture the expression on his face, but I had a pretty good guess at it.

If my guess was anywhere close to being right, then the woman did a brave thing. She opened what turned out to be the door to the kitchen and ushered me in.

As she shut the door quietly behind her, I heard the slamming of another door across the hall.

The eyes still looked bewildered . . . and something else. They were plain sore from the perpetual crying, the endless rubbing with her hands.

She sat on a stool and I wanted to put my arm round her, hold her hand for a while. I wondered if anyone had done those very simple, very important things since her daughter had disappeared. I doubted it.

But then neither did I.

'Mrs . . . ?'

'Skelton. My husband's name was Skelton. My brother wanted me to change it back again after my husband had his accident, but somehow I didn't like to. I don't know why. It would have been wrong. A kind of betrayal almost.'

She looked at me and she had the expression of someone who was expecting to be shouted down.

'Is that silly of me?' she eventually asked.

'No,' I said, 'I don't think that's silly. It might be a little unusual in these days, but it's none the worse for that.'

I hadn't held her hand but I had said that and she tried a weak little smile.

'I wanted to ask you about Cathy, Mrs Skelton. Was she happy? Can you think of any reason why she might have wanted to have run away?'

The look of bewilderment returned.

'But she didn't run away, she's been . . .'

'I know, Mrs Skelton, but let's suppose things were different. Can you see her wanting to run away?'

The mother seemed to shrink far away, back into herself, back into who knows what thoughts.

When she said something at last it was: 'Of course not. Why, Cathy had everything she wanted here. A nice home, pocket money. She was doing well at school. She had a lot of friends. She . . .'

I had to interrupt again. I didn't want to risk big brother coming in too soon.

'How did she get on with her uncle, Mrs Skelton? What did she think of him?'

'Oh, Crosby thought the world of Cathy. Always did, right from when she was a little girl. He would do anything for her.'

And right on cue Blake came in. She hadn't answered my question and I didn't know if it had been on purpose. I wouldn't know now. At least, not yet.

Blake was standing there holding a photograph album.

'With everything else we talked about, Mr Mitchell, I forgot to show you what Cathy looked like. If you would like to take this with you and bring it back in the morning . . . ?'

He handed me the album and I stood up and accepted it.

'Don't worry, Mrs Skelton,' I said, 'I'm sure it will all be all right.'

She didn't look up or move. I walked past her and shut the door behind me.

'That wasn't what you were just saying to me,' said Blake as I stood doing up my coat.

I gave him a good ten seconds of my best stare.

'You're not her mother,' I said.

As I shut the front door behind me I felt somehow better for that; even though I hadn't put my arm round her.

-3-

I left the house with the photograph album in my hand and a nagging pain in my head. There was a lot going on inside that place which I didn't like, which I didn't understand—yet. Well, I was sure as hell going to understand it and I didn't think that when I did anyone was going to be any the happier.

I stood on the kerb and looked back at the house. Solid. Respectable. Prosperous. How many people would give how much money, how much time to be in there? I mean, that sort of thing is what we spend our lives striving for, isn't it? To get more than our fellow men. More money, more comfort, more land, more happiness . . .

I spat down into the gutter. Happiness, shit!

The people in that house were as happy as a family of stoats which can't get round to hunting food for fear of being eaten by one of its own.

Mummy stoat, daughter stoat, secretary stoat—I wondered which ones dear old uncle Crosby stoat sank his teeth into and how often?

It seemed to me like a house which was about to explode. And then along came a nice little kidnapping, very conveniently, to act as the detonator.

Makes you think, Mitchell, doesn't it? I asked the question to myself as I climbed back into my car.

But I wasn't so busy with the conversation that I didn't see the upstairs curtain opposite twitch a little. There was a flash of light from the room beyond and a suggestion of dark hair. Then nothing but curtain.

Just nosy neighbours, I guessed. Anyway, I thought I'd sit there in the car a while to make sure. After a minute or so, the curtains parted once more. Why the hell didn't whoever it was switch the light off behind?

Good question. Possible answer: our peeper didn't mind being peeped at herself.

Why herself? Well, this time you could see a little more than a head of dark hair. A shape that was definitely female in what had to be her honeymoon nightie revisited. And she wasn't too hasty in letting the curtain fall back into place. Not this time. Not now that she knew I was looking.

I remembered this movie I'd seen once . . . or was it twice? There's this cop who drives around a small southern town in the U.S., each night the same route, the identical patrol. Each night he passes the same window. Each night the blind is raised. Behind it there's a young girl, well-built, itchy and aching from the heat, letting the man see her body, letting him know what she wants him to do to her. If only he'd be man enough to get out of his old police car and get on over to her room.

She was asking for it. She got it. So did the cop; he also got a whole lot of trouble—including killing a guy and getting caught for it by this smart-arsed black cop.

Just a movie. The curtain fell back. I turned the key in the ignition and ran the motor a little. It was a quiet engine. I could hear the car at the far end of the street start up, then wait.

So somebody was watching. The thing was—were they watching the Blake house or were they watching me?

I made a turn with the aid of someone's drive and headed for home. The headlights that shone in my mirror as I drove along the main road answered my question. My first question.

The second one was: who were they?

I didn't think it would be too long before I found out. They weren't trying to keep themselves much of a secret.

There were several things I could have done, including driving along to West End Central and taking a nightcap with my friends in the force. In the end I did none of them: except go on home.

I pulled the car into the lay-by and looked in the mirror. A pair of lights flicked down from head to side; an animal waiting in the night. Between where I now was and my front door there was some concrete, some grass and a little more concrete. Either they were going to let me cross all that and get inside or they weren't. Either they wanted to know where I hung out or they wanted more. Either they were going to stay in their motor or they were going to come out after me.

I opened the car door.

They did the same.

That settled a lot of things. I didn't want to get my front door kicked in, so I made the walk real slow. I was half-way across the grass when they caught up with me.

The street light on the corner told me all that I wanted to know. Whoever they were, I didn't think they were cops, although with recruitment what is is, you never can be certain. But they were big enough and ugly enough and I hoped they weren't going to ask a lot of questions that I wasn't going to want to answer.

They stood there not saying anything, trying to look intimidating. I had this dreadful feeling that one of them was going to say something like, who the hell are you, buddy?

The one in the dark blue overcoat stuck out his chin and did his best to talk without opening his lips. As a ventriloquist the boy had possibilities, but as a scriptwriter he was nowhere.

'Who the hell are you, buddy?' he said.

I looked at him with a certain amount of disbelief: they didn't make movies like this any more. Did they?

'I'm losing track,' I told him, 'but I'm rapidly beginning to think that one of us is in the wrong picture. I haven't heard lines like that since Warner Brothers started parodying their own material.'

He looked at me as though I'd said some dirty words. To him, anything with more than four letters in it was a dirty word.

He glanced across at his pal and stuck his chin out even further. This time he even opened his mouth a little. Given time he might even make it big.

'Look, smart-arse, never mind with the fucking about. Answer the question!'

Jimmy Cagney never said anything like that.

I still didn't answer his question: I asked another one instead.

'What wants to know?'

'I do, stupid! Who do you think?'

I grinned at him. 'I wasn't sure if it was you or your dummy there. In fact, I'm still not sure which of you is the dummy. On second thoughts, maybe you both are. So who's pulling the strings?'

He didn't like that at all. I could tell by the way he snarled and screwed up his face in a fair imitation of anger. Also, there was something about the way he formed his fingers into a fist that made a bunch of bananas look like one of Carmen Miranda's ear-rings.

Any minute now he was going to throw a punch at me and it was going to be a good one. He had to be able to do something.

The shoulders under the blue overcoat heaved themselves into the air like a whale breaking the surface of the water.

'I'll ask you once more, buddy, who the fuck are you?!'

'Well, if you put it like that,' I said pleasantly, 'the name's Mitchell. Scott Mitchell.'

'And what do you do? Aside from trying to get your face pushed in for talking clever?'

He really was improving now he'd got started. A sort of clockwork action man: wind him up and he'll play for hours.

I reached inside my coat for my wallet. Or I started to. The fist hit me once below the ribs and I staggered back, winded. The silent type grabbed for my right arm and swung it up behind my back as though he was trying to find out if I was double jointed. I wasn't. My mouth opened and I yelled out. Blue overcoat showed me his fist again. That close to my face it was really impressive.

'Shut it!' he hissed.

'Then tell your friend to stop taking my arm off at the roots.'

'Leave him,' he ordered.

He left me. My arm swung down and hung there, moving slightly like a useless propeller blade.

'Don't reach for anything again,' he said.

'I was getting my wallet. I have this nice line in business cards.'

He grunted. 'We'll see.'

He nodded to his friend, who frisked me in a pretty professional way. Then he lifted my wallet and began to go through it. Not for long. A huge hand was stuck out and the wallet lost itself in that.

There were no prizes for guessing who was Hardy and who was Laurel in this team.

He took out one of my cards and examined it. Then he jammed it back and looked at me hard.

'So what are you investigating now?'

'Nothing. I'm collecting my dole money regularly every Tuesday morning.'

The fist unbunched itself and the fingers grasped me by the coat lapels. He pulled me close to his face and I caught the stink of old salami like a sudden slap.

'If you're not working, then what were you doing at Blake's house tonight? And don't waste my time with smart-arsed answers!'

'Just a social call.'

'Huh! A social call at a time like this?'

'A time like what?'

He hit me again. This time I made it all the way down to the ground and thanked the laws of gravity that I landed on the grass and not the concrete.

Nobody made a move to pick me up—which had its good points. At least it meant they weren't about to knock me down again in a hurry.

'I keep telling you not to get smart! Now just what sort of social call would a bum like you be making on a guy like that?'

'Well, not exactly on him. I was seeing his secretary. She's staying there at the moment. I called round to ask her out to dinner.'

'Like hell!'

'That's funny,' I said, 'how did you know?'

'Know what?'

'That that was exactly what she said.'

The look in his eyes told me if I had been standing up he would have knocked me to the ground. So sitting there was saving him trouble: even though it was giving me a quick dose of pneumonia.

'Okay, buddy, now listen and listen good. You remember how easy it was for me to get you down there. And that's just a little taste of what might be to come. You keep out of Blake's affairs. Let things carry on as they are. If we see your face round him again, you'll get such a working over that your old man wouldn't recognise you. That's supposing you know who he is!'

He turned on his heels and muscled himself down the pathway, his talkative companion following along behind. I stayed where I was until they had turned their car round and I had got a look at the number plate. Then I picked myself up and brushed the seat of my pants. I had been right: the grass was damp. My chest was aching. It was past midnight. I went inside.

As I was midway between the living room and the kitchen, the phone rang. I stayed where I was and listened to it. There used to be a time when phone calls meant good news, meant voices that I wanted to hear: one voice I wanted to hear.

But that was yesterday. Or was it a few hundred years ago? I couldn't remember which.

The phone kept ringing. I walked back into the living room and picked up the receiver. As soon as she said my name I recognised her voice.

'Hello, Miss Miller. Isn't this kind of late for a social call? Or are you operating an early alarm system to make sure I don't miss that breakfast you're going to cook me?'

'Neither,' she said. 'I just wanted to . . . to apologise for the way Crosby was tonight. He's not himself at the moment.'

'Who is he then?'

'Mitchell, I was trying to be nice. Don't get smart.'

'Why not?' I snapped. 'Maybe it's about time that I did.'

'Why? What's happened?'

'Nothing important.'

She managed to sound anxious. 'Are you sure? I phoned before and there wasn't any answer. I couldn't understand why it took you so long to get home.'

I felt my side and winced a little. 'I just had a visit from two real nice guys who wanted to chat a while and punch me around for practice. Like I said, nothing important.'

'But are you all right?' Now she did sound worried. The only thing was, I wasn't too sure whether she was worried on my account or for other reasons. She wasn't saying.

I said, 'I'm fine. It's nothing that a minor operation, half a mile of bandages and a couple of bottles of pills won't cure.'

'Now you're not being serious.'

'You're right,' I said. 'There's only one kind of treatment I need and if you were here you might be able to oblige.'

She made a low whistling sound.

'Now who's getting saucy?' she asked.

'I don't know,' I replied. 'Is old Crosby creeping up behind and goosing you?'

'Mitchell, that's a cheap remark!'

'I'm a cheap detective.'

'At your rates?'

'Remember my rates for this job are special.'

'Then could you arrange a little high-class chat to go with it?'

I paused for breath. This sort of thing was more wearing than being knocked around by some big guy in an even bigger overcoat.

'Look,' I said, 'can we call a truce?'

'Call anything you like,' she said, 'only look after yourself, will you? And think about what I said—Crosby didn't mean to behave like he did.'

'Did he tell you to phone and apologise for him?' I asked. 'Or are you using your secretarial initiative again.'

'You don't make things easy, do you?'

'No-one makes things easy, sweetheart. Not any more. Not even for folks with lots of money in the bank and houses on Millionaires' Row.'

'Now you sound bitter and jealous,' she retorted, anger rising in her voice.

'Bitter, yes, but jealous, never. Not any longer. I'm not a kid any more.'

'What does that mean?'

'Skip it. It's too long a story to tell over the phone . . . and too boring.'

She mellowed her tone. 'You should have stayed the night. Then you could have taken your time and told me. That and all sorts of things.'

A pause, then she said, 'Why didn't you stay?'

'I was afraid of sleepwalking . . . all the way to your room.'

'What's wrong with that?' she asked, and the voice was really low and soft now.

'I was afraid of who else I'd find there apart from you.'

She called me a very rude name and slammed down her phone so hard that the sound echoed in my ears for several minutes afterwards.

I shook my head all the way to the kitchen and carried on shaking it while I made coffee.

The album Blake had given me was full of the usual kind of stuff. Cathy as a baby dressed in white and either sitting up in her pram or being held by various adults—all, I noticed, female.

Which was odd. If her father had been killed when she was one year old then there could have been a picture of him with her, holding her. Maybe he just didn't like holding babies; maybe he was always behind the camera; maybe . . .

There was Cathy with her first skipping rope, Cathy with her dolls, Cathy with her kitten, Cathy in her school uniform, blonde hair, brown satchel, a brace across her teeth. Underneath that picture it said her age: ten years.

Then she got older. Uncle Crosby began to appear more and more frequently. At the seaside, building her a sand castle. In the country, holding the reins of her pony. In the garden, splashing her with water from a hose pipe while she held her hands to her face, her bikini patterned over her growing body.

The next page was empty. There had been a photograph there, you could tell from the shading on the paper and the slight tears where the mounts had been removed.

I stared down at the blank page for a long time, trying to imagine the photograph that had been stuck there, then removed. Removed or fallen loose?

It had to be the former. Then the next question was, by whom? And what had been in it?

My mind shot up lots of partial answers but none of them seemed right, none fitted. I wondered who had that photograph now. Supposing it still existed.

I turned over another page, and another. Shots of Cathy as a teenager, wearing long dresses with her hair pinned up; wearing tee shirts and jeans. Cathy at fourteen, fifteen, sixteen. All the while growing more attractive, except . . .

There was something in her eyes that wasn't right. With Crosby Blake it had been the mouth, with his niece it was the eyes. They were dark and something more; they looked at the camera yet somehow failed to focus on it. Almost as though they were staring back inside Cathy herself, looking at something there which she could never leave alone, never forget.

I wondered what it could be. When it had happened. What had happened.

Carefully, I thumbed backwards through the album, then forwards again.

The eyes in the early photos were all right, quite normal, alive and girlish. Then suddenly, they were the eyes of a young girl no longer. They knew, they had seen and what they saw was driven down deep within her. Yet still she could see it although no-one else could. Still she looked at it, not wanting to, yet unable to prevent herself.

The change came after the empty page, after the missing photograph.

I put down the album and looked at my watch. It was well past one o'clock. The coffee pot was empty again. I walked slowly upstairs to bed.

Something woke me up around four. Something that screamed at me inside my head, but screamed without a sound. It had woken me up before, that same scream. I'd never heard it yet, only sensed it, the terror of it. The mouth wide open, the lungs bursting: silent horror like a drowning man seen through the glass sides of an aquarium.

I sat up in bed and knew that my body was covered in sweat. Whatever my dream had been it hadn't been pleasant. But it had told me something; all I had to do now was understand it.

I closed my eyes and tried to bring it back. The projector clicked into action. I was back in an old house. There were a governess and two young children, a boy and a girl. Fear filled each room. The woman's fear. Fear of the two children. Fear that showed in her face when she looked into their eyes.

Eyes that stared at her, through her, as though seeing something, someone that she could not. Knowing things that she did not know; things that they should not have known.

My legs were suddenly cold, cold as ice. My skin felt oddly sensitive. The hair at the back of my neck tightened; my scalp began to itch with a prickly feeling.

The children were staring past the governess, staring straight at me. I blinked and rubbed my eyes: they were still there. Staring still.

The governess lifted the boy up from the floor.

'Time for bed,' she said, as though afraid no longer. She carried him out of the room.

The little girl remained. She was wearing a long garment, white. A nightdress. She walked slowly towards me.

'Aren't you going to take me to bed?' she asked and all the while she looked deep inside me.

She put up her arms to be lifted and I bent down. The little arms flung themselves around my neck and clung on tight, almost choking me. When I loosened them, the face was almost touching mine; the eyes, dark and large, were burning into my face. She smiled a strange smile.

'A good night kiss?' she asked.

I lowered my head over hers and felt her breath on mine. It should have been warm, but it was cold, cold and musty like the damp air at the centre of an old wood.

I put my lips to hers gently, but immediately her mouth opened wide and she drew me inside. I felt her small pointed tongue pushing itself between my lips . . .

That was when I had heard the scream. That was when I had woken up.

I thought about trying to get off to sleep again, but decided against it. I was going to have to leave for Blake's place early as it was.

My legs pushed out over the edge of the bed and my feet found the floor there beneath them as usual. This morning, at this time, nothing would have surprised me. Even a bottomless pit.

Don't tempt providence, Mitchell. They're probably saving that for later. They. He. Whoever runs this thing. I mean someone must. Nothing could get as fucked up as life just by accident.

I thought I could try standing up. That's better! Easy does it now! Take the stairs one at a time. Good. Now don't splash the water into that kettle too loudly.

I took my coffee into the living room and pulled the photo album over from the table. Turned to the blank page. I looked at it for a long time and waited until things settled down in front of my eyes, until they stopped revolving round in my head like a roundabout that was chasing itself hard into oblivion.

Finally it slowed down enough for the people to get off. There were only two passengers. One was Cathy Skelton, the other was her uncle. I turned through the pages until I came to the most recent picture and slipped it from its mounts. I'd stand a better chance of finding out where the missing lady was if I knew what she looked like.

Perhaps.

An hour or so later I dialled Tom Gilmour's home number. It rang ten times with no answer so I put the receiver down and waited half a minute then tried again. The third ring did the trick.

The voice at the other end sounded as though it was owned by a grizzly bear that had got its head caught tight in a noose. I was glad to be out of reach of its claws.

'What stupid mother is calling me at this godforsaken hour?'

'Steady, Tom,' I said, 'I could be the Commissioner.'

'Like a monkey's tit, you could!'

'Take it easy, Tom. You'll never make your pension at this rate.'

He told me a few things I could do with his pension, which seemed unusually charitable for a man who had only just been rudely awoken from hard-earned sleep.

'Anyway,' he finally growled, 'why aren't you over at the Blake place?'

'I'm on my way,' I said. 'There were a couple more things I wanted to ask before I went.'

'Get on with it then.'

'When this thing broke the other day, did you check Blake out?'

There was a short silence at the other end and I tried to work out what the expression on Gilmour's face might be.

Then he said, 'We asked a few questions. At the time there didn't seem to be any point in going further. Are you suggesting there is?'

'No. I'm not suggesting anything. I only wondered if there was something you knew about him which might help.' I let out my breath, then added, 'It might be interesting to know how he made all his money in the first place, though.'

Gilmour didn't say a thing for a while. Perhaps he was one of those people who don't like to talk early in the morning.

'One other point,' I added after a while, 'do you have some-body watching the house?'

'Shit! Of course we have someone watching the house. What the mothering hell do you think we're playing at?'

I didn't tell him. I said, 'But not from the house directly opposite?'

'No, smart guy, not from the house directly opposite.'

'And you're not using two heavy looking musclemen, one of whom could be deaf and dumb and the other wearing a few dozen yards of blue overcoat?'

'What the hell are you talking about?'

'Okay, okay, forget it. But, Tom, if your man there doesn't log the fact that those two characters were sitting in the street in a green Zodiac last night and that they followed me away, then you'd better find out if he's asleep on the job or just on the take like nearly everybody else.'

People were always hanging up on me in the noisiest possible ways. I'd have to take a Dale Carnegie course in telephone tactics if my ear drums were going to survive.

I went out and started scraping the frost from the windscreen. Maybe I should use the garage more often. I'd probably wait until the weather changed.

It was still dark and the street light shone brightly above my head. I was beginning to feel hungry. I wondered if she was a good cook, too.

-4-

In the event she didn't cook the breakfast, Mrs Skelton did that. I should have guessed. However, it left Stephanie free to wander around the place looking cool and beautiful. She was wearing black pants, which hugged her hips and her bottom as though they really cared. Above the waist, she wore a white blouse with loose sleeves and a high, open collar. Over this there was a black waistcoat. Her hair and make-up were perfect and she looked like she'd been up for hours.

It was six thirty precisely.

Crosby Blake sat at the other end of the table, head down behind last night's paper. He was obviously content to ignore me for the time being, which suited me fine. It meant I could concentrate on the food.

Stephanie may not have cooked it, but she had passed on my order with the expected efficiency. Normally I was an orange juice and coffee man, but I guessed I could get used to this kind of living without too much difficulty. All I needed was somebody around permanently to provide the necessary service.

I was in the middle of biting into the last mouthful of kidney when Blake banged his paper down on the table and stomped out of the room. Twenty minutes to phone call time and he was beginning to feel every passing second.

In his shoes I might be feeling the same but I wasn't wearing his shoes and so there were things I had to do. Like settling him down or sorting him out or doing something that would ensure he didn't crack up on the phone and ruin the whole play.

I wiped the juices from the plate with a piece of bread and stuffed it into my mouth. Then I went looking for Crosby Blake.

I found him in the living room. He was sitting alone in the dark room and the stereo was on. Someone was playing the piano, slowly and with feeling. Blake's hands were to his face when I walked through the door and they didn't move until I had sat down opposite him.

When he spoke, his voice was quieter than last night, as though all of the confidence had been knocked out of him.

He said, 'You must think I'm reacting in a very stupid way?'

I shook my head and said that I didn't think that at all. It was no time to hammer him even harder. Not that I was beginning to like him; I just needed his co-operation a while longer.

'Look,' I said in my best reassuring manner, 'you're going to be okay when this call comes through, aren't you?'

He nodded and added nothing.

'Right. Good. But let's go through what happens. As soon as the phone starts to ring, you count up to six, then pick up the receiver. I'll take up the extension phone at exactly the same time. That's important. We don't want him to hear two phones being lifted. Then you just have to listen to the instructions very carefully and if anything isn't clear, stop him and get him to repeat it. If you can, at the end, ask him if he'll go through things one more time. Say you don't want to make any mistakes in delivering the money. Have you got all that?'

He looked at me with eyes that were tired from too much worry and too little sleep.

'Why the last part?'

'The longer you can keep him talking, the more chance there is of the police tracing the call. At least, they should be able to cut it down to an area, even if they don't have time to pin-point the exact phone.'

He heard me but I wasn't too sure how much he understood—or cared at that moment.

'There's one more thing,' I went on.

'What's that?'

'Proof.'

He looked at me without a sign of understanding.

'You must ask for proof.'

'Proof of what?'

'Proof of Cathy still being alive.'

The tired eyes closed; the hands returned to the face; behind us unseen fingers struck notes in quick succession.

I reached forward and pulled his arms down. Stared at him hard. At first he looked as though he was going to hit out at me, then as if he was going to cry. In the event, he did neither. Just looked back at me, strain showing in every line and in the set of his oddly thin mouth.

'Look,' I said again, 'there are two reasons why you must do that. Firstly, if whoever this is is any kind of professional he'll expect it and if it doesn't come then he might be suspicious. Secondly, for Cathy's own sake. Let's presume she's still alive—and remember we have no way of knowing if that is so—then there's nothing to stop the kidnapper changing that situation before he collects the money. That way it would be easier for him to disappear afterwards. For one thing, she wouldn't be able to identify him.'

The hands pressed down on the face, the knuckles turned white.

'So you want some kind of proof—positive proof—that's she's alive and you want it before you part with the cash. And as close to that time as possible.'

He peered at me through his hands, trying to take in what I was saying.

'But won't he release her at the same time as he takes the money?' he asked.

'It's doubtful,' I told him, 'that's too dangerous as far as he's concerned. The thing to do will be to leave her somewhere and what we'll get in exchange for the ransom is the place spelled out for us. That's all.'

Blake said nothing more, but looked at his watch. I checked mine. It was five to seven. He stood up carefully, as though afraid he might keel over at any moment.

Without another word or a look he walked out of the room and shut the door behind him. At first I thought that when he left he took the emotion with him.

But he hadn't. There was still the piano playing its disembodied way round the still dark morning of the room.

The music rang louder, fragmented, like small birds diving and fluttering, unsettled, over a field of corn. The keys hammered out odd little journeys of the heart.

I knew that Crosby Blake wasn't the only person who had lost someone. My mind went back to another time, another place. I was looking anxiously along a road, empty in the dusk. Always empty now.

The phone had sounded twice before it had fully registered. By the fourth ring I was by the extension. After the sixth I lifted the receiver.

Blake said the number: then nothing.

An awareness of someone at the other end, the faintest sound of a breath being drawn: then the line cut off: dead.

It had been less than a minute.

I expected him to be more shaken than ever, but the abrupt click of the receiver being replaced at the other end of the connection seemed to have jolted the life back into him.

Some snap had returned to his walk and the eyes were brighter now.

'What does that mean?'

I looked back at him. I didn't know. I said so.

'I thought that was why you were being paid—to know things.'

He was right. It was just that I didn't know all of the answers: at the moment I didn't even know most of the questions. And his sudden change of manner surprised me. In a way, it was as though he was relieved.

In which case maybe he should be telling me what the phone call had meant.

Instead of that, he asked me again.

'Well,' I hesitated, chewing a few ideas gingerly around the edges, in case one of them should snap back at me, 'the first thing is that we can only presume that it was our man.'

'Come on, Mitchell,' he interrupted. 'It's pretty unlikely that anyone else would call at the exact time. Especially with a strange call like that.'

'Right,' I agreed, 'though remember that our kidnapper was supposed to be talking about ransom demands—not doing his deep breathing exercises. You sure you haven't got a hidden admirer who goes in for dirty phone calls?'

The look in his eyes told me that he hadn't. It also told me I'd better come up with something else if I wanted to stay on the payroll.

I tried.

'The possibility is,' I said, 'that he wants us to know that he's still around and to assume that he still has Cathy and is interested in doing a deal. Only for some reason we don't know, he doesn't want to talk about it at the moment.'

'That's great!' said Blake, pushing his fists down hard into his jacket pockets.

'It could be worse,' I offered.

'How?'

'He needn't have called at all.'

Just at that point the phone rang again, jolting in upon our conversation when neither of us expected it. Stephanie appeared from nowhere and picked up the receiver first.

I went for the extension but she stopped me with a wave of the hand.

I saw her face wince a couple of times as though someone was whistling loud down the line. Then she put the instrument down and turned to face us.

'Was it him?' demanded Crosby, the colour fading fast from his face once again.

'No,' Stephanie shook her head of fair hair from side to side.

'Who was it then?' I asked.

'That policeman.'

'Gilmour?'

'That's the one. He doesn't exactly have an orthodox way of talking to the public, does he?'

'Tom doesn't have an orthodox way of doing anything. What did he say?'

'Well, in between mistaking me for his mother every few words, he asked if we had heard from the kidnapper. When he learnt what had happened he said he wasn't surprised.'

'But did he say why not?' asked Blake anxiously.

'Not exactly,' Stephanie replied, 'but he did suggest that we changed our reading habits this morning and got hold of a copy of the Comet.'

Blake and I exchanged glances. We thought we knew what had happened: the imposed silence had been broken.

'I'll get one,' said both Blake and Stephanie at the same time. I stopped them both with a gesture that would have made a traffic cop proud.

'Let me. I'm the one who's getting paid to run around.'

They didn't argue with that so I left.

The Comet wasn't a paper that normally wasted its readers' time by insulting their intelligence with too many long words. Life happened in thick headlines and exclamation marks and anything that couldn't be dealt with in that way didn't exist.

They didn't have much in the way of either facts or rumour this time, but that didn't worry them. They just sank the headline an extra half-inch down the page.

Enough to make sure that our friendly neighbourhood kidnapper couldn't miss it.

SCHOOLGIRL KIDNAPPED!
A Comet World Exclusive

Three nights ago vivacious young sixth-former Cathy Skelton was snatched from her luxury North London home.
Her mystery kidnapper broke into the house in fashion-
able 'Millionaires' Row' in the middle of the night and
whisked her away into the darkness. Since then nothing
has been seen or heard of her.

It is understood that the kidnapper has contacted
Cathy's uncle, Crosby Blake, to make his ransom demands.
Mr Blake is a retired businessman of considerable wealth.
He amassed his fortune from a wide range of transport in-
terests and is believed to still exercise considerable control
over his former empire.

Police in charge of the case are playing their cards ex-
tremely close to their chests. Last night they were not prepared to make any statement about the kidnapping, not
even to confirm that such a crime had, in fact, taken place.
However, it is confidently believed that they have several
definite theories as to the possible identity of the kidnapper, who may be a man they already wish to interview in
connection with other serious crimes.

There is no suspicion of there being any political motive behind the kidnapping of the schoolgirl victim.

My stomach turned over inside and I thought a while about
what the effect of all this might be: on whoever the kidnapper
was: on Cathy. I didn't like either thought.

When I parked the car and made to get out, the bedroom
curtain across the street dropped back into place. Sometime soon
I would have to go visiting. For now, I slammed the door shut and
walked up the drive towards the house.

It was lighter and somewhere a solitary small bird was setting up a conversation with itself.

Not all little birds sang as sweet; not all little birds sang to themselves. I wondered what Tom Gilmour was thinking and saying at this moment. I wondered who had sung and who had listened. I walked through the door which Crosby Blake held open for me and handed him the paper as I did so.

Stephanie still looked beautiful, but the beauty was rather saddened, flattened by the morning. For some reason I gave her a smile; for some reason she returned it.

I went on into the kitchen and played around with the coffee grinder, trying to think what the two of us could be so happy about. Finally, I gave up and went to find Crosby.

He was sitting in that room again, the curtains still drawn over against the light. The same record was playing. He had the look of a man who has seen the earth crumble away underneath himself and can't understand why he hasn't yet tumbled after it.

It was just a matter of time.

I sat down opposite him again and said, 'What is it?'

He looked up abstractedly, not really seeing me.

'The Hammerklavier,' he said.

'What?'

'The sonata,' he said. 'Beethoven.'

Jesus! All I needed was a music lesson!

I said, 'That wasn't what I meant.'

He said, 'Oh.'

I got up and left him sitting there, staring into space and lost in his own thoughts.

Stephanie was finishing the job I had started with the coffee and some of the crispness had come back into her blouse.

'Would you like some?' she asked.

I shook my head, partly in surprise to find that I was shaking my head. Mitchell refusing coffee. It didn't happen often. But nor did my great ideas and when they did I knew better than to waste them.

'Look,' I said, 'your boss is lame with depression, introspection and a few dozen other self-indulgent things. If the phone goes again, you'd better try to handle it. As soon as anything does happen, especially if our boy rings back, I want you to get in touch. Try me at my office. If I'm not there, then keep trying. And phone Gilmour as well.'

She looked able to handle it. She looked able to handle most things. Including me. But that, like the coffee, would have to wait.

'Think you can cope?' I asked.

She smiled. 'Sure.'

There was something about the way she looked, standing there in the middle of that brightly polished kitchen. I didn't know what it was but it made me go towards her and take hold of her arm and lean down my head and kiss her hair.

'Take care,' I said.

'You take care,' she replied as I walked out the door.

I should have turned back but I didn't. Just kept right on heading for the front door. I had things to do; there were people I wanted to see before anyone else got to them. And I wasn't cut out for a modem remark of 'Brief Encounter'. Perhaps I didn't like the idea of railway station buffets.

Dave Jarrell had been around a long time: as long as me. Ever since I'd known him, he'd made some kind of a living from peddling odd bits of news to papers and magazines. His pockets spilled over with broken stub ends of black Sobranie and empty match boxes. In the midst of these movable ashtrays there were always numerous scraps of paper bearing hastily scribbled notes in a florid, artistic hand.

He always seemed to be wearing the same black corduroy suit, which grew increasingly threadbare and scuffed. Its front was a mixture of tobacco stains and the droppings from the bottoms of the innumerable pints of draught Guinness that he got through in a normal working day.

Jarrell wasn't just a slob: he was a fat slob.

I guessed that he punished the scales at between sixteen and seventeen stone and that was when he was living carefully. Because he was over six foot tall, he sometimes gave the impression of being able to fill a normal sized room all by himself.

Not that he was often in rooms alone. Dave was a compulsive talker—just as he was compulsive about most things that he did—and there was never any shortage of people who were willing to listen. For he didn't only talk; he talked well.

The listeners came in three basic groups. There were the reporters and would-be hacks who came round for whatever tasty morsels they could gather from the fat man's table; there were the ardent little left-wingers in their beards and badges, anxious for evidence of the decadence of the ruling classes; there were the quiet, pretty boys who sat in the corners of his room until everyone else had gone and then went to bed with him.

It was still early in the morning and I wondered whether any of the first two sets had arrived; whether any of the third were still around.

I rang the bell three or four times before I decided that it wasn't working. Then I knocked politely on the door. Still nothing. He could be out, but it wasn't likely. Not unless he had changed his ways. And I doubted that.

This time I banged the door with the side of my closed hand and after a moment or two there were sounds of someone moving around inside.

I could hear muffled voices, then the door opened a couple of inches and came to a halt at the end of its chain. Unusually careful, I thought, then looked at the half a face I could see.

Not more than eighteen, fair curly hair still tousled from sleep, the eye was blue and the mouth which opened to speak was full and oddly red.

'Yea?'

It didn't open for long. Long enough to catch the sharpness of cockney.

'Dave Jarrell.'

'Wot about 'im?'

'I want to see him.'

'S'pose 'e don't want to see you?'

'Too bad.'

'Right!'

He pushed hard on the door, but I was ready for it and forced the underside of my shoe between door and jamb. He looked oddly surprised. Pushed nevertheless. My foot held and I leant on the woodwork. Something was going to give and the mood I was in it wasn't going to be me.

'Look,' he said, 'why don't you piss off?'

'Why don't you stop pushing on the door and let me in like a good boy?'

I kicked hard against the bottom panel and there was a fierce cracking sound. Then another voice from inside the flat: 'What the fuck is going on out there?'

Very intellectual, I thought. Must be the company he's keeping.

'If you'll tell your boy friend to stop pretending he's Supergirl for a minute, I'll come in and tell you.'

'Mitchell?'

'That's right.'

'Why didn't you say so?'

'I didn't get the chance.'

'All right. Let him in, Mick, before he takes the door off the hinges and eats it for breakfast.'

The boy shut the door, undid the chain and opened it wide enough for me to get through sideways but no more. Something told me that he didn't like me too much.

I don't know why. If I'd been that way inclined I could have quite fancied him.

'I've had it, anyway,' I told Jarrell as I walked into the flat and started to search for a chair that wasn't covered in clothing, old newspapers or spilt ash trays.

'Lucky you!' said Jarrell in the camp voice he adopted when-ever he thought the occasion demanded it.

'I meant breakfast.'

'Of course; you're off everything else at the moment, I suppose.'

I shrugged my shoulders and thought that he might be right. It was so long since I'd got myself laid that I could have been excused for thinking someone had slipped in during the night and performed the operation.

I made a mental note to call Sandy and succeeded in finding somewhere to sit.

Jarrell wandered between the main room and the tiny kitchen, holding a large brown teapot and offering to make me some of his fine brew. I said no. I'd been caught like that before.

His tea was thick and strong and acted as the finest laxative I'd yet come across. Three cups of that and you were running for the nearest gents like a ferret up a trouser leg.

'Well, Mitchell, if you don't want tea . . . and you don't want Mick . . . what have I got that you could be after? Don't say it's me after all this time!'

I made a face and pretended to throw up over the side of the chair.

'That's nice, init?' said Mick.

'Mitchell always has had the most charming manners. When he was in the police force they always made him head flunkey at the Commissioner's Ball.'

Jarrell came into the room with two mugs to tea, gave one to Mick and sat by the table, brushing things aside to make room for his tea and his elbow.

'Well, my fine friend, what is it?'

I pulled the copy of the Comet out of my pocket and threw it across at him. He sipped at his tea and glanced at the front page.

'What am I supposed to be reading?'

'The front page.'

He did so and grunted. 'Usual muck. What about it?'

'Only that it shouldn't be there.'

'Why not?'

'The law put a silencer on the whole thing. Like they did with that Cypriot girl a while back. Same tactics. Beat the ransom down while you're investigating, then get the girl safe, hand over the money and pick up the kidnappers before they've had time to spend it.'

Jarrell waved the paper at me from his pudgy hand.

'Where did this come from then?' he asked.

'That's what I've come to you for.'

He looked hurt, then perplexed, then contrite. But he didn't say anything.

'You got a bleedin' cheek,' said Mick.

'So will you have if you don't keep your nice little nose where it belongs!' I didn't have anything against him, but I didn't have time to waste either.

'Where's that then?'

'Right up against Dave Jarrell's arse for all I care. Just sit there and drink your tea like a good boy.'

He jumped to his feet and came for me across the room.

'Don't be silly, Mick,' Jarrell warned.

He was too late. The boy reached down a hand towards my jacket and when his fingers grasped the front of it I hit him in the chest with a right uppercut that loosened his grip and sent him back a couple of paces. Then I stood up quickly and crossed with my left.

It was okay but a bit too much like working out in the gym with a punch bag; not a very heavy one at that.

He dropped to the floor and stayed there, groaning quietly to himself as he rubbed his chin.

'I did warn you,' Jarrell said to him and sipped some more of his tea.

I sat down again.

'What about it then?' I asked.

He shrugged his shoulders and tried a look of abject innocence.

'It wasn't me, Mitchell, honest.'

'Okay, so it wasn't you. I'll believe that for now. I will. Whether Gilmour will is another matter.'

The expression changed to one approaching physical fear. I didn't think masochism was Dave Jarrell's bag at all.

'This is his case?'

I said it was and he whistled softly from between pursed rather rubbery lips.

'Then whoever wrote that piece for the Comet had better look out, as well as whoever grassed.'

'Exactly. So there are two things. One, there's a chance you might know where the cough came from or you might hear something in the next day or so . . . if you listen good and hard. Two, you might know who did that hack muck and where he might be hiding. Cause if he isn't hiding, then he's too much of a fool to have lasted even till now.'

Jarrell poured himself another mug of tea and thought; apart from the almost audible sound of the cogs ticking against each other inside his brain, there was only the noise of the blond boy, still moaning on the floor. It obviously wasn't his scene either: masochism, I mean.

'Well?'

'I haven't heard anything, Mitchell, but I might.'

'And if you do?'

'If I do, I'll let you know.'

'Good. Now what about the reporter?'

'Their crime stuff's usually handled by Ivor Jacobs.'

I reacted to the name and Jarrell noticed.

'You know him?'

'Used to. A lot of years ago. It doesn't matter.'

'Well, if there was a tip-off he would have handled it. As for hiding out, I don't know. The thing isn't signed and the Comet wouldn't let on to the cops. Newspaper ethics. They won't tell you where the tip came from either.'

I stood up. 'Ivor will.'

'How can you be sure?'

'He's another guy who doesn't much like being hit.'

'You've done it before, then?' Jarrell asked.

Yes, I'd done it before. It had been at a party and we'd both been around eighteen. Ivor had been dancing with the girl I was with and getting his paws a bit too close to her arse for my comfort. So I'd asked him to step outside. I was a gentleman in those days.

When he'd refused, I'd knocked him down there and then and started to mash him into the red Wilton carpet.

It hadn't gone down very well. Kids didn't do things like that at respectable parties in Golders Green and get invited again. It hadn't even done me any good with the girl . . . whoever she'd been. Not so much as copping a quick feel that night.

I walked around Mick's pretty body and looked back at Dave Jarrell, still at the table drinking his tea.

'You won't forget to call me?'

He waved his mug at me and some of the brown liquid slopped down on to his trousers. He didn't appear to notice; it couldn't have been very hot.

'On my word of honour, Mitchell. My word of honour.'

I went through the doorway and shut the door hard behind me. There was a splintering sound as the bottom section of wood split further.

I considered it all the way down the stairs but I still couldn't figure what Dave Jarrell's word of honour was worth. Maybe I'd find out.

Maybe I'd find out lots of things. Some of them from Ivor Jacobs: one way or another. I hoped it would be the other.

-5-

It was late morning but the darkness as I drove northwards made it seem like dusk. I switched on the car radio and some idiot told me how many shopping days there still were till Christmas. I flicked the knob and enjoyed the silence. That was the kind of information I could do without.

What I needed was far more substantial, more difficult to come by—and you usually had to do more for it than reach out your left hand a few inches.

Something had started nagging away at my brain like the rough edge of a broken nail. I didn't know what it was for sure, but whatever it was nearly took me through the set of lights showing red in the gloom.

At the last minute I stabbed down hard with my foot and grabbed for the hand brake. The car did its best to stand up on end and someone behind me barely screeched to a standstill a few inches from my rear.

If only people would watch what the hell was going on!

What the hell was going on?

I didn't know, but I did know that the reason the car following hadn't seen the lights either was that they were more interested in watching me.

The smart one was still wearing his blue overcoat, but today he'd added to it a cute little hat with a narrow brim that perched on top of his head like a dark golf ball on an oversize tee.

His friend was driving and as he tucked his car in behind me again, there was something shining in his eyes that made him look suspiciously as if he was alive after all.

But I discounted that. They were just making better dummies this year.

For a while I wasn't sure whether I wanted them to know I was going to Ivor's or not. If they'd picked me up at the Blake place again, then that meant they already knew about Dave Jarrell. Perhaps it wasn't a good thing for them to know too many of my contacts; just in case, they did have it in them to turn nasty.

As if they would!

I swung left off the main road and made a few desperate efforts to lose them. But taking corners on two wheels wasn't really my thing and for a dummy that guy could handle a motor well enough.

This kind of thing was all right in glorious technicolour with cars chasing one another up and down hill, suddenly flying off into space and landing again with a bumping of springs and a squeal of wheels.

But Golders Green isn't San Francisco and I'm not Steve McQueen. I'm not a cop and I certainly don't have Jacqueline Bisset waiting beside the road wearing a yellow dress that looks good even through the gathering petrol fumes. Even if she was waiting to say goodbye.

My goodbyes hadn't come that way at all. There had been no searching looks, no anxious fumblings for words. She had known what she wanted to say all right and she had used the telephone to say it.

Oh, I mean I suppose I'd known well enough, though there had been weeks when I'd hung on to every last vestige of hope. Like a drowned man who still splashes his arms vainly when he's already dead.

And rumours eddying round his body pick his bones with the keenest of whispers.

Only I hadn't had to rely on rumour: not for long.

Nor whispers.

Her voice had been clear and strong. She had never sounded more confident, more sure. Only afterwards had she softened slightly, said that she shouldn't have told me on the phone, should have been there to hold me, help me.

But we both knew that wasn't true.

If we had been together it wouldn't have got said: again. That had been the trouble. For months she must have wanted to say those words, to cut the rope that bound and let me slip silently into the waiting sea. Being close enough to touch, to pull me back, she had not been able to.

And so the telephone was different; the telephone was better; she couldn't see me waving . . . or drowning.

Five minutes of sharp turns and sudden accelerations and still the other car wouldn't disappear from my rear view mirror. I wasn't in a nice mood at all and this sure didn't help.

In fact, I was feeling lousy. More than that, I was feeling mean and lousy. Maybe I'd have to do something about that.

I stopped trying to lose them and took the main road that led down into Hendon. Alongside the main gates to the park, I pulled up and sat there, watching to see what they would do.

They parked opposite and the driver stared across at me. I showed him one upright finger, then got out of the car and locked the door.

The class of people there seemed to be around, I wasn't going to take any chances of having my car pinched.

There was a call box a few yards down from the entrance to the park. I went in and fumbled in my pockets for a coin, dialled a number. There wasn't much to say and I said it very quickly; but not too quickly for it not to be understood.

Then I walked into the park.

Beyond the tennis courts were the kids' swings. In this sort of weather, neither of them were exactly overused.

One small coloured boy, about four years old, was trying to push the long swing-boat and then clamber up on to it, but he wasn't having much success. After four or five attempts, he gave up and stood looking at the woman sitting on the bench opposite.

He pushed his red bobble hat back from his curly hair and then drew it across the front of his face, either wiping his nose or the tears that were forming in his eyes. Then he jammed the hat back on again at a wry angle and turned back to the swing.

The woman got up from the seat. She was short, white; long fair hair hanging over the edges of a grey duffle coat.

She walked over to the boy and lifted him on to the centre seat. She went to one end and began to push until the thing was going through the dull air at a good rate.

The swing cut back and forth across my vision, slicing thick lines out of the two men who stood on the edge of the grass, not stepping yet on to the gravel. Not coming for me. Waiting still.

I didn't mind. There didn't appear to be that kind of hurry.

The woman tired of her efforts and let the long swing come to a halt.

'Come on, Chiedo,' she said. 'It's time we were getting home.'

The boy didn't make a move, just sat there, legs stretched wide across the wooden plank, staring at her.

'Chiedo! Come on!'

He looked as though he was going to let the tears come again, but instead he grinned at her and scrambled down to the ground. She took hold of his gloved hand and the two of them walked over in my direction.

She looked at me and I liked what I saw in her face. I smiled my best smile at her. Her eyes flickered on to mine suspiciously for a moment then she looked away again, past me and towards the park gate.

Now there was no-one between the two hoods and myself; nothing but the empty roundabouts and swings.

I stood up.

The big one hunched his shoulders and called across to me. 'You don't listen, do you? You clever guys are all the same.'

'Sure,' I shouted back, 'we're all brighter than the stupid ones.'

He jutted out his chin and one large fist emerged from an even larger pocket. 'Meaning?'

'Meaning whatever you can manage . . . stupid!'

That did it. The other fist came into sight; it was every bit as big as the first one; the only difference was that there seemed to be a number of heavy rings on its fingers.

'We warned you, Mitchell, and you didn't listen. Well, perhaps you'll listen to us now.'

They started to move across the gravel. Behind them I could see faintly the house lights from the far side of the park. It really was a dark afternoon. And getting darker with each step they took.

'Who's paying you?' I asked.

I hadn't expected an answer and I didn't get one. They didn't even hesitate; simply kept coming at me. They must have thought that I was as easy as a stuffed teddy bear.

I waited until they were within good spitting distance, then made as if to go to the right. The little one came after me. I turned sharply on my left foot and moved my right side in towards him. My right arm followed through behind.

He shouted out something I couldn't quite catch. Maybe a mouthful of fist wasn't doing anything to improve his diction. Such a shame! It was the first time he'd tried to say anything at all.

His friend wasn't so shy.

'Right, bastard!' he shouted at me and this huge paw reached out for my shoulder. I let him have the shoulder. I also let him have the same bunched hand his colleague had sampled. He didn't like it much either.

I looked back at the little one in time to see him feeling around inside his coat. He could have been looking for some sticking plaster to put over the cut on his lip, but I wasn't taking any chances.

I jumped at him and he fell backwards, the two of us rolling over on the harshness of the gravel. I yanked the arm clear and banged it down on to the ground. Then lifted my knee and rammed it down hard into the muscle inside the lower arm. He opened his mouth in a gasp and I moved my knee quickly upwards.

There was a loud, sharp click as his teeth cracked together and his head jerked backwards. I was just enjoying the sound when something strong and powerful lifted me up into the air, twirled me around like a berserk crane, then dropped me without ceremony on the edge of the roundabout.

I moved my face away from the right-angled iron bar that was gently caressing it and blinked. A two-handed hammer blow was thundering down towards my head. I ducked and rolled . . . but fast.

The blow landed on the wood of the roundabout and a hollow echo boomed out. I reached up for one of the legs and pulled at it. It was like trying to shift one of the columns of the Eiffel Tower. The only thing that budged was the muscle across my own chest.

This obviously wasn't getting me anywhere.

I jumped up as quickly as I could, just in time to meet the other one coming in at me.

He was easy: I could play with him all day. My right hand was homing in on his face like a guided missile.

I took his falling body in one hurdling stride and kept on going. Something big and ugly was following me. I let it, until I came to the edge of the playground and the line of kids' swings that dangled from their lengths of rusting chain.

Then I pulled myself round on the end support and turned a sudden circle. As I did so, my foot shot out. It caught the guy in the blue overcoat right below the third button and almost doubled him in two. Almost. It took a second kick to do that.

There he was down on all fours and I was staring around behind me, looking for his mate. I saw him all right. He was scurrying away across the grass like a furry animal.

Maybe he'd left his sticking plaster in the car, after all.

The shape in the blue overcoat was showing signs of wanting to return to combat. I looked at the line of swings and smiled to myself.

Well it was a playground wasn't it?

Why shouldn't I have a little fun?

I took hold of one of the swings and ran backwards with it. As he clambered to his feet and started to come for me again, I took a couple of fast paces towards him with my arms outstretched, then let go with as much effort as I could muster.

All those Sunday mornings in the bowling alley hadn't been wasted after all!

The edge of the seat struck him full in the face. His mouth spread wide as though trying to swallow it whole, then gave up in a splinter of shattered and broken teeth. The swing came away and I had this sudden vision of two shocked, wide-open eyes and beneath them an equally open mouth, whose lips were blubbering forth bubbles of fresh blood.

He staggered forward and into the swing's return flight.

This time it hit him below the belt. Not so viciously, but still hard enough to send him face first across it. It was as though an unseen pair of hands had carefully folded the blue overcoat in two.

The body swung back and forth twice more, before it overbalanced and was tumbled forwards. The face struck the gravel almost soundlessly. With only the strangely soft sound of skin being grazed away from the inside of the nose and the bone that surrounded the right eye.

I hastily glanced back across the park. There was no-one to be seen. The second guy had not bothered to return. I wondered what blue overcoat would think about that when he came round. Whenever that was.

For the moment, he was dead to the world: around the eye that had lost its skin a bright circle of blood was staring up at me, seeming unreal in the premature darkness.

There had been questions I had wanted to ask him, after all those he had tried on me. But it didn't seem as though he was going to be saying much for a while.

Perhaps he and his buddy could change places.

Again, I looked around me. If he wasn't coming back by himself, then that probably meant he had gone for reinforcements.

I knelt over the unconscious body, all the while trying not to stare back at that enlarged socket of blood.

There was a wallet in his inside pocket and I pulled it clear and went through it . . . carefully. But however carefully I did it, there wasn't a single useful item there.

I swore and pushed the wallet back. His head moved of its own accord and the eye inside the ring of red flickered once. I didn't like it.

So I lifted him clear of the ground by the neck and slammed the head backwards, down on to the ground. Twice.

After that, the eye didn't try to open again.

I began to go through his pockets.

With the third one, I struck lucky. It was a business card of sorts. In gothic lettering it advertised the Club Internationale, Gerrard Street.

I wondered if Sandy knew anything about that place. I wondered if she had got the coffee brewing yet.

When I stood up the wind cut across the flat surface of the park and into my back like a sudden razor. The lights at the far side could be picked out more clearly now.

When I walked away from the swings, towards the road, it was like walking across years of wasted promises. I thought of the wooden edge opening the man's mouth with the senseless greed of a ravening shark. I thought of the little boy, perched somewhere between tears and smiles; finally treating his mother to shining teeth and dark eyes that glistened. I thought of a telephone ringing, of knowing who it would be and what would be said, yet picking it up nevertheless.

Something ached and it wasn't my bruised knuckles.

The coffee was more than ready and from the look that Sandy gave me when she opened the door, I guessed that she'd resigned herself to finishing the whole pot without my assistance.

So I smiled at her and gave her the sort of quick kiss on the lips I reserved for my nearest and dearest. It didn't get used very often.

It didn't impress Sandy, either.

'Don't think you can get round me just like that, Scott. I'm getting fed up with the way you use me as a coffee shop and quick stopover between better things.'

Her green eyes gleamed and I knew that she was as aware as I was of how good she looked when she was angry. Or pretending to be . . . either way it didn't matter. What did matter was the way her red hair hung richly down, the shine of her skin.

Sandy wasn't young; she had been around; been used and abused; she was still one of the most attractive women I had ever seen. Until she took her clothes off.

Not that that had always been the case.

Her body had earned her living for a long time. On the game when most girls are still at school, Sandy had finally seen the sense of selling herself in another way and had begun work as a stripper. She had been great . . . until one evening she had been visited by a large black guy with a nasty habit of waving round an open razor.

The scars on her head had disappeared under the new growth of hair, but the two long lines down her body were still visible. The raincoat brigade wouldn't pay to see her any more.

She'd got a job handling strippers for some of the clubs, a kind of agency thing. It was okay but she obviously didn't think as much of it as she had of performing herself . . . and she couldn't forget the scars which made that impossible.

She saw the traces of them every morning, every evening.

Sandy had got them for asking too many questions in dangerous places; questions she had been asking on my behalf.

And now I was here to get her to find out something else.

I looked at her as she sat on the edge of the bed, bright green dress sprayed over the white bed cover. She raised the cup to her mouth and drank the bitter coffee, looking at me over the edge of the rim.

She said, 'It's been a long time, Scott.'

I nodded. 'I was thinking that earlier.'

'That you hadn't seen me for a while?'

'Sure, why?'

'Just to see me?'

'Yes.'

The greenness of her eyes was brighter, keener; she put down the cup and I noticed the length of her fingers, remembered how they felt on my body.

It was enough only to see her and I would be aroused. After all this time that had never altered, diminished. It wasn't love, nor anything like it: it was sexual, animal attraction.

I knew it: she knew it.

Usually we both enjoyed it. Today, from the way she was acting, I wasn't sure.

'It couldn't have been that you wanted something out of me?'

'Coffee?' I suggested.

'Or a quick lay.'

I tried to ease things with a half-smile. 'I don't know about quick.'

It didn't seem to do any good.

'Or something more?'

'More?'

Sandy stood up and came over to where I was sitting nursing my cup in both hands. She stood over me and for a moment I thought she was going to strike out and send either the cup or my head flying.

'Christ, Scott! You're a bastard!' She said it quietly, but with feeling.

I looked at her face but didn't argue. How could I?

'You spend all of your time using people,' she went on, 'that is, when you're not sitting around feeling sorry for yourself.'

I didn't know what had happened to her last night or what had caused her to try getting out of bed through the wall, but something had made her less than happy all right.

I reached up for her hand and took it in mine. Squeezed it. There was as much response as from a statue . . . except that a statue didn't have warm blood running through its veins.

And now that I'd touched her . . .

I stood up and kept hold of her right hand; slid my right arm around behind her back and pulled her towards me. Her breasts against my chest, I moved my mouth the short distance down to the front of her neck. Kissed her slowly, tenderly.

For a minute I thought I had it all covered.

But I'd forgotten that Sandy was left handed.

The slap caught me around the back of my ear and bounced back off the bone at the rear of my skull. I jumped and let go of her other hand. She had to be ambidextrous!

At least both ears would be red.

'What the hell was that for?' I asked. It really was my day for asking stupid questions.

'What the hell do you think it was for?' she blazed back at me. I thought that she was going to strike out again, but she stood there smouldering away instead.

'But, Sandy . . .'

'But shit! No sooner do I finish telling you about the way you use people than you get on your feet and try the same thing again. Well, let me tell you this once, Scott Mitchell, and you'd better listen good. I don't mind you dropping in on me for the occasional cup of coffee, I don't even mind the occasional fuck. But I will not be treated like some bloody slot machine . . . especially when you don't even put the money in! You're such a smart guy that you think a little fiddling with those famous fingers of yours will get things working for nothing.'

She paused and I couldn't do anything but stand there feeling like a circus midget down a deep hole.

She didn't pause for long.

'So next time you want something out of me, you can pay like everyone else does. You got that?'

I nodded stupidly. I thought I had it all right.

'Which means fifteen pence for a cup of coffee, ten pounds for me and everything else on top.'

She stopped again and stood there looking more beautiful than I had ever seen her. I wanted her now as much as I ever had, probably more so, but I wasn't risking getting slapped again and, anyway, I didn't have that kind of money to throw around. Not on my own behalf.

'What's it to be then, Scott? Apart from the coffee you've already had.'

I took the coins out of my pocket carefully and counted them out into the palm of my other hand. One five, three twos, two ones and five halves. I put them down on the table alongside the bed.

'You can keep the change,' I said.

Sandy didn't move. I did. I turned around and headed for the door. My hand was on the handle before I turned back to face her; she hadn't altered her position.'

I reached back into my jacket pocket. Put the card from the Club Internationale down alongside the money.

'Anything useful you can find out about that place, I could do with. Especially why whoever runs it might not like me poking my nose around where others keep clear. Maybe around some guy with a lot of bread called Crosby Blake.'

She still didn't move; only those green eyes following me back to the door.

'Come up with anything I can use and there'll be a fiver in it for you.'

I pulled the door to behind me and walked down the stairs. I'd known Sandy a long time. Maybe too long and maybe not too well.

What the hell! I didn't have time to stop and figure it out . . . not now.

Not ever.

-6-

There was one letter on the mat inside the outer door of the office. I picked it up as delicately as if it were a flower. There weren't that many pink envelopes that came through the letter box that I could afford to be blasé about them.

I unlocked the door to the inner office, threw my coat at the rack and pulled the chair round by the desk. I was going to enjoy this. From the third drawer down on the right hand side, I took out a slim paper knife. The handle was dark wood, the blade had two arcs cut out of it close to its base, then tapered away smoothly to its tip. I inserted the tip under the edge of the envelope and slid the knife across the fold.

It was a very satisfying feeling.

I put down the knife and removed the card from the envelope. It was pink, too. I read it very carefully, savouring every word. It said:

SU VENNER DESIGNS
Attract the attention of both old
and new customers with personally
designed stationery and business
cards that reflect your own
especial character and personality.

Then there was a nice logo and an address and telephone number.

Perhaps that was what my business was lacking: the right kind of stationery. That was why the right kind of people weren't flocking over the threadbare mat to hammer on my door and pay me handsomely for solving their problems.

Now I knew the answer there need never be another worrying day in my professional life.

I held the card between two fingers of each hand and very lovingly tore it in two. Then I dropped it down into the waste paper bin, watching the pink petals float on to the grey enamel.

I pushed back the chair and stuck my feet up on the desk. It was still too early in the day to be drinking, so I reached out from where I was and was just able to finger open the drawer with the bottle of Southern Comfort in. Sadly, I couldn't reach the glasses. I tipped the neck of the bottle between my lips and enjoyed the orangey taste as it swam lazily around my mouth.

The right kind of people, I thought. If they were that then they wouldn't come into my office at all. The kind I got were mostly timid and frightened and wanting help to stop bigger guys leaning on them, husbands or wives cheating on them, bigger fish feeding on them.

Or they were rich enough to have money oozing out of their arses and used to buying their way out of any little trouble that their arrogant thoughtlessness had got them into. So they came round and strewed notes all over my desk and expected me to lick their feet and lap up their shit while I was down there.

Oh, yes, I was called on by the right kind of people!

I took another swig at the bottle and rinsed my mouth round with it, trying to get rid of the taste of bitterness. Not that I should be feeling bitter. I was the guy who spent all his time using other people, remember?

Then the phone rang.

I picked it up and said, 'Hello, sweetheart, this is Su Venner Designs.'

'What the fuck are you playing at, Mitchell?' growled Tom Gilmour's voice from the other end.

'I've decided I'm in the wrong line. What I want is something a little more sensitive, a trifle more artistic . . . in keeping with my personality.'

'Will you cut that pansy crap and give me a straight answer?'

'Sure, Tom.'

'Right, then what the mothering hell are you doing in your office instead of being with Blake?'

'I'm sitting with my feet up on the desk drinking Southern Comfort from the bottle and waiting for inspiration to strike me.'

'Well fuck you . . . sweetheart!'

And the phone went dead.

I took another drink.

The phone rang again.

This time I picked it up and said nothing. Sometimes it paid to play safe.

There was a silence, then a voice saying, 'Is that Scott Mitchell's office?'

I thought about it for a while and decided that it still was. I said, 'Hello, Stephanie, where are you?'

'I'm at Crosby's house.'

'That's nice.'

'Mitchell, I didn't phone you up so that you could make your usual sneering remarks.'

'Oh,' I said, 'you want a special kind of sneering remark. That comes more expensive.'

'Mitchell!'

'Sorry, but everyone seems to be into charging for everything all of a sudden. What's your price?'

'More than you can afford.'

'I believe it.'

There was a silence. Maybe she was thinking of offering me some kind of discount.

Then she said, 'I thought you might like to know what's happened.'

'Okay,' I replied, 'try me. What's happened?'

'Nothing. No more phone calls. Nothing.'

'That's great. The sort of progress that throws my adrenaline into a mad fit of excitement. You'll keep me informed if nothing else happens later?'

'All right, I'm sorry. It's just that . . .'

'I know, it was a long while since you talked to me and your tongue was in danger of getting blunt.'

'All right, I said I was sorry. What more do you want?'

'We both know the answer to that, but we also both know I can't afford it.'

'Mitchell!'

'You've said that before.'

'What do you want me to say?'

'You could tell me the name and address of Cathy's friend. The one she spent the evening with on the night she was snatched.'

'Hang on a minute,' she said.

While she was gone I wondered if they were being pestered with newsmen and TV cameras and if not, then why not. But she said that nothing had happened. If the others were letting the Comet get away with their scoop free of competition, then Tom Gilmour had someone up high pulling a lot of heavy strings for him.

'It's Lyn Cameron. Thirty-five, Gladstone Avenue.'

'Okay, thanks. And, by the way, have you had anyone round from the press asking questions, taking pictures?'

'Not as far as I know. The police arranged for a press conference at the station so as to keep as many people clear of the house. There could be photographers around in the street, I don't know.'

'Fine. I'll be round later. Thanks for ringing with the news.'

This time I beat her to it and got the receiver down fast.

It was a long time since I made a call on a seventeen year old schoolgirl and I didn't want to miss a minute of it.

Gladstone Avenue was a street of detached houses that were a couple of leagues down from the Blake place, but still high enough on the social register to put them out of my class.

Which was what Lyn Cameron was . . . out of class. Until I knocked on the door and she answered it, it hadn't occurred to me that she shouldn't be there at all. Should probably be off in some stuffy schoolroom somewhere going over the finer points of some poet or other. Then why had I just got in the damn car and driven round?

Who knows? But there had to be some occasions when my instincts worked correctly.

'Hello,' I said, 'my name's Scott Mitchell. I'm a detective working on Cathy's disappearance. I understand she's a friend of yours.'

The girl didn't move out of the way to let me in. She was a well-built seventeen and although uplift bras were out of style that didn't seem to bother her any. Perhaps she wasn't fashion conscious. She wasn't silly, either.

She said, 'Shouldn't you show me a warrant card or something?'

I reached for my wallet. 'It's not a warrant card because I'm not the police. I'm a private detective.'

I gave her one of my cards, suddenly conscious of how very ordinary it looked. I'd have to give Su Venner a ring after all.

The girl looked at the card and handed it back to me.

'That doesn't prove anything, does it?' she said. 'Anyone could have one of those printed for next to nothing.'

I sighed. 'You could phone West End Central police station. They'll check me out.'

'But they'd only tell me a Scott Mitchell existed. That still might not be you. You could have knocked him out and stolen his wallet.'

I grinned at the thought. 'I might have knocked him out, but I wouldn't be so stupid as to waste my time stealing his wallet.'

'Okay,' she said, 'I'll risk it. Besides, a bit of excitement wouldn't be a bad thing.'

I followed her through the hall and into a small room that was obviously her own.

'Do you think that's what your friend Cathy thought?' I asked.

'What?'

'That she could do with some extra excitement.'

Lyn wrinkled up her nose for a moment. 'I don't know. Anything was possible with Cathy.'

'How do you mean?'

'Just that I'd known her for a long time and yet I hadn't. Does that make sense?'

I thought that it made sense all right and I told her so. I sat down on a wooden chair and she sat on the bed. On the wall behind her there was a large colour poster of Elvis Presley, looking slightly paunchy in a white suit flashed with blue embroidery. He was trying to look mean and evil, but to my eyes he only succeeded in looking comfortable and cuddly. I wondered what he looked like to Lyn's eyes.

On the table beside my chair there was Allen Harbinson's photo biography of the singer; pinned to the wall was a badge that was a replica of one of his early records—a single on the yellow Sun label called 'Good Rockin' Tonight'.

In those days, yes; today, I wasn't sure.

I could ask her what she saw in him, but there probably wouldn't be a coherent answer. People were attracted to other people for the strangest of reasons and mostly they couldn't be explained. There didn't seem to be rhyme or reason.

Someone had liked me once and I'd never been able to believe that until it was too late.

I wondered who Cathy had liked.

'Did you know enough about her to know what she thought about boys, men?'

'Not really. I mean, she didn't agree with me about Elvis,' she laughed. It was a good laugh, open and without affectation: I hoped that nothing would happen which would make her lose it.

'But she must have talked about men she did fancy? There must have been boys she saw?'

'The only boys Cathy saw were strictly at a distance. Her uncle saw to that. He seemed to think she should have been a nun or something. There was time enough for her to see boys when she'd finished at school, he said.'

'Weren't there any boys at school?'

Lyn shook her head. 'Sorry. Strictly private, fee-paying and single-sexed. Even the gardener's a woman . . . of sorts.' She laughed again.

'How about on the way there or going home?'

'No way. That uncle of her's had her taken there and back by taxi. If he could have sent her into the loo with someone to watch her I think he would have done.'

'So she accepted all this, did she?'

Lyn's face lit up. 'Did she? She hated it! But she was waiting until school was over and she got away to university. Then she was going to cut loose and break every law and taboo that existed. She was really going to throw over the traces and spit in her dear uncle's face with a vengeance.'

'Why didn't she just leave home before that? Lots of girls do.'

Lyn gazed past me at the wall. 'Cathy couldn't do that. She liked her comforts too much. She liked money. Her uncle may have kept her away from boys, but other than that he'd let her have anything she wanted. Cathy wasn't going to let go of that in a hurry.'

'What about when she got to university?'

'She had that covered as well. He was letting her have some kind of endowment when she was eighteen.'

'How much?'

'Twenty thousand pounds.'

I sat back and let out a long, low whistle. That was a large amount: large and interesting.

I asked, 'She didn't say anything about the money that evening?'

'Sorry. We spent all of the time going over school work. That and my usual efforts to get her to listen to some of my Elvis. But she couldn't take it at all.' She smiled. 'I'm not being much use to you am I?'

I wasn't sure how useful she was being, but there were a whole new brand of ideas fighting for space in my head. That twenty thousand could be a coincidence, but then again . . .

I took out a card again and gave it to her.

'Hang on to this. If anything does occur to you, give me a call. Okay?'

I got up and she showed me towards the door. I was on the outside step when she remembered.

'She did say something once, about a man she found attractive. He was one of the drivers who took her to school and back. But then he was switched round for someone else. Maybe he got another job altogether, I don't know. Anyway, she didn't say anything about him after that.'

'How long ago was this?'

'Oh, some time. Cathy would have been fifteen. It was towards the end of the summer term and her birthday was in October.'

'You don't remember the man's name?'

She laughed. 'How could I forget?'

'What do you mean?'

'It was Burton. James Burton.'

I looked confused.

She explained: 'He was the guitarist on a whole batch of Elvis records. There was no way I was going to forget him!'

Was Cathy, I wondered?

'Thanks, Lyn, you've been great . . . and keep laughing.'

I walked away down the path and for the first time in a long while I felt as though I was starting to make a little sense out of things. I just hoped I wasn't deluding myself again.

The office of the taxi company was in a side road close to Tufnell Park underground station. The sign over the door was blinking off and on accidentally, as though contemplating whether or not to short out altogether.

I pushed open the door and found myself in a scruffy little room with black seats pushed back against the walls. The plastic coverings had been torn and pulled from the cushions in a number of places and bits of tatty foam were poking through. On and around a low, long table a large number of empty plastic cups were stacked in piles or lying on their sides. There were cigarette ends everywhere, even some in the ashtrays. Magazines were strewn around over much of the floor and seating. The walls were adorned—if that's the right word—by the kind of pin-ups that went out of date when pubic hair stopped being painted out.

Whatever it looked like, it wasn't the prosperous place I'd been expecting. I walked through the mess, trying not to disturb it with my big feet.

Behind another door I found the cab controller. He was sitting in front of a blue telecommunications set-up. In front of his face was a microphone covered in blue plastic up to the grid at the top. His right hand held the mike stand, thumb poised above a red button.

Alongside him, by his left hand, there was a small switchboard, with two phones on the table before it. He was talking into one of these.

'Right. There'll be a cab there in five minutes.'

He put down the phone and spoke into his mike, his thumb holding the red button firmly down.

'Any cab near Holloway Road?'

'Seven.'

'Say on, Seven.'

'Turning down from Finsbury Park.'

'There's a Mr Turner waiting outside the old cinema on Holloway Road, by the pet shop. Got it?'

'Right.'

'Okay, Seven.'

The thumb released the button. Another voice came through: 'Four.'

He pressed the button down, then sensed my presence. Looked round. Went down on the button twice quickly. The calling stopped.

He swung round in his chair and looked up at me. A little guy of around forty-five. Sort of hunched-up by too many years over cab wheels and microphones.

'What are you creeping around here for?'

'I wasn't creeping around. You were too busy to notice me.'

'Yea. And I'm too fucking busy to waste time. Outside!'

He turned back to the set. I took a couple of quick paces towards him and pulled him round hard in the chair. I didn't have much time to waste either.

'What the . . . !'

'Shut it!'

My voice cut across him and he did as he was told. Till he tried to push himself away from me and reach down into the deep drawer alongside where he was sitting. That was naughty.

I told him so with a punch to the head which sent him off the chair and down on to the floor. He didn't look as though he liked that very much.

I opened the drawer and took out an old-fashioned car jack. I picked him up off the floor and pulled him towards me so that I could see the frightened look that jumped in his eyes. I rested the edge of the jack alongside his face.

'Now you don't want to get too close to this nasty looking bit of iron, do you?'

He didn't say anything, but he shook his head quickly from side to side.

'Good boy. Now, tell me about a driver called Burton. Jimmy Burton.'

His expression didn't change. There was no obvious sign of recognition.

The phone rang, then stopped, then started again. A voice came through the set from one of the cabs: 'Four. Four.' Then another: 'Nine.'

'How do you shut them up?' I asked, easing the metal across his cheek.

'You . . . you press the button a couple of times. It makes a row in the cabs, shows I'm busy.'

The phone rang on; a light started flashing on the switchboard. Four and nine kept trying, one voice overlaying the other.

I reached across and pressed the red button half a dozen times, very rapidly. The voices stopped. The phone stopped. The light continued to show, together with a slight buzzing which I hadn't noticed before.

'James Burton. Come on! You must know more than numbers.'

He shook his head. 'No, I don't, honest. I never see them at all, they only call in. Besides, so many of the drivers are casual how, not like . . .'

I interrupted him, 'Not like in the old days.'

I dropped the jack to the ground with a heavy clanking sound. That way it was easier to hit him in the stomach. At the same time I grabbed hold of his shirt so that he wouldn't go flying across the office.

He should have bought better stuff. It came apart in my hand and he hit the table holding the switchboard with a hasty bang which sounded as though it had hurt his back a lot.

One of the phones fell to the floor; the receiver was jolted off the second one and it hung down close to his face, the constant live tone sounding in his ear.

'You'd better tell, me, or I'm going to do more than that. A whole lot more.'

He looked up at me as though he was trying to decide whether or not I meant it. I thought he might be in need of a little more proof. I grabbed for him and brought him to his feet for long enough to knock him down again. This time I scored the second phone, too.

'Burton,' I reminded him.

'He . . . he used to drive for us. Regular, like. Haven't seen him for a long time. Nine months, maybe.'

'Was he sacked?'

'No. Just came in and asked for his cards one day, so I heard. Don't know why. Didn't seem to have another job, though. One of the fellers said he was trying to scrounge some cash off him on the rank a month or so back.'

'Where does he live?'

The little guy shook his head. 'Don't know that, do I?'

I went as if to go for him again. His eyes blinked shut and his arms came up to cover his face.

'There's an address book in that drawer. His might still be in there, I don't know.'

I found the book and then the address. I'd just copied it down into the little note book that all good private detectives carry around with them, when there was this jarring against the back of my head.

It was the car jack.

Some guys never gave up. You had to hand it to them. So I did.

I spun round and threw up my left arm, knocking the weapon from his grasp. While I was doing that, my right fist was closing in on his face with some speed. I hit him between the end of his nose and the top of the chin. He felt surprisingly solid: for a second.

His body bounced back from the wall and one eye was strangely open as he came back on to the same fist. I tried to shut it. I think I succeeded.

He folded to the floor and didn't move: not as much as an eyelid.

I thought that would do. There didn't seem to be anything else to keep me hanging around in that dump. Not until I opened the door, that is.

He was still wearing the same blue overcoat, though it was looking a trifle soiled. But then, you should have seen his face.

It was patched together with so much sticky tape that you got the impression that if anyone reached out and pulled it off, the whole face would crumble away into little pieces.

Not that I was about to try.

His right hand was out of his pocket and extended towards me. And in its grasp was what looked remarkably like a Walther P 38.

-7-

We stood there looking at each other for a long while. I was wondering whether I was going to make some kind of fool move and he was waiting for me to try it. I could tell from the way he held the gun so lovingly that he wasn't just waiting for it; he was praying for it.

I decided that I wouldn't give him that pleasure. At least, not yet.

So I eased my hands well away from my pockets and stood there waiting. I'd let him lead for a while and reckon on making my tricks from his mistakes.

I only hoped he didn't wait too long before letting something slip. Establishing losers was all too easy.

'I said you were the sort of dope who didn't listen to good advice. Well, sucker, now you're going to get yours!'

At least I knew what he'd been doing since last we met—aside from visiting his friendly neighbourhood out-patients department—he'd been down to the Biograph to see a few more old movies.

'Look,' I told him, 'why waste your time here with me? With dialogue like that you should be in pictures.'

'Wise guy!' he snapped.

'See what I mean?' I said.

Perhaps we both should have been in pictures.

'Where's your pal?' I asked him. 'Still running?'

'Never mind him.'

'I don't. I just thought that you might.'

'Cut out the crap and turn around.'

I shrugged my shoulders. 'It's the best offer I've had today.'

'It's the only one you're likely to get.'

Well, yes, I was right. He did get better when he got going. I thought I'd do as he said. He was still holding the gun and looking as if he'd like to use it.

I turned round to face the wall and waited for him to frisk me. But he didn't bother with such niceties. He hit me with what I thought was probably the butt of his gun. I didn't have time to dwell on it.

The dirt of the floor rose up to meet me with alarming speed and I nestled my cheek to it lovingly.

When I started to come round it was already dark. I made the mistake of lifting my head too quickly and something at the back of it seemed to hit me like the kick of an angry mule.

Don't worry, I told myself, hang on in there with your hands and knees on the ground and your head down and as time passes it will all get a little easier.

I knew I was right. Only I wasn't certain if I had that much time. I wasn't certain if I had any time at all. Maybe I'd used all of my time up. Maybe Cathy Skelton's time was used up too.

I asked myself if there'd been another phone call to the Blake place and if so what it had said.

There was no way of knowing the answer. And no way of finding out while I was stuck in that stupid position down on the . . .

Where the hell was I, anyway?

Gradually I looked up and around. The big guy had been good enough to drop me down alongside a couple of tracks of disused railway line. I could see the outline of a bridge, with a street light at its corner.

Great! He'd probably taken me to the edge and rolled me over.

All that it needed was for a train to shuffle its merry way along the line and then I'd be feeling even better.

But from the state of the track the line wasn't used any more and as I looked more closely, I could see that the end of the tunnel under the bridge had been bricked up.

I shook my head to clear it but only succeeded in making it nearly fall off.

Apart from the phone call, there were two thoughts nagging away at me.

First, if the heavy mob weren't keeping me out of Blake's business because of anything to do with the kidnapping, then what were they frightened I'd turn up?

And second, if my friend with the overcoat and the patchwork face had found out from the cab controller what I'd been looking for, then had he paid Jimmy Burton a call himself?

Well, sure as hell I wasn't about to get any answers where I was. I straightened myself upright and winced a few more times. I wanted to feel the back of my head, but didn't think I'd enjoy what I found, so I resisted the temptation and began to clamber up the bank towards the road.

The sodium lighting didn't help my eyes any, but from between the slits I could see where I was. He could have thrown me this far from the taxi office.

Which meant that I could probably make it as far as Burton's place before I fell over again. The only thing was, my car didn't seem to be where I thought I'd left it.

And I wasn't about to call a cab.

I started to walk down the slight hill away from the bridge, trying not to notice the passers-by who glanced across at me open-mouthed, then hastily looked away again, trying to pretend that they hadn't noticed anything out of the ordinary.

The traffic lights at the crossroads changed in time for me to keep walking. Past the station with the flower stall and paper stall outside.

I looked at the headlines, but there was nothing at all I wouldn't have expected. They were all carrying the basic story of the kidnap, with pictures of Cathy and smaller ones of Crosby

Blake. The stuff the police seemed to have released was minimal, with an attempt to give the impression that the whole thing was very much under control.

I carried on walking.

Anson Road was a turning off to the left that dipped down a hill, with blocks of council flats on one side and once superior Victorian mansions on the other.

The house I was looking for was down on the bottom corner, after the road had twisted round. It was on the right hand side of a crossroads, standing back from the pavement. A turret-like attic stuck out from the roof and the whole appearance was of some small-scale attempt at the baroque.

It was dark enough for there to have been plenty of lights on, but none were showing. I edged open the wrought iron gate and turned sharp left in front of the rock garden.

I preferred flowers myself.

The path took me round the side of the house, between a privet hedge and an area of dark soil with nothing apparently in it but worms. Though they weren't apparent either. I simply assumed them to be there. Like I assumed I would eventually get round to the back door. After another two corners, I did.

It was locked. Of course. No point in making things easy for intruders.

I walked back to the front. There were two entrances. One up a flight of stone steps; the other down more steps and under the first set.

The door at the top of the stairs had panels of oddly coloured glass set into it. Alongside it there were four tarnished brass fixtures into which the residents could slip cards bearing their names.

None of them had availed themselves of this magnificent opportunity. I guessed that whoever did live there was shy.

If it was still James Burton, then maybe he had good reasons.

I pushed on a long white bell push. What else would you do with it?

There didn't seem to be any sound from inside the house so I went back down the stairs and tried the door to the basement. No cards; no bell; no knocker. I tried the handle just in case.

And what do you know? It was locked.

Well, if I had to break in, then it was best done round the back where not so many people might notice.

I was half way along the back wall of the house when I heard a sound. I stopped and turned. The skin down my right thigh had instantly gone cold. A small pit hollowed out in my stomach.

In the darkness I could see that the garden seemed to rise up steeply in the far corner. There was a small tree there and a number of bushes.

And something else.

Someone?

It might be nobody important and there might be nothing to worry about. Then again, it might be pally with the Walther or it might be the mysterious missing taxi driver—the one with the same name as Presley's guitarist—the one who had driven Cathy Skelton to and from school for a while and whom she had fancied. He might even have a gun himself.

It might be a cat. I liked cats. I listened for the noise again. If it was a cat then it was a big one. Still, I wouldn't hold that against it. If it was a cat . . .

The first half of the garden I covered slowly, cautiously, ready to drop down or throw myself to one side if necessary. If I had sufficient warning.

Nothing happened.

The rest of the way I went as fast as I could.

Bare branches scratched at my face and a piece of root tripped me as I tried to get up the steep little slope as quickly as I could. There was something crouching at the top, jammed into the corner between two walls of brick. I couldn't see clearly what it was but I kicked out at it hard and it shifted and made a noise that made it sound like a man. I swung my foot back and tried again. It was a man all right.

I pulled him to his feet and he grabbed at me, but it may

only have been in fright. Whatever the reason, it was enough to make me lose my balance and I went backwards, taking him with me.

We tumbled together down through the sides of the bushes and a branch or something like one hit the back of my head, making me wince as the sharpest of pains cut down through my head. Still, I didn't let go. After all this, I wasn't going to lose him easily: whoever he was.

We rolled on to the grass and he was up on one knee first, trying to free himself from my hands. He half-way succeeded. I jabbed the front of my head into his stomach, which was a pretty silly thing to do, though at the time there didn't seem to be any alternative.

He fell forward on top of me and I made the effort and stood up, taking him with me. I shook him over the back and listened to the remaining breath bounce out of him.

Then I pinned his arms to the ground with my knees.

I couldn't see his face too clearly in the dark but it didn't look the kind of face a young girl would fall for.

But like I said before, you can never tell about that sort of thing.

I tried it anyway. I said, 'Burton? James Burton?'

He nodded his head up and down.

'Let's go into the house. You and I have got things to talk about.'

He nodded again and I let him get up, slowly, then followed him towards the back door.

The door was sideways on to the house and led into a kitchen. I sort of wished that it hadn't. Hygiene wasn't a word my new friend was too familiar with. I snapped on the electric light and blinked a couple of times to get used to it.

A plastic bin over by the sink was trying hard to hold twice as much rubbish as it was designed for and wasn't doing too bad a job. A mess of coffee grounds and potato peelings was plastered all over the swing top and a vivid splash of something red enlivened the front. I hoped that someone had spilled a bottle of ketchup.

The sink appeared to be trying for a world record for containing the most dirty crockery. A pile of old cardboard boxes was stacked alongside one wall and there were numerous bottles standing on end and lying on their sides.

But none of this mattered. What did was the stink.

It was strong enough to make my eyes smart and I had to swallow hard to stop from retching.

'For Christ's sake! Do you live in this?'

He stood there and nodded his head, eyes squinting as though it was the first time in a long while that he had been in such a bright light.

I pushed him towards the kitchen door. 'Let's get the hell out of here!'

The kitchen led into a hallway; stairs to the left, two doors to the right. He went automatically to the second door and I followed him through. This time when I reached for the light switch nothing happened.

'You some kind of mole?' I asked him.

He stood there and as far as I was aware he was looking at me, but maybe he couldn't see any more than I could, which was damn all.

Occasionally, the lights from a passing car slid round the room and I caught a quick glimpse of his face, of chairs and a table, an empty fireplace.

'You got a bulb?'

He nodded again.

'Get it.'

I watched him through the door and wondered if he'd try to run, though somehow I didn't think that he would. Where the fuck would he run to?

He came back with a bulb all right, and pulled a chair into the centre of the floor to stand on. I walked over and started to close the curtains. No point in making this thing too public.

When I turned back into the room, the light was swinging

still from the end of its flex, sending alternating pools of light and shadow over the threadbare carpet, the worn furniture, the dingy wallpaper.

He stood just on the other side of the light. He was wearing a soiled white tee shirt underneath a mulberry coloured cardigan that sported a hole in the left sleeve and a button sewed on with purple thread. He wore thin blue jeans with a pee stain above the crotch and frayed bottoms. They were a couple of inches too short above brown boots that hadn't seen polish for so long they wouldn't even have been able to greet it like a long-lost friend.

He had a darkish beard which was straggly and wild and a moustache which drooped hairs round his top lip. His head was almost completely bald on top, with a gathering of lank strands that hung greasily down the sides and stuck out over his ears. Off the centre of his forehead there was a red spot. His cheekbones were a mass of blackheads and small pimples. A vein at the side of his head stood out jaggedly, pulsing away while all the rest of him was still.

Jesus Christ! This was what a fifteen year old kid had found attractive?

'Sit down!' I told him.

He sat down. I sat down. That was great. Now we were ready for a cosy fireside chat. I hoped it wasn't as empty as the fire, or as cold.

'Okay, sunshine. Let's start with an easy one. What were you doing up behind the bushes?'

He didn't jump to answer so I gave him a little prompting.

'Well, it was a bit late to be taking cuttings and I don't think you were looking for owls because you didn't have your glasses with you. So what was it?'

Still no answer, no response at all. He continued to sit there and look at me and his face was so full of dumb self-pity that I could have jabbed my fist into it a few times for the joy of jolting him out of it.

But maybe I was being hard on him; maybe he had something

to feel real sorry with himself for; I hoped that it wasn't what I feared it might be.

'Right. Let's try something a little more likely. You were in the house around the end of the afternoon and it was getting good and dark, the way it does now. Suddenly, without notice. There was a knock on the door and you went over to one of the windows and peeked out. You didn't like what you saw. Maybe you didn't know his name, but you'd seen him around and that was enough. A big guy who hung around the cab office sometimes, big and nasty and used for throwing someone else's weight around for them. He might even have thrown a little of it at you in the past.

'Anyway, you don't want to stick around to see him and he's not the kind of guy to let a shut door put him off. So you head off out into the garden and hide behind those trees. He uses his bit of plastic and lets himself in, turns the place over and finds nothing. Leaves. You get back into the house. A while later, I arrive and start snooping about. You play the same game. Only this time you're not quite so careful, or perhaps my hearing's better. Whichever it is, it doesn't matter. The result's the same.

'I've got to you first. And you'd better be glad about that. It could have been your big pal and it could have been the cops. It still could be either. So you'd better sing to me before either or both of those others come and beat the living shit out of you.

'And I don't think you'd like that very much, would you, Jimmy?'

He didn't answer that one either, but the vein in his head began to throb all the more fiercely, which told me as much as I wanted to know.

'So what's it to be, Jimmy baby, are you going to take your chances with me, or wait and see who finds you on your hands and knees in the trees next time around?'

'How . . . how do I know that you're not with them? Either of them. How do I know you won't pass me over to them when I've talked to you?'

I shook my head. 'You don't know, Jimmy. But if I were you I'd take that chance for now.'

His head sank down between his legs and for a moment I thought he was going to faint. But slowly he sat up straight again and the holes where his eyes were were as empty-looking as pits in the snow.

'Where is she?' I asked.

'Not here.'

'But she's alive?'

He almost jumped in the chair. 'Of course she's . . . I mean, there's no way . . . nothing I could do to hurt her.'

His head went down again.

'Oh. Christ!' I said, 'This isn't going to be another tale of true love gone wrong, is it? Spare me that crap!'

'Don't you . . . don't you . . . just don't, that's all.'

Which was pretty clear, but not clear enough. I wanted a whole lot more and I wanted it fast. But one look at him told me that the only way I was going to get it was to start him off gently and let him tell it his way, with only the gentlest of promptings from me. I realised that but I wasn't making any rash promises to anybody . . . about the prompting being gentle, I mean.

'Come on then, Jimmy. Let's take it more or less from the beginning. I know that you used to drive her to school and back, but that was a couple of years ago. What happened since then?'

'I don't . . . it's not . . . where to start. You see when I was driving her to school, she . . . I don't know . . . there was something about the way she looked at me when we arrived or when I picked her up. It was as if she . . . well, as if she liked me, you know?

'I didn't do anything, say anything. How could I? She was the boss's niece. Anyway, she was half my age. Then one day she started talking to me. Not about anything in particular. What she said didn't matter. I wasn't really listening. It was her eyes. They used to be flat-looking as a rule, but when she spoke . . .

'No, I didn't bother with what she said. Just looked at her. I think . . . I think she was the most beautiful girl I'd ever seen.'

The head went back into his lap, cardigan hunched across his shoulders. After a while he hadn't moved; I reached forward and lifted him up. Tears were running down his face, noiselessly, endlessly.

He looked ugly and stupid and pathetic.

'Did you get in touch with her, or she with you?' My voice was hard and fast.

He didn't bother to wipe his face, simply stared at me as though his eyes were melting.

'Well?'

'I drove her for a term, then I was switched. That was the normal thing. I didn't mind. After all, nothing had happened. Then . . . it was a long while later . . . I suddenly knew that I was missing her. After that, there was no way I could stop thinking about her. I started hanging around places where I thought I might see her. Outside the school, her house. Times when she'd go out shopping with her mother. Anything.'

'She knew you were doing this?' I asked.

'Yes. She knew. She saw me and looked right through me.'

'That didn't stop you?'

'No. It couldn't have. And besides, she was with somebody else all the time. So I convinced myself that even if she wanted to speak or smile then there was no way in which she could have.'

'So you let all this build up inside you until you were totally obsessed with her and then you decided that you'd snatch her, get some cash from her conveniently rich uncle and head off into the hazy romantic sunset together.' I was smart. I had it all figured out.

But I was wrong.

He reached out and touched my hand. His fingers were thin, cold; I let them rest there until the coldness had begun to get through to me, then pushed them away.

'I didn't think that. Never. I knew it was hopeless. Maybe that was part of the trouble. Maybe I should have gone round to her place and knocked on the door . . .'

'Oh, Jesus! Come on! You'd have got pitched out on your third-rate arse so fast there wouldn't have been time for you to fart! Who do you think you are? Some fucking knight in shining armour who wants to rescue the fair maiden from the wicked king?'

He closed his eyes and opened his mouth and slowly let out a deep breath as though I had just punctured his last vision. Well, if that was so, then it was about time.

The only thing visions were good for was hiding the truth. You had to imagine the real and not the illusion if you were to have any chance at life. Only it was too late to show Jimmy Burton that simple fact. Much too late.

'What did happen then? Cause someone's been phoning up and asking for a whole lot of money on the understanding that Cathy's been kidnapped and that someone has to be you. So you'd better level with me fast.'

'All right. One day she was in town with her mother; they were in this place drinking tea or something and she smiled at me when her mother wasn't looking. A little while later she gave me a note. It was when she was on her way out. It told me to meet her.'

'Where?'

'Near her school. She . . . I don't know how, but she just seemed to be able to come out and see me.'

'What happened?'

'We went for a walk. She told me about Crosby, her uncle. Told me that he . . . he was always after her, around the house. You know what I mean. She said that one night, when her mother had been away, he had . . . had . . .'

The hand came out searching for mine again and this time I allowed it to stay there. I needed to hear the rest of the story.

'He had gone to her room and . . . and forced her to make love to him.' The words tumbled out in a rush, falling over each other in their haste.

'He raped his own niece?'

'Yes.' The voice was so quiet that it seemed to be coming from another person, another room, another nightmare.

'Why didn't she tell someone . . . her mother, the police?'

'She was frightened. Crosby said that he would give her this money when she was eighteen if she . . .'

'If she kept putting out for him?' I suggested.

'No! She never did anything like that again! Never! She swore it to me. It was because he was afraid she'd tell people, because he felt guilty . . . I don't know.'

'Then why the kidnap? Why the ransom for the same amount?'

'He'd begun to get after her again, tell her that he couldn't keep away from her, had to have her. She kept her bedroom door locked and stayed out of his way. That was when he threatened to withhold the money. She . . . she didn't like that.'

'She liked money,' I said.

'What's wrong with that?' The vein was bulging through his skin again. 'She was used to living comfortably.'

I waved my hand round the room. 'Not like this.'

He didn't answer that. But at least his hand was back where it belonged.

'She suggested that we get the money by pretending that she had been kidnapped. And then we would go away.'

I stood up and glared down at him. 'Christ! You did think it was all fairy tales and happy endings, didn't you. What a . . . !'

He interrupted me. 'She loved me. She said so. She wouldn't have come here otherwise, would she? She wouldn't have slept with me.'

Burton stood up and faced me. For the first time that evening he looked as though he had achieved something he could be proud of. Had done something he believed in, could believe in himself for.

'You don't believe me, do you? Well, it's true. That was what she said when she asked me to help her. She said I could sleep with her, make love to her, if I did what she said. She said she wanted me.'

I sneered at him. 'Sure. She wanted you. She wanted you as long as you were going to help her get some money. Then how long do you think you would have lasted? She sold herself to you like any other cheap tart, any other whore. The only difference is that her price is higher!'

The vein seemed as if it would burst; the red spot glowed more brightly; his fists clenched. He stood there in front of me and pulled himself straight. He was around the same height as myself. I thought I had said enough to needle him into taking a poke at me and I hoped that he would.

I wasn't sure why, but more than anything else I wanted the excuse to knock him around the room.

He wasn't going to let me down. He swung his arm faster than I thought he would and the blow was strong enough to send me back into the edge of the table.

But I didn't mind that. I didn't mind that at all. He was coming for me again and I slid under his right arm and my face was close enough to his for me to see clearly the foul pallor of his skin. I brought up my fist into his stomach and moved quickly to one side so that his head didn't jerk down into my own. I caught him with a left as he dropped forward and he grabbed for me and held fast.

It took my knee to free myself from his hold. He spun round on the edge of the armchair and slid across the floor until he landed in the sideboard. There was a crash of crockery from inside it and when his body rolled off, the doors opened and broken and cracked saucers and plates splintered out.

I picked Burton up and his lip was cut from where my knee had gone hard into his mouth. One eye had a swelling already rising up above it. He didn't seem to have much fight left in him, which was a shame. I don't know what I thought I was doing, but it could have been some fool idea about knocking the sense back into him.

I wanted to show him the stupidity of building a dream of a life round a young girl. So I hit him. Then I hit him again. I wanted to punish him for his delusions. Maybe I wanted to punish myself.

After a while there didn't seem to be any point in hitting him any more. I laid him across the torn fabric of the armchair and walked out into the street. I needed the fresh air: also I needed to make a phone call.

There didn't seem to be any danger of Burton getting up and running for it while I was away.

A few hundred yards further down the road I found a call box. Crosby Blake's voice came on the line. I told him who it was and he didn't seem too happy.

'Where are you? The idea was that you would be here when the kidnapper called, or at least be within touch. What do you think I'm paying you for?'

I was beginning to wonder.

'Never mind where I am,' I said. 'Have you had a call?'

'Of course I have.'

'When?'

'During the afternoon.'

'And?'

'He said he would overlook the fact that the news had been leaked if I would find the money by tomorrow morning. I said that I would and he said he would call later this evening to make the final arrangements.'

'You told the police?' I asked.

'Yes.'

'That's fine.'

'But listen, Mitchell, will you be here when he calls again?'

'No.'

'Why on earth not?'

'I don't think he'll be phoning.'

I put down the phone quick, thought for a few seconds, then dialled another number.

By the time I got back into the house, Burton was sitting up and shaking his head.

'You got any scotch anywhere? Or brandy?'

He shook his head. 'There was some whisky. Cathy finished it.'

'So she boozes as well! What kind of school is that she goes to?'

He got up and looked as though he was going to try to hit me again, but this time I wasn't interested.

I said, 'Sit down and don't waste my time. Besides, I want some more information.'

He thought about it, then sat back down. Perhaps he was starting to learn sense after all.

'What do you want to know?' he said resignedly.

'The most important thing?'

'What's that?'

'Where Cathy is.'

He stared up at the light, shut his eyes tightly, then looked down at the floor.

Oh, no, I thought, he doesn't even know that.

He confirmed it. 'I don't have an idea.'

'Shit!' I said. 'What sort of kidnapper are you, anyway?!'

He didn't have to answer.

But in a way he did. He said, 'She stayed here for the first two nights. Wouldn't come down from the room upstairs. Wouldn't get out of the bed. I brought food up to her. And stuff to drink. All the while she told me about the phone calls, the things to say. Then when I went out to make the call and saw the newspaper I got frightened and wanted to forget the whole thing. She wouldn't let me. Said all we had to do was change the plans slightly. Get the money as soon as possible.'

'But just in case anything went wrong, she was getting out while she could?'

'No. Yes. I don't know. It made sense if she left here and met me after I had the money.'

I said, 'It never occurred to her you might take the cash and run?'

His look answered that one for me as well. She had never been more certain of anything in her life: and rightly so.

'How were you going to get in touch?'

'After I picked up the money, tomorrow morning, she was going to call me.'

'Where?'

'At a call box in Liverpool Street station.'

'And you've no idea where she is?'

'No.'

He got up and wandered out of the room, only just managing

to negotiate the doorway. I followed him through the hallway and up the stairs. He went into one of the rooms: a bedroom. Looked at the bed. Stood there for maybe five minutes, simply staring down at the tangle of sheets and blankets, the pillows without covers.

Then he turned around and walked past me as if he didn't know I was there. He went on into the bathroom. I let him alone for a few minutes more and then went in.

Burton was sitting on the edge of the bath, staring at his own face in the mirror. I wondered what he saw there, what he thought about it?

On the back of the sink there was an open razor. The blade was starting to rust along the edge. I looked down at the blade, then at Burton, then at his reflection.

There was a knocking on the door downstairs. I thought I knew who it would be. I went out of the bathroom, shutting the door behind me. I didn't look back.

Downstairs, I let them in. I could see the bulge of the Magnum Tom Gilmour had brought back from New York, sticking out through his jacket. I tapped the butt and said, 'You won't be needing that. He's upstairs in the bathroom. Thinking about putting an end to it all.'

Gilmour pushed past me but I called after him.

'Don't worry,' I said, 'he won't actually do it. He's just enjoying thinking about it and how fucked up he is. He wouldn't have the guts to cut his own toenails with a sharp pair of scissors.'

Gilmour snorted and turned away, continued up to the bathroom. I walked past the two other cops at the door and down into the street. I wasn't as certain about Burton as I had made out: maybe I didn't want to stick around and see if I was right or not. Though I couldn't think why.

It was late when I got back to my place. A quick shot of Southern Comfort didn't do anything to bring me round. I sat slumped in the chair and tried to think clearly but it was no use. I was too tired and there were still too many loose ends.

What was the use of being a great detective and finding the

kidnapper first if that didn't finish anything? It only seemed to start things off all over again.

What I needed was another break. That didn't seem about to happen, so I had another drink instead.

And then someone knocked on the door.

There were times when I thought that was all my business was about. People knocking on your door or calling you on your telephone. Usually you didn't know who it was going to be and when you found out you wished you hadn't. More often than not it was trouble.

I remembered this movie. There was a cop who was honest so his buddies didn't like him overmuch. They gave him all the tough assignments; sent him in first and sat back, waiting for him to get blown away.

One time they were after some narcotics bust or other. There was a doorway on a landing. This cop, he went through that door; at least, his arm did. Someone grabbed it on the other side. While they were holding him they shot half of his face away.

Nice guys.

Nice movie.

The knocking sounded again.

I walked over to the little table and pulled open a drawer. Took out a Smith and Wesson .38. I didn't carry it often, but there were times . . .

I wondered if this might be one of them.

Carefully, I slipped the bolt back and took hold of the handle with my left hand. In my right I held the gun and it was pointed straight into the centre of the doorway.

I pulled it open fast and pointed the gun some more.

He stood there with his mouth open and his face still managed to look pretty.

'What can I do for you, Mick?' I asked.

'Dave wants to see you, don't 'e. Reckons as 'ow 'e's got somethin' for you.'

-8-

Half-way up the stairs, Mick started running. I couldn't understand why, but I ran after him anyway.

He was a lot younger than I was and he got into the place first. Found Dave. I stood inside the door and leaned back against it. Mick was kneeling in the centre of the room, kneeling beside a fat, flabby body. Holding it. Crying over it.

It.

I asked myself if he was alive or dead. Went over and made to take hold of his wrist, but Mick turned on me savagely and pushed my hands away.

'Get out! Get out, you bastard! Leave him alone. Leave him with me.'

'I want . . .'

'Why don't you think about something else? Not what you fuckin' want!'

He stared up at me and his eyes were still full with tears; he looked at me with something akin to hatred; turned back to the broken and bruised body he was cradling and gazed down with disbelief and something close to love.

I got up and walked away. But I didn't go out of the flat. I went into the kitchen and put on the kettle. Then I looked for the brandy; poured one for myself, drank it down and poured another, then one for Mick. The kettle was starting to make the familiar sounds: I went back into the kitchen and found a tin of ground coffee.

When I took the coffee through he was still kneeling there. I put the cups down and went over and stood behind him, looking down. Then I reached past him and tried again to find a sign of life in Dave's body. This time the boy did nothing to try and stop me.

A pulse moved gently against the tips of my fingers, gently like the beatings of a tiny, dying bird. Coming from that huge body, how could it be enough?

Yet I wasn't surprised. They would have been very good, very professional. And what they were doing their best to protect was not quite important enough to kill for. Not yet.

I went over into the corner of the room and rang for the ambulance. Then I went back to Mick. Picked him up by his shoulders and led him to a chair. Set him down; carefully. Gave him the coffee, the brandy. Went back to Dave.

Both eyes were closed, the flesh round them puffed up and swollen purple. The lips were cut and caked with coagulated blood. The skin on the right cheek had been torn away by something hard and abrasive and what had burst through seemed unnatural, unreal—the stuffing from a child's doll.

A bump rose through the hair near the back of the head and clots of red had matted the strands together in random patches.

I knew that if I removed his clothes and looked beneath them, there would be more bruises, more cuts, more blood. But I didn't want to see them.

The ambulance would soon be here. I went over to where Mick was sitting, coffee and brandy beside him. Neither had been touched. He sat there, numbed and still.

I squatted down beside him and lifted the glass of brandy to his lips. After a few attempts, I got him to drink a little. He coughed a couple of times, his eyes watered again. I gave him some more, then set the glass down.

'Mick. Mick.'

He turned and looked at me without seeing me at all.

I reached up and touched his arm; ran my fingers slowly up and across his shoulder; felt the soft, cold skin of his face. The edge of his mouth. The first curls of his hair.

'Mick.' I said. My voice was soft, caressing. 'Mick. What was he going to tell me? What was it?'

He was still looking at me; still staring through me to the beaten shape that might be dying, might already be dead.

I pushed my hand further up into his hair and moved myself closer to him. I felt his head edge away as his neck stiffened then something broke within him and he collapsed forwards, down into my arms, sobbing against me.

In the distance I could hear the siren approaching.

I held the boy to me and whispered in his ear: 'What was it, Mick? What?'

I released him enough to be able to see his face.

His lips opened and moved. There was no sound. I continued to hold him, look at him. He tried again. This time words came.

'It was about Blake. 'E used to be mixed up in some racket for bringin' wogs into London, illegally. Pakis mostly. Used to come in from over the water in 'is charter planes, land at some disused aerodrome, then do the rest of it in 'is vans. Dave reckoned as 'ow it was still goin' on.'

He stopped abruptly. He'd said it all. Without inflexion, without thought. Just repeated what he knew.

In the silence I knew that the ambulance had arrived downstairs.

I let go of Mick gently and he stayed where he had been when I was holding him. I reached for the glass and drank what was left of his brandy. I let in the ambulance men, then went over to the phone again.

I didn't think Sandy would be in, but after four rings she picked up the receiver and said her name.

'Hello,' I said, 'it's Scott.'

'Yes,' she said. 'I know.'

I moved the earpiece a few inches further away from my face. The kind of chill that was coming down the line would freeze me as easily as a couple of nights in the Arctic.

'Look. That place. The Internationale. Is it a Pakistani hang-out?'

'It could be. I don't know.'

There was a pause. Behind me, the ambulance men were lifting Dave's body on to a stretcher.

I said, 'Look, Sandy, keep away from the place. Don't go round there asking questions for me. It might be nasty.'

'Don't worry,' she replied. 'I haven't and I won't.'

The door to the flat shut. I looked at the chair where Mick had been sitting: it was empty. From where I was standing you couldn't tell the new stains on the carpet from the old ones.

'Was there anything else?' Sandy asked.

There wasn't. I replaced the receiver and headed for the street. I knew where I was going and that it was stupid to go alone. I knew that I should get on the phone again and call Tom Gilmour and get at least a little back-up. Also knew there was no way in which I was going to do that. At least, not until it was over. One way or the other.

People were pushing me on one side. They had their reasons and they were usually good ones. I realised that but knowing it didn't make any difference, didn't make it any better. Not that I minded being on my own. It was what I'd always wanted: nearly always.

It was good. It had definite advantages. It meant you had all the time, all the space, all the money, all the food that should have been in the cupboard and all of the dust that collected underneath the bed.

It meant that you could go to bed alone: wake up alone: walk the lonely streets without anyone by your side: walk them all the way to a lonely death.

What difference did that make?

In the instant of death we're all alone, all reaching out for someone we can no longer see or touch.

Alone.

It was cold and getting colder. I hunched up my shoulders. It was always fucking cold. And it would soon be Christmas.

Great! Fucking great!

The Club Internationale was one of a score of such places within spitting distance of the centre of Soho. If anything, it was a little larger, plusher than most. The cellar was given over to a discotheque, the kind that is invariably filled by foreign students, most of whom gained admission from a free invitation given out in Oxford Street. The money for that operation came over the bar.

There was another, larger bar on the ground floor. Dark decor, a few subdued coloured lights strung around the walls; low tables and high prices. A number of girls who'd seen better nights sat at strategic intervals. There were a few men sitting around, mostly in small huddles, as though uncertain of whether they should be there at all.

At the far end of this room there was a bead curtain draped across a doorway. Above it, a sign: Private Members Club. That was where I wanted to be.

There would be some gambling; not very significant on the surface, but the stakes would be higher than I could manage. A little friendly conversation and a lot of hard bargaining. Bargaining about cafés and about slot machines; about hairdressers and sweat shops that turned out clothes sixteen, seventeen hours, a day; young boys and not so young girls; the traffic in dope and in human beings—so much a kilo, so much a head. The dope was better handled: it brought more on the market.

I had one hand between the beads when the coloured boy from behind the bar put his hand on my shoulder. Not roughly, not yet.

'Members only, sir.'

I turned and faced him. He looked Indian, but I couldn't tell for sure. Not more than twenty years of age and handsome if you liked that sort of thing.

He smiled. 'It is private club, sir. Members only.'

He lifted his hand and pointed upwards, looking at the notice above the door.

He was still looking up when I hit him. Just once. He rocked back on to the edge of the bar, eyes dark and open wide. I thought he was going to make it and that I would have to clip him again. But I didn't. He leaned back on the bar and slid down it to the floor.

In the bar, no-one moved. The huddles moved even closer together. Painted faces failed to shift their masks.

On the way up the stairs, my right hand shifted for a second to the butt of the Smith and Wesson that was clipped to my belt. It gave me a sort of inner ring of confidence.

There was another door at the top of the stairs, with a bell push and one of those tiny spy-holes. There wasn't a handle of any kind. I pressed the bell and waited. Something moved behind the tiny circle at the door's centre. I did my best to look like the cop I used to be. The eye still stared out, uncertain. I reached for my wallet and gave him a quick flash of a warrant card that was more years out of date than I cared to remember.

It worked. The door opened and I was in fast. I stood in front of him and pulled my jacket back far enough to let him see the gun. He saw it but his expression didn't change.

I spoke quickly, quietly: 'You're going to take me in to your boss. No fuss. No trouble. Right?'

He still didn't alter his expression, but he did think about it for a couple of moments. Then he said, 'Yes.' What an accommodating guy!

He turned away and walked past a few tables. I kept close to him and we made it to the office without anything else being said. There were a few cursory glances from the others in the room, but nobody appeared too worried.

He knocked twice then went in. Again I stuck with him and leaned back against the door so that it shut with a satisfying click. My left hand reached out and slid down the catch on the lock. But I couldn't do anything to prevent the warning that must have come from the guy's eyes.

The Pakistani behind the big desk shifted his hand to the drawer at his right. I shifted faster. With my elbow I got rid of the one standing by me, then leapt for the desk. I landed flat across it, the heel of my open right hand catching the well-rounded broad chin underneath the bone and slamming his teeth together with a clear cracking sound. My left hand banged down on the front of the desk drawer: the bejewelled fingers were still inside it.

There was a crunching noise, quickly followed by a scream of pain. I hit him again and let go of the drawer. He went backwards and came out of the swivel chair on to the carpeted floor. I grabbed the gun from the drawer in time to stick it into the doorman's face. I don't think he liked that very much.

At least, this time his expression changed. I preferred it as it had been before.

'Against the wall!' I snapped at him.

I stood to one side of him, so that I could watch all that good class material still writhing around on that expensive carpet. I frisked him and was surprised when he was clean. Turned him round and motioned him into the corner. Then I helped the boss man up from the floor.

He slumped his greased head down on to the surface of his desk, so I tucked the point of his gun underneath his chin and lifted it gently up until he was facing me.

'I'm Scott Mitchell. I think you've been taking an interest in me. In some of my friends as well. And I want it to stop.'

The head tried to slip down again and I pushed the gun harder, until it was half an inch into the fat of his neck. He was sweating hard and his eyes were black with fear.

'The guy with the blue overcoat. What's his name?'

For a moment I thought he wasn't going to tell me, but that would have been silly. He obviously came to the same conclusion.

'Cole. Billy Cole.'

'Okay,' I said. 'Call him.'

The eyes expressed surprise.

'I said, call him!'

The barrel of the gun sank further into the fat, sweaty neck. Chubby fingers reached out for the telephone and pulled it towards him.

'Tell him you want him round here and you want him here fast. Don't tell him anything else.'

The hand shook a little as it held the receiver, but he was a good boy and did as I said.

I stood up from where I was leaning across the desk and backed off a little. His gun was still in my hand and it was still pointing at his head.

'Right. There's just a couple more things. The first is this: my only interest in Crosby Blake is to do with his daughter. I don't care a twopenny fuck about whatever nasty little rackets you and he have been in together; I don't even care if you still are. If it wasn't you then it would only be somebody else.

'The second thing is: keep away from me. If you ever send anyone after me again or if you get to any of my friends then I'll be back here and I'll ram this gun right up your arse before I pull the trigger!

'Is that clear?'

From the way he looked back at me I thought it was clear. I emptied the chamber of his gun and tossed it back to him. He failed to catch it cleanly and it bounced off the top of the desk to land silently in the pile of the carpet. No-one moved to pick it up.

I pointed at the one in the corner.

'Put your arms down. You're going to lead me out of here and let me through the outer door just as though I've been paying a nice friendly call. Then you can both forget about me. Otherwise, apart from what I'll do to you, I shall take great delight in passing on what Dave Jarrell told me to the cops. Got it?'

They had it. He came over and let me out of the office, then out of the upstairs room just as he was told.

When I got down into the bar, the barman was back on his feet and serving a couple of customers. I stood and looked at him and he looked back at me. There was nothing in his face to show that he had ever seen me before. Not even a bruise.

*   *   *

I figured that there was only one way he could come so I parked my back against the wall and waited. The guy outside the strip club gave up inviting me into the all-live show of a lifetime and left me alone. Anyway, I didn't have to wait long.

He parked his car half-way up the pavement and it still managed to block a good bit of the street. When he walked across towards the club he managed to look as big and as dangerous as he usually did.

I waited until he was outside, then shouted down the street to him. He froze, thinking maybe that I was calling him out there and then. I saw the right arm dip towards the pocket.

He saw that I was just leaning back against the wall, nothing in my hands which hung down alongside my body. He came slowly towards me.

When he was almost there, I moved easily away and turned into the alley that ran along past the side of the strip club. Apart from a dim red light at the far end, it was dark. The cobbles dipped at the centre to allow a thin stream of water and refuse to lie there unmoving. Here and there were empty wooden vegetable boxes from the market.

I went a dozen paces in before I bothered to turn around. He was standing at the entrance, partly silhouetted against the neon lights that flashed on the wall behind him and across the street.

'You got things to say, pal?' he asked.

I shook my head. 'In a while,' I said, 'when I've taken you apart and before I send for someone to put you together again. Supposing that I bother.'

He laughed and the large frame shook with his amusement. He obviously thought I was making an oversized joke. I hoped that he wasn't right. He began to walk down towards where I was standing. Waiting.

I thought I'd clip him with a good right hand to warm him up, but he was obviously warm enough already. An aim came up and swept away my punch as though it was brushing away a cobweb. Then he hit me. I jolted back and fell awkwardly on my elbow, the breath jerking out of me as I did so.

The shape came closer and a leg lifted then came down fast. I tried to roll out of its path, but the heel caught me on the hip and a searing pain went through the bone. He lifted the foot to try again.

I dived forwards for it and hung on. He swayed uncertainly for a couple of seconds before falling backwards with my arms still wrapped about his thigh.

Something hit me hard on the back of the neck, trying to knock me clear so I moved my hand up the short distance into his crotch. The fist was clenched fast and I put all the weight of my shoulder behind the blow. Both blows. He called me several very nasty names and the punches stopped pounding at my neck.

It was time to stand up. I did so by way of a hand in his face, my fingers searching for his eyes, thumb jabbing down at his mouth. This time he screamed rather than shouted and I kicked between his still spread legs.

Then I took hold of the lapels of his famous blue overcoat and lifted him to his feet. He sure was a heavy guy.

I had to punch him three or four more times before he fell on to the cobbles again and I could drag him back up.

Only he came up with his Walther stuck in the middle of his hand. I was close enough to chop down at the forearm and swivel my body to one side in case he fired off a shot. He didn't. He didn't drop the gun, either.

I hit down at the arm once more, but this time I held the wrist fast at the same moment. The pain jarred through me sharply enough, so I didn't like to think what it did to him. But the gun did fall to the ground and bounce into a shallow pool of water. He reached down for it and my knee caught his body at an angle across his chest and drove him over to the wall.

He staggered back, arms flapping out in a vain effort to maintain his balance. He hit the wall and started to rebound back and downwards. I met him on the way and hoisted him up high enough to smash my fist into his face and enjoy the feel of his nose crunching up beneath my knuckles.

I grabbed his arm and the collar of his coat and spun him round, then threw him at the brick wall with all of my strength. This time there was no bouncing back. His face cuddled up to the harsh surface as though he wanted to go to sleep. But it was still too early for that.

I yanked one arm high behind his back and with my other hand I took a grip on the back of his neck.

There were things I had to say to Mr Billy Cole.

'Listen, you big dope! You've been leaning on me for too long and too hard. You had your chance the other night when you came at me with a gun in your paw and there was nothing I could do about it. But you thought a good going-over would be enough to keep me quiet. Well, this is to show you that you were wrong. There's only one way you could have kept me from getting to you and that was to press the trigger of that nice little gun of yours. And now it's too late for that even, because when I've finished with you the cops are going to pick you up for what you did to Dave Jarrell and you'll be inside for a nice long time.'

I pressed down with my right hand and moved his face over the brickwork, opening up the cuts that I had made in the playground.

'If there's one kind of bum I can't stand, Billy, it's the dumb heavy boys like you who think the world owes them a living just because they've got a few muscles and aren't fussy how they use them. Well, I am. And I don't like what I saw of Jarrell's face. He may have been a fat poof as far as you were concerned, but whatever he was he was doing me a favour and I don't like people who do me favours getting roughed over for it. So this is to let you know what it feels like. And when you look at yourself in the mirror next . . . when you can finally get your eyes open wide enough to see anything clearly, you'll know what it looks like as well.'

He tried to push himself off the wall and swing round at me, but I simply hoisted his arm a little higher and his head automatically dropped down. I extended my right arm straight, keeping a firm grip on his neck. Then I folded the arm towards my chest, bringing his head back. I repeated the process half-a-dozen times, until it was like bashing a bundle of dirty washing against the wall instead of a man's head.

I pulled him round and looked at him. In the darkness it was difficult to see the features of the face for blood and shreds of skin. I pulled at him and threw his body down into the middle of the alley. His face landed in the water, soiled tissue paper from the fruit boxes lying alongside his head.

Then I went over and picked up the gun. It was my night for emptying other people's weapons. I stuffed the Walther back into his pocket and walked back into the street.

The tout was still calling out for custom for his strip show and from the noise that spilled out of the Club Internationale when I went past business was going on very much as usual.

I looked down at my knuckles in the light that changed colour and intensity above my head. They were raw and bleeding slightly from the punches that I had sent into his face. It had been a good job the wall had been there to do most of the really nasty work. I'd forgotten to bring my gloves. It was a long time since I'd worked anyone over that well and I'd forgotten the mechanics of the thing.

Maybe I should get in a little more practice. Maybe I should get back to what I was being paid for. Cathy Skelton still hadn't been found . . . as far as I knew.

I went into a bar and bought myself a double Southern Comfort, then made my way to the phone.

Tom Gilmour said that they hadn't turned up anything about the girl, but that now the supposed kidnapper had been found they were releasing as much to the media as they could in the hope that someone would have seen her recently and would come forward. He asked me if I had any ideas as to where she might be and I said that I didn't, which was true. I might have had a few thoughts as to how I might find out, but for the time being I was going to keep those to myself.

'Listen, Mitchell,' he said, 'do you think that guy is telling the truth when he says everything was the girl's doing? The planning, the whole bit.'

'Sure,' I told him. 'Don't you?'

'I guess so. But, Christ, she's only seventeen.'

'How old was that girl who threw herself past you off a building in New York? You don't have to be old to make pretty big decisions. How old are your average terrorists? Girls with bombs in their bags and sub-machine guns for excess luggage.'

'Shit!' he said, then rang off.

I rang the Blake house and a woman answered. It was a moment or two before I realised that it was Mrs Skelton. She sounded quiet and I was sure that she had been crying.

'Is Crosby there?' I asked.

'No,' she replied, 'he went out about an hour ago.'

'And his secretary?'

'She's hardly been here all day. I think it was starting to get her down. She went home to rest.'

'Where's home?'

She told me and I wrote it down.

'Mrs Skelton,' I said, 'you sound very upset. Has anything more happened.'

'I don't think so. Not since that poor man was caught.'

'Poor man? You mean the kidnapper?'

'Don't, Mr Mitchell.' Her voice was on the edge of tears once more. 'Crosby told me what the man said about Cathy after he had spoken to the police. He told me all about the things Cathy had got that man to say and do . . . the things she had agreed to do for him . . .'

Her voice trailed off into nothing, to be replaced by quick, breathy sobbing. I waited until she had controlled herself enough to answer my next question. I thought that she might be able to answer it better than anyone.

'Mrs Skelton. Your daughter, would she have been capable of doing all those things, of striking out against her uncle in that way?'

There was a silence. I didn't think she was going to be able to say anything. I thought what I was asking of her was impossible.

But the voice came very slowly and with only the slightest of tremors. 'Cathy used to love her uncle. She would go everywhere with him, do anything he asked. Until . . . I don't know. Almost overnight it seemed, she changed to him. Not just to him. To me. To everyone. It was as though she had grown out of childhood and happiness and suddenly found herself in a different world which she didn't like or want to like. And so she shut herself off from it.'

'You've no idea what might have caused this change? What might have triggered it off?'

She thought and then said no, that she hadn't.

'And you've no idea where she might be hiding now?'

Again the time taken for consideration; again the negative reply.

I told her that she wasn't to worry, that everything would be all right. It should have sounded fine. Should have sounded true. I don't know what it came out like down at the other end of the phone, but inside my own head the words rang hollowly, like so many useless lies.

But why shouldn't Cathy Skelton be all right? Who would harm her now? Who knew where she was?

I left the bar and thought about where I had parked my car. Then I remembered that somebody had borrowed it from near the cab office. I could always call the local station and see if it had been taken for joy-riding and left somewhere.

I didn't. I hailed a passing cab and gave him Ivor Jacobs' address. Now that the news had broken officially he might be back in circulation and receiving visitors.

And Spurs intercept that, the ball is up to Bobby Smith, Bobby Smith inside now to White, White back through to Smith, taking it right down along the line, across the goal, a header there—it's in the net! It's in the net!

'That's a beautiful goal by Dyson! They upset Smith, but that's a beautiful goal. Smith lobbed that right across the whole defence, across to the left wing and there Bobby Smith, who made the first goal, pushed it into the back of the net, lobbed a beautiful centre over and Dyson went into it, eight feet up, son of Ginger Dyson the jockey, and he slashed that with his head into the net and now Spurs are two up.'

I moved easily across the hallway. The football commentary went on from the speaker attached to the wall at the bottom of the stairs. As I opened the door to the living room, the excitement began to fade from the man's voice and the cheers of the crowd died away. But the game wasn't over yet.

I put on the light and looked around. A lot of furniture, a couple of walls packed with books and tapes and records. On the side wall three large framed photographs: I walked over and read the inscriptions. For one of them it hadn't been necessary. I knew Marilyn Monroe when I saw her. This one was titled 'The

Legend and the Truth.' Black and white. Marilyn sits on a chair in
the foreground; she is wearing a black slip, or it might be a dress.
That much isn't clear. What is clear is the expression in her eyes.
They look wide and tired and hurt the way a child might . . . an
animal, even. For too long she has been treated as either or both
of those: child or animal.

The head is slightly raised and tilted to one side; the shoulders
are rounded, slumping forwards. She has rested her hands on her
knees and her legs are slightly apart. But there is nothing sensual
in this. She is only trying for comfort.

Aren't we all?

I stood back and looked at the other photos. Both men. A
skinny footballer in a white shirt with a cockerel on the front; a
man named Tommy Harmer. The other shows a man in left profile. His head leans backwards and his forehead is so high that it
looks like a ski slope in winter. All that intelligence in one man!
The slope of the head is repeated almost identically on the nose.
He's wearing those skinny wire frame glasses that were fashion-
able all over again a few years back. The thing I don't like about
him is the thin pursed lips. They make him look like some kind
of puritan, some kind of religious nut. His name, apparently, is
Gustav Mahler.

From the other side of the door, the sports commentator is
still doing his best to keep up with the play and to convey what's
going on.

Myself, I'm not too sure.

I started trying the other rooms, upstairs and down. No Ivor.
I was almost at the front door again, when I noticed a door under
the stairs. I figured it was only a broom cupboard, but what the
hell?

The handle was small and round and made of something that
felt cool and smooth. It also opened the door easily.

Ivor Jacobs was inside. He was sitting on a stool with headphones on his ears and his hands were all over a glorified switchboard full of plugs and dials and a lot of other things I wasn't too
familiar with.

He obviously hadn't heard me until I'd pulled open the door and he didn't look too pleased at the intrusion. Which was too bad.

He pulled the phones from his ears and attempted a half-smile which only got a little way towards succeeding.

'It's Mitchell, isn't it?'

'You're doing well, Ivor. For a newspaper man you've got a good memory. I want to test it a little more. Can you come out of there, or are you only paying rent on this bit of the house?'

He tried the smile again and reached out and turned a switch to the right. The voice behind me cut out abruptly in mid-word; the cheers and singing were suddenly no longer there.

Ivor got up and ducked his head to get out of the tiny studio he had had built into the cupboard.

'I was just transferring some tape from reel to cassette,' he explained. 'It's so much easier to store.'

'What was it?' I asked. I didn't really care, but if he was prepared to be friendly then perhaps I could get what I wanted without having to turn nasty about it. And I was fed up with hitting people.

Especially, I didn't want to hit Ivor, who was only around five foot six and looked as though a strong wind would play havoc with his navigation.

Ivor led me into the living room. 'It's the sixty-one Cup Final,' he told me enthusiastically, his beard moving up and down as he spoke. 'Spurs beat Leicester by two clear goals. It was the double side, you know. And they won the Cup in two consecutive years.'

I gave him a look that was meant to be a mixture of admiration and interest. I didn't know whether it worked or not. Probably it didn't matter. Like most enthusiasts, Ivor was keen enough to provide his own dynamism. He automatically assumed that everyone else would be as keen as he was.

'You do a lot of recording, Ivor?'

'Yes,' he nodded, 'as much as time allows. All kinds of things: music, talks, commentaries . . .'

'Telephone conversations?' I suggested.

'Well, that . . . that depends on what you mean.'

'I mean you have an attachment which enables you to record any incoming call. Either one that comes straight through to you here, or which is transferred from your office.'

Yes, sometimes it is useful to . . . to make certain recordings of important conversations . . .'

'But until the call has begun you can't know if it's going to be important or not.'

'What do you mean?' He was starting to look flustered now and his eyes were searching the room as though looking for a way of escape.

'I mean that you at least start to record every call that is put through to you. If it isn't any use then you switch it off and later erase what was recorded. Right?'

He didn't say anything, but I knew from his expression that I was working along the right lines.

'Now, you can guess what I'm interested in, can't you, Ivor?'

'No. Well, not really. I don't see what . . .'

'There was a story in your rag the other morning.'

'A story?'

'A story, Ivor. Don't get all coy with me! It was something none of the other papers carried, something there was a clamp down on. But you got something special, didn't you? Something that you weren't going to let slip if you could help it. So you got round your editor, who'll do anything to scrape up a few more readers, and got it all over the front page.'

He stared past me for a moment as though concentrating on the pictures on the wall. I wondered which one he was looking at and what kind of inspiration it was giving him.

He shifted uncomfortably in the seat and I thought that it was time to pile on some pressure so I stood up and reminded him of how much taller I was. Taller and heavier. Possibly he could even remember what it had felt like all those years ago at that nice polite party . . . I hoped he would remember. Then I wouldn't have to do it again. My knuckles were still sore.

'It was a good scoop,' he said apologetically. 'No newsman would pass that sort of thing up.'

'Not even after what the police had warned might happen?' My voice was getting steelier with every syllable and his eyes were growing wider with apprehension.

'What warning was that?'

'I've told you before not to be coy with me. The guy who snatched the girl said that if anything appeared in the press then she would be killed.'

'No.'

'Yes!'

I reached down and he pushed himself back into his chair. But not far enough. I lifted him to his feet and still had to bend down a long way to look into his eyes.

'You knew damn well the risk you were taking, but you went ahead, regardless.'

'I didn't think it was that much of a risk.'

'Not that much of a risk! Not for you. You weren't the kid involved.'

'You can never trust nutters like that. You know that as well as I do.'

'Who says he's a nutter?'

'Aren't they always?'

'I don't know. What's a nutter anyway, Ivor? Some people would say that a grown man who spends his spare time listening to recordings of old football matches isn't exactly sane and sensible.'

He ducked away from me and went over to the window. He stood in front of the brown curtains and looked at me. I couldn't be certain what he was thinking, but I could guess that it wasn't all that charitable. I did think he wanted me to go. Which was good. It meant that he might be more willing to tell me what I wanted to know.

After all, if you've got the kind of ethical grasp which enables you to go against a firm warning that printing a story might endanger a young girl's life, then what price the so-called ethics about disclosing sources of information.

In that sense I thought that Ivor was probably like me. He played the game as it came and figured out the consequences afterwards.

'So who was it, Ivor?'

'Who?'

'The informant. The mysterious caller. The break out of the blue which gave you the names and addresses which the cops were withholding and without which you had no printable story.'

He was just standing there and I could almost see the little wheels turning over inside his head, as the pros and cons of telling or keeping quiet were considered in detail.

'Who was it, Ivor? Who wanted the story published and came to your paper because they knew it was the most likely to pull the kind of cheap stunt it did?'

He was still thinking it over. But I sensed that time was running out. Mine and maybe that of a lot of other people, too.

'Come on, Ivor.' I started to walk towards him. 'All I want is a name.'

I was almost up to the curtains. The beard was looking decidedly droopy. I was going to get what I wanted. Only then did I query whether I did really want it; the confirmation of what I had been thinking for some time now.

But there was no going back: there never is.

'I don't know a name,' he said. 'But I can play you the tape of the call. It was put through from the office.'

I followed him back into his cubby hole underneath the stairs. It was as cute and cosy as a nesting box for a couple of hoopoes.

He handed me the headphones and searched along the shelves for the right cassette. I slipped the phones down over my ears and waited. There was a hiss of blank tape sliding over the head, a couple of mechanical clicks, then the voice.

Something very unpleasant hit me in my stomach and tried to force some of its contents up into my throat. It wasn't a fist and it wasn't a boot: just a tone, a nuance, a vocal gesture. It hadn't even helped that it was what I had been half-expecting.

If you know you're due to get into the ring with Ali and that there's a better than even chance he'll hammer all hell out of you, that doesn't keep your body up off the canvas or stop your eyes from closing over.

I didn't really want to keep listening to the end, but something made me do just that. There might be something else on the tape that I ought to know. But nothing more was given away. It had all been very precise, very professional, very business-like.

As I would have expected.

I took off the headphones slowly and handed them back to Ivor.

'Is it someone you know?' he asked.

'That would be telling, Ivor,'

'Come on, Mitchell, after what I've just done for you. That could cost me my job. At least give me a break in return.'

I came out of the little studio and stretched myself back to my proper height. No wonder Ivor's growth had been stunted.

'Sorry, Ivor,' I said, 'professional ethics you know. Never disclose anything which might prejudice a client.'

He followed me to the door. 'Christ, Mitchell, you're still as big a bastard as you ever were! You won't ever change.'

I reached out and patted him on the head. Why not? I was prepared to be friendly. That was the kind of guy I was.

I had walked maybe half a mile before a cab came by with his sign lit up. The driver was a skinny guy in his early twenties, with long blond hair which ran down to his shoulders. He wore a green jacket and the fixed smile of a man who knows he's already driven two hours too many and is trying to live with the fact that there's still another two to go.

I gave him the address and sat back. I wondered if he was already on his way to another call and if that made me another of his mouldies. But instead of looking at the meter, I lay my head along the top of the seat and closed my eyes. I was tired.

I was tired of many things. Tired of getting a lot of crap from people who told me everything but the truth. Tired of having to peel away mask after mask and still not knowing when you were down to the real thing—until you had scratched your way through a layer or two of skin and your fingernails were stained with blood. Tired of having to slug my way from one situation to another, without ever really being sure of why I was doing it or even where I was going.

I was especially tired of people with too much money and too little sense whose blind stupidity got them into a maze of callous lies which they then used more money to try and get out of—by hiring me.

Scott Mitchell: shit-eating Theseus to the over-privileged!

There weren't many others who could afford even my miserable fees. I felt like a guy with a sensitive nose who was forever doomed to spend his days and nights toiling in a sewage farm.

'Well fuck them! Fuck the whole cruddy lot of them!'

I had opened my eyes and I saw the driver glance over his shoulder and give a sort of funny grin. I didn't know if he'd heard what I'd said but it didn't matter anyway.

I checked to see where we were, then closed my eyes again and tried to relax.

My years in the police force had taught me a lot of things. Most of them bad. But some useful . . . like getting into other people's property with the minimum of difficulty and without disturbing the occupants.

Supposing there were any.

I flashed the torch at the bedroom door for a second and thought about it. The bed might be untouched, unoccupied; or it might contain a curled sleeping form. I didn't think I wanted to know: yet.

There were things I wanted to check first. Like the photograph. It had to be here somewhere and I didn't think it would be very hard to find. I guessed that whoever had taken it had not only wanted others not to see it; I guessed that they looked at it more than a little themselves. For whatever reasons.

I was right. It was in the centre drawer of the writing desk, and there was only a pad of paper on top of it. I stood and looked at it carefully in the light of the torch.

Cathy Skelton was sitting on an ornamental garden chair, all wrought iron and white paint. Behind her were fruit bushes, behind them, disappearing into the sunny distance, fields. She was wearing a white dress that was short enough to leave most of her legs uncovered as she sat astride the chair. She had good legs for a young girl and at their centre there was a patch of a different colour which could have been her pants but didn't have to be.

She was looking straight into the camera and smiling. She looked happy: very happy. It looked to have been taken a few years ago. She could have been fourteen, probably not any more.

I flicked off the torch and I was disappointed though I hadn't known what I thought I would find. But as it was, the photograph didn't tell me all that I still needed to know.

I stood there in the dark and thought about the place and wondered where it was.

Then I thought about the smile and wondered why she was looking so happy.

I thought about who had been holding the camera and receiving the smile.

I thought for so long that suddenly I was no longer in the dark.

Someone had come silently into the room and switched on a light.

I turned round to look at her.

She was standing in the doorway wearing a green lawn nightshirt with a narrow white stripe. It might have been meant for a man but the way that green was doing things to her eyes, it looked even better on her. The light which shone from behind her kind of helped as well.

The outline of her legs was clear all the way up to where they joined the rest of her body and it was there that I was centring my attention.

For the moment.

I raised my eyes and took in the shape of her breasts as they swelled out against the material, nipples already hardening for whatever reason, whatever excitement.

She had pulled her hair round so that it swung alongside her cheek on one side only.

She had a smile on her face and a neat little. 32 in her right hand.

She looked as if she could use it; would use it. Standing there like that she looked as though she could use anything . . . or anybody. And when she was done they'd come round and ask to be used again.

'Why, Mr Mitchell,' she said, the smile broadening, 'I thought you were a burglar.'

I smiled back. Why not keep the party happy for as long as possible? 'I am.'

'I see. And what have you come to steal? Should I be afraid?'

'That depends?'

'What on?'

'On what you've got that's worth taking?'

She pouted and came a couple of steps towards me. But she didn't lower the gun or move it away from the direction in which it was pointing.

'Can't you see anything you fancy?' she asked.

'Sure,' I said. 'I can see a lot of things. Things I expected to find and some that I didn't.'

She had stopped walking and was staring at the photograph in my hand.

'Don't tell me you have a preference for little girls, too?' she said.

I shook my head. 'Not ordinarily. Not this little anyway. I prefer something a little more experienced.'

'Well, now, Mr Mitchell, that's what I've been waiting to hear you say ever since I first called you on the phone.'

I knew it was a lie, but she had started coming for me again and I didn't care. I tried hard to keep my eyes on the gun, but other things kept distracting me: the dark triangle that was barely visible through the nightdress, the pressure of her nipples against the green material, the fire in her eyes.

Suddenly she was too close for me to be able to focus on anything and her arms were around my neck and I was kissing her and it was as good as I had always known it would be.

Her mouth opened and the warmth of her lips spread over mine; then her tongue was living in my mouth, living and darting,

darting and flickering like some soft and swift creature that had just been given life. I could feel her breasts pressing against my chest and one of her legs slid itself between my own.

I felt myself stiffen against her and she responded by pushing even harder, against me. Her mouth moved from mine and found my ear. She alternately whispered and drove her tongue into it while my hands eased over her back and came to rest on her bottom. I pulled her into me and moved my head away so that her mouth came back on my own.

Then I kissed her hard and long and all the while I was trying not to notice the vein which thumped and thumped at the side of my head.

It wasn't any use: not after a while.

I moved my left arm round and the fingers of that hand sought out her wrist; closed on it hard so that she would not be able to turn her nice little gun on me. When I had done that I stepped away. Stepped far enough away to be able to slap her.

I slapped her across her face with my hand outstretched, first with the back, then the front. The cracks sounded loud in the quiet of the room, in the quiet of the night.

There was no other sound: she didn't cry out or shout or say a word. But the fire in her eyes changed. It still glowed, but with a different kind of heat.

My left hand increased its pressure and the gun fell to the floor.

'You're a bastard, Mitchell!' She spoke as though her words were made of finely honed steel.

'People keep on calling me that,' I told her. 'It's enough to make my old man turn over in his grave.'

'Don't try and be funny,' she said.

She needn't have worried.

I pushed the picture at her and she averted her eyes. I took it in the fingers of my right hand and pulled it back, forcing her to look.

'Don't be shy,' I said. 'You must have looked at that enough before doing what you did.'

'What was that?'

'Phoning that paper and leaking the details so that they would print a story. So that whoever had taken Cathy would carry out his threat and kill her. That would have been perfect for you, wouldn't it? She was the only thing in the way between you and Crosby Blake. I don't know whether you wanted him for his money or because you loved him or both. But you wanted him, all right. That was why you stayed around for as long as you did. Always efficiently there, never quite sure why he didn't make the passes at you that you anticipated. Never certain why it was that even when you made a point of leaving your bedroom door open nights you stayed at his house, he didn't come calling. Until you realised that he might have been taking nightly trips in another direction.

'That was more than you could take, wasn't it. A woman like you being passed over for some silly kid. So you hung around thinking it was a crush that would wear off and it didn't. Then when this happened you had the perfect opportunity to get rid of Cathy and be on hand to give Crosby Blake all of the consolation he was undoubtedly going to need.'

I stopped talking, looked at her. There was nothing more to say.

She wasn't about to deny anything. Now that she no longer needed to use me, she probably thought I was beneath any contempt she might have to feel.

'What do you intend to do with all this supposition, Mr Mitchell?' she finally asked, as though daring me to give her an aggressive answer.

'Nothing,' I said, 'if you tell me one thing I don't know.'

Her eyes widened: 'Don't tell me there's something you don't know. You, the great detective.'

I ignored what she said and showed her the photograph again. 'Where was this taken?'

She considered it for a couple of moments, then told me. 'It's a cottage in a village called North Creake, in Norfolk. Crosby has a weekend cottage there. When that was taken, he had taken her for a holiday.' She pronounced the word 'her' as if she was saying something only just mentionable. Then she added, 'Her mother didn't go that time; it was just the two of them. No wonder the bitch looks so gormlessly happy.'

I still had hold of her left wrist. I let it go and moved back towards her. I let my head travel the short distance that was still between us and then I was kissing her again. She stood there like a statue, but somehow I didn't seem to mind. As I moved my mouth over her's I could taste the blood that ran down her lip from where I had slapped her.

Then it was enough. I walked past her, the photograph held tightly in my hand. I think I was trying to tell myself that it didn't matter, but I couldn't be clear even about that.

It was cold and I wasn't going to be able to get a cab. I hunched up my shoulders again and listened to the sound of my own shoes on the wide pavement.

– 10 –

By the time I got home it wasn't only my feet that were aching. All down my legs and through my arms ran some dull throb that I tried to shake but failed. My head was as thick as curdled vomit.

I didn't know what had grabbed hold of me, but whatever it was I could have done without it. All that I wanted to do was curl up in front of the electric fire and sleep for a long, long time.

Instead I went into the bathroom and began to run a hot bath. Then I poured myself a large brandy; drank some; coughed; wiped my eyes clear; fumbled in the phone book.

The car hire office at the airport was open and after a lot of bad hassle they agreed to have a car driven round. I don't know why they were worried; it sounded as though they were going to charge me plenty.

I put my feet up and sipped the brandy. After a while my eyes began to flicker and I couldn't keep them open any longer.

The guy with the car banged on the door enough times to rouse all of the neighbours several times over before I came round and let him in.

He told me that the last thing I looked fit for was a long drive so I agreed with him and phoned for a cab to take him back.

When he had gone I made a flask of black coffee and walked out into the night.

There was a good chance I'd get there without putting the car into a ditch or driving it headlong at some poor jerk coming the other way. If I pulled into a lay-by every time I felt my eyes going and rested up for ten minutes, then I should make it. And by first light.

Apart from a scratch on the right mudguard and an argument with the woman in the all-night café about the contents of my bacon sandwich, I did okay.

It had been light for around half an hour when I drove along the only street that North Creake seemed to possess. Even then, they had to put something approaching a racing bend in the middle of it. But perhaps when all you were driving was sheep it didn't matter.

The cottage was on the left hand side at the far end of the village. It had the normal stone faced walls and with its white paint on the window frames and the orange blinds behind them, everything seemed nice and cosy. The perfect country retreat.

Both doors were locked, but the back one was forced open without too much persuasion. It led into a kitchen with one of those wooden dressers along one wall and a pine table against the other. Directly opposite me was the door which led into the front room.

I swallowed hard, then pushed it open. A couch, some chairs, a lot of bottles and other knick-knacks, dried flowers in the fireplace. Nothing else.

I went up the wooden stairs and into the front bedroom.

The bed was an old-fashioned four-poster with brass ends and a white candlewick bedspread which reached down to the floor. The blind was down. I walked round the edge of the bed and let it up slowly.

Outside the rows of ploughed mud in the field were reflecting the early light from their edges. As I stood there the brightness grew until it formed a glistening spray. I closed my eyes and for an instant the inside of my head was lit by a memory: the edges of a girl's hair as she bent across a lamp.

Then it was gone.

I opened my eyes again and turned back from the window. Back to the bed.

She had been lain carefully upon it, as though someone had put her gently down to rest. She was wearing a white nightdress that was split from between the top of her breasts to above her waist. This was tied across in several places by bows of white lace. Her eyes were closed and there was no sign of worry on her face. From the angle at which her head lay I could see that her neck had been broken.

I wondered what she had been thinking when it had happened.

I stood gazing down at her for a long while: but other than that she was young and beautiful and dead there didn't seem to be very much to think about her. Not now: not any more.

I went back down the stairs and poured out the last drops of the coffee. I swallowed them back, then went out to the car.

I still had quite a way to go.

It was mid-morning. I knocked on the door and waited. As I stood there staring at the expensive wood I could already see those strange, thin lips.

And then the door opened and he was standing there himself, wearing some kind of quilted smoking jacket and looking like a second lead from a Fox movie of the early forties. All he needed was the neat, dark moustache.

A thought struck me. Maybe that was why they all had moustaches. Maybe they all had funny lips.

They moved.

He said, 'This is a surprise, Mitchell. I wasn't expecting you.'

'Weren't you?' I snapped as I pushed past him and into the hallway. 'What kind of an idiot did you think you'd hired anyway?'

He shut the door firmly, yet quietly, and stared at me with the appearance of someone who is used to expressing his authority through a glance.

Not with this guy he didn't.

'I don't understand your meaning, Mitchell, but I do resent your attitude.'

It was all that I could do to stop myself from slugging him right then but I was afraid that once I started I wouldn't be able to stop. And he wasn't worth getting put away for.

'Let's get somewhere a little more private,' I said, 'then we'll make things clear enough. Too clear for your liking.'

I pulled open the door to the room where we had first talked, where he had sat listening to all that Beethoven or whatever it was, where he had hatched who knew what thoughts?

Crosby Blake moved past me and I closed the door behind us.

'I've seen her,' I told him.

He wasn't bad. The sudden turn had almost the right amount of surprise in it. The voice when he next spoke had something approaching the correct querulousness. But it was already too late for all that.

'Where is she?'

'You know where she is, Blake. She's laid out on the bed in the cottage where you left her.'

The eyes blinked, the mouth tightened even more; his right hand made a vague flapping movement by his side, then was still.

'What . . . what do you mean?' He was still trying, but the command was almost gone from the voice. He looked strained, broken.

'She's lying on that nice white bedspread with a twisted neck. Or had you forgotten? So soon.'

'But I . . . why should . . . there was no . . . I loved her. Loved her!'

He screamed the last words in my face and as he did so he moved towards me and I thought he was going to strike out. But instead he began to crumple slowly towards the floor, knees giving way, body folding under him until he was at my feet and all I could hear in the room was the quiet ticking of the clock and a strange choked sobbing sound which came from his throat.

'You loved her all right. If that's what you want to call an emotion that screws you up so much you'll kill because of it. Her running away from you and trying to get back the money you'd once promised her—you would have stood for that. But the man's testimony of how she got him to do as she wanted, of how she had given herself to him in payment. That was something you couldn't stand. She had to be yours and yours only.

'You had this twisted vision of her as a mixture of virgin innocent and lover. But that vision would only admit her as your lover. If it was anyone else, then the whole thing fell apart.

'So you drove up to where you guessed she would be and she was there all right. I don't know if she tried to get round you; I don't know if you tried to come to terms with what she had done to you . . . to herself. Either way, the result was the same.

'She's seventeen years of age and she won't get any older. Ever.'

The moaning increased and he moved his arm until the ends of his fingers rested on the leather of my shoe. I looked down as though I was staring at a number of pale white slugs. I eased my foot away and turned round.

I shut the door behind me and went over the hall to the telephone.

For the rest of that day and all of the night, I was alternately sitting and standing in front of a number of police officers at West End Central. My bones ached worse than ever and my head throbbed like someone was perpetually kicking at it with a steel-capped boot. They weren't but in its own way it was as bad. If I slumped forward in my chair and they could see that I was almost beyond staying awake, they made me stand up. When I swayed enough to make it seem that I might fall over, they pushed me down on to a chair. And started over again.

Tom Gilmour was my friend and he was the biggest bastard of the lot.

But by about five the following morning, it was beginning to look as though they might be going to believe everything I had told them and let me go.

When Tom finally said I could get the mothering hell out of there, he gave me the other bit of good news. My car had been found: it was wrapped round a lampost on the Southend road and looked to be a total write-off.

'I'll get someone to drive you back,' Gilmour said grudgingly.

I looked at him blearily and it took me several minutes to get him in focus. 'Sure. Only I'm not going straight home. I want to go to the Blake place. There's something in the medical report on Cathy that I want to tell her mother.'

He stared at me as though I really was all those kinds of idiot he had spent the last endless hours telling me. But he agreed.

Mrs Skelton came to the door straight away, although it was still very early. From the way her face was shaping up she hadn't had any sleep at all and she'd spent most of her time crying.

Until we were in the kitchen and she'd poured me a cup of tea I didn't say anything. Then I told her what I thought she would want to know.

'Mrs Skelton,' I said, 'I've just come from reading the doctor's report on your daughter. I thought you'd want to know one of the things it said. There's been a lot of dirt thrown about one way and another, a lot of claims and a lot of accusations. There'll probably be a whole lot more before the trial is over.

'But the doctor was positive about one thing. Whatever she or anyone else said, Cathy was a virgin.'

She gazed at me and her timid, tired face broke into tears once more. I wanted to hold her, but somehow I couldn't. So I sat there until the crying had stopped and she had wiped her reddened eyes yet again on her apron.

I got up and made to go.

She said after me: 'Thank you, Mr Mitchell. You're a good man.'

I knew it was a lie, but it wasn't until the coldness of the early morning hit me that the warmth of it was driven away. Sometimes you needed lies like you needed a good overcoat: it was when they became a straightjacket that you had to watch out. Though by then it was usually too late.

I looked up at a red post office van as it drove past me. The sign on the side told me to post early for Christmas. I didn't think I'd bother.

They didn't deliver cards back into the past.

ABOUT THE AUTHOR

John Harvey (b. 1938) is an incredibly prolific British mystery writer. The author of more than one hundred books, as well as poetry and scripts for television and radio, Harvey did not begin writing professionally until 1975. Until then, he was a teacher, educated at Goldsmiths College, London, who taught literature, drama, and film at colleges across England. After cutting his teeth on paperback fiction, Harvey debuted his most famous character, Charlie Resnick, in 1989's *Lonely Hearts*, which the English *Times* called one of the finest crime novels of the century.

A police inspector noted for his love of both sandwiches and jazz, Resnick has starred in eleven novels and one volume of short stories. The BBC has adapted two of the Resnick novels, *Lonely Hearts* and *Rough Treatment* (1990), for television movies. Both starred Academy Award–nominated actor Tom Wilkinson and had screenplays written by Harvey. Besides writing fiction, Harvey spent over twenty years as the head of Slow Dancer Press. He continues to live and write in London.

THE SCOTT MITCHELL MYSTERIES

FROM MYSTERIOUSPRESS.COM
AND OPEN ROAD MEDIA

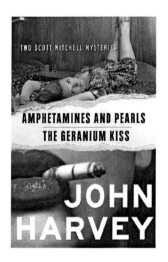

MYSTERIOUSPRESS.COM

INTEGRATED MEDIA

MYSTERIOUSPRESS.COM

Otto Penzler, owner of the Mysterious Bookshop in Manhattan, founded the Mysterious Press in 1975. Penzler quickly became known for his outstanding selection of mystery, crime, and suspense books, both from his imprint and in his store. The imprint was devoted to printing the best books in these genres, using fine paper and top dust-jacket artists, as well as offering many limited, signed editions.

Now the Mysterious Press has gone digital, publishing ebooks through **MysteriousPress.com**.

MysteriousPress.com offers readers essential noir and suspense fiction, hard-boiled crime novels, and the latest thrillers from both debut authors and mystery masters. Discover classics and new voices, all from one legendary source.

FIND OUT MORE AT
WWW.MYSTERIOUSPRESS.COM

FOLLOW US:
@emysteries and Facebook.com/MysteriousPressCom

MysteriousPress.com is one of a select group of publishing partners of Open Road Integrated Media, Inc.

THE MYSTERIOUS BOOKSHOP, founded in 1979, is located in Manhattan's Tribeca neighborhood. It is the oldest and largest mystery-specialty bookstore in America.

The shop stocks the finest selection of new mystery hardcovers, paperbacks, and periodicals. It also features a superb collection of signed modern first editions, rare and collectable works, and Sherlock Holmes titles. The bookshop issues a free monthly newsletter highlighting its book clubs, new releases, events, and recently acquired books.

58 Warren Street
info@mysteriousbookshop.com
(212) 587-1011
Monday through Saturday
11:00 a.m. to 7:00 p.m.

FIND OUT MORE AT:

www.mysteriousbookshop.com

FOLLOW US:

@TheMysterious and Facebook.com/MysteriousBookshop

OPEN ROAD

INTEGRATED MEDIA

Find a full list of our authors and
titles at www.openroadmedia.com

FOLLOW US
@OpenRoadMedia

CPSIA information can be obtained
at www.ICGtesting.com
Printed in the USA
LVOW11s1518271016
510547LV00001B/155/P